PRAISE FOR CHARLIE N. HOLMBERG

THE NUMINA SERIES

"[An] enthralling fantasy . . . The story is gripping from the start, with a surprising plot and a lush, beautifully realized setting. Holmberg knows just how to please fantasy fans."

—*Publishers Weekly*

"With scads of action, clear explanations of how supernatural elements function, and appealing characters with smart backstories, this first in a series will draw in fans of Cassandra Clare, Leigh Bardugo, or Brandon Sanderson."

—*Library Journal*

"Holmberg is a genius at world building; she provides just enough information to set the scene without overwhelming the reader. She also creates captivating characters worth rooting for, and puts them in unique situations. Readers will be eager for the second installment in the Numina series."

—*Booklist*

THE PAPER MAGICIAN SERIES

"Charlie is a vibrant writer with an excellent voice and great world building. I thoroughly enjoyed *The Paper Magician*."
—Brandon Sanderson, author of *Mistborn* and *The Way of Kings*

"Harry Potter fans will likely enjoy this story for its glimpses of another structured magical world, and fans of Erin Morgenstern's *The Night Circus* will enjoy the whimsical romance element . . . So if you're looking for a story with some unique magic, romantic gestures, and the inherent darkness that accompanies power all steeped in a yet to be fully explored magical world, then this could be your next read."

—Amanda Lowery, *Thinking Out Loud*

THE FIFTH DOLL

Winner of the 2017 Whitney Award for Speculative Fiction

"*The Fifth Doll* is told in a charming, folklore-ish voice that's reminiscent of a good old-fashioned tale spun in front of the fireplace on a cold winter night. I particularly enjoyed the contrast of the small-town village atmosphere—full of simple townspeople with simple dreams and worries—set against the complex and eerie backdrop of the village that's not what it seems. The fact that there are motivations and forces shaping the lives of the villagers on a daily basis that they're completely unaware of adds layers and textures to the story and makes it a very interesting read."

—*San Francisco Book Review*

The Will and the Wilds

ALSO BY CHARLIE N. HOLMBERG

The Numina Series

Smoke and Summons

Myths and Mortals

Siege and Sacrifice

The Paper Magician Series

The Paper Magician

The Glass Magician

The Master Magician

The Plastic Magician

Other Novels

The Fifth Doll

Magic Bitter, Magic Sweet

Followed by Frost

Veins of Gold

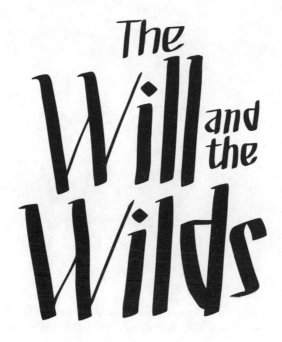

The Will and the Wilds

AUTHOR OF *THE PAPER MAGICIAN*

CHARLIE N. HOLMBERG

47NORTH

Text copyright © 2020 by Charlie N. Holmberg LLC
All rights reserved.

Published by 47North, Seattle

www.apub.com

Amazon, the Amazon logo, and 47North are trademarks of Amazon.com, Inc., or its affiliates.

ISBN-13: 9781542005005
ISBN-10: 1542005000

Cover design by Micaela Alcaino

Printed in the United States of America

To Andy, my silently brave sister who always follows her heart.

CHAPTER 1

Most mystings find the smell of lavender repulsive.

A chill wind snakes its way through the wildwood, whispering of misfortunes to come. My hands pause against moist soil between oon berry and rabbit's ear in my mysting garden as I turn to face it, listening. It's the height of summer in Fendell, but one can never be sure what will emerge from the wildwood, or when.

But the stone dangling from the silver bracelet around my wrist is quiet, assuring me the wind is simply wind. Still, I feel the instinct to move, to stretch out my legs, which have cramped from tending my herbs, so I stand and brush my hands across the apron over my skirt. Stepping out the narrow gate, I wind around the house to the open cellar door, which leads to the earthy room where thousands of mushrooms grow. There are always some ready for harvest, while others are just sprouting from their mulch and soil.

"Papa?" I call down into the darkness. "I'm finished. We can go."

"Go where?"

"To the market. You asked this morning. You're collecting the mushrooms?"

A pause. "Oh. Yes. Here I come."

A moment later the ladder creaks, and my father emerges from the shadows, a thickly woven basket hanging from the crook of his elbow. Gray, white, and brown mushrooms fill it, matching the speckling of his beard. He's kept the mushrooms sorted, which will save us time in town.

"Come." I take his hand and brush soil from his knuckles. "Remind me to get some lye."

He won't, but I know he appreciates the sentiment.

The people of Fendell will never know the truth behind my father's weakened faculties, though it is a grand story, the sort a bard could sing a dozen verses about. Papa was a swordsman for Lord Eris, and when I was but a babe, he was recruited into the king's army to answer the threat of a mysting army intent on conquering the mortal realm. A rare threat, as mystings can only withstand our plane temporarily before it begins to consume them, just as the monster realm would consume us. But he heeded the call, and after the threat was quelled, he stole into the monster realm and thieved a charm from a warlord there. Something to protect his daughter against the mystings, as mystings had killed her mother.

The stone, dark as old blood, or perhaps wet rust, swings from my bracelet as I lead my father into town. I don't think the realm of monsters damaged his mind enough for him to get lost on such a simple path, but I won't chance it.

Fendell opens before us. It's not a place one gradually strolls into, but one that happens suddenly. Follow the dirt path parallel to the wildwood, and homes and shops, wood walls and stone fences burst into being. The path widens to a road lined with linen tents and wooden stalls selling the day's wares. A large well sits near its center, and above it reaches a two-story tower. The town watch only rings the tower bell to warn others when mystings are spotted leaving the forest. It hasn't sounded for nearly six months. Not because mystings aren't nearby, but because they go unseen. Fortunately, large groups of humans repulse most mystings. It is the lone traveler that need be wary.

The crowd is abrupt and busy, and stepping into it is like falling into deep water, with the same currents and garbled sounds.

The Lovesses' booth is one of the closest to us in the market, and perhaps that's why my father chooses to do business with them. Or maybe he favors them because the Lovess family doesn't side-eye us as much as the others do, marking us the strange, reclusive pair who live so close to the wildwood, too far from the protection of the town. The man whose mind slips more than it stays, and the girl who knows more about mystings than any person should.

I take the basket from my father and approach the long tables beneath a white linen tent to keep off bug and breeze. The eldest Lovess son manages the rows of fruits and vegetables, and I offer him a smile as I near. He returns the gesture, and it warms me through. Tennith Lovess is of an age with me, twenty, and is as fine a boy as Fendell could produce. Kind in heart and young in face, with arms and shoulders that tell of hard work on his family's farm. He is fair in his bargaining and treats Papa well. I'd respect him for that alone, even if he weren't wonderful to look at.

"What have you today?" He leans over the table to take my basket.

"I'm afraid I haven't counted them."

"That's fine." His fingers dance over the mushrooms, his lips moving silently as he counts the harvest. "Had someone not a quarter hour ago asking for these. Glad to have them."

He sets the basket down and retrieves a bag of coin. He counts out eight coppers and passes them to me. His warm and calloused fingertips brush my palm, sending tingles across my skin.

"Thank you."

He smiles, but I mustn't linger. My father has crossed the road and is staring intently at a chicken. I take his elbow. "I do need lye. Thank you, Papa."

"Yes. Don't forget." He nods.

I walk him down the road. We're mostly overlooked by the town. I pay no attention to the folk, for I've learned, mostly, not to care for the opinion of others, as they have never cared for mine. Though we have lived in Fendell for all the life I can remember, many of the people here are strangers. I know the wildwood better than I know their faces. The fact should sadden me, but it doesn't. And yet, when I pass two young men laughing with each other, I grit my teeth against a pang of jealousy. Ever since my grandmother's passing, there has been little laughter in my home. My father is too nostalgic and forgetful for jokes, and perhaps I am too prudish to make my own.

Pulling my attention from the lads, I approach the soap maker and select his least expensive lye. I have lavender in the mysting garden if I want to smell fair, and it helps that many species of mysting find lavender repulsive. I offer my coin. Papa pulls me toward another vendor, gesturing to a goat shank.

A cool sensation, like that of melting snow in the first weeks of spring, runs up my arm and dances across my shoulders, causing me to shiver. The silver bracelet around my left wrist feels heavy, and I swing its dark, egg-shaped stone into my palm. It's cold as deep soil against my skin, leaving me with no doubt.

There is a mysting nearby.

Though I've cultivated an interest in mystings, planted by my grandmother years ago, I shudder. Monsters are only ever fascinating from afar. I lift my head from the butchered meat my father examines and look around, acutely aware of the sound of my own breathing. We are in the heart of Fendell, surrounded by townspeople and their homes. It's unlikely a mysting will show itself in such a crowd, but the suddenness of the chill concerns me. As though the creature entered the plane nearby, and didn't merely wander within reach of the charm's senses.

How close is this one? I massage the stone, coaxing its answer.

My father notices my stillness right away. "Where?" he asks. "What?"

The only faces I see are human, a few of them peering back at me with confusion, or maybe disdain for the odd girl and her senseless father. They are easy to forgive. They do not have a Telling Stone. They do not know what I know.

I shake my head in response to my father's question. I'm unsure. My father quits his purchase and, with his hand on my back, leads me away from the market.

"Let's head home," he murmurs. A breeze picks up bits of his dark-blond hair and tosses them across his eyelashes. A few strands stick. Some of my own darker locks brush against the stubble of his jaw. With my pinky finger I pull them free, letting the hair fall back against my chin.

I slide away from him just enough to grasp his calloused hand—a hand that once knew the weight of a king's sword, but no more, thanks to me. "Papa, home is this way." I tug him south.

He pauses—"Yes. It is."—and follows me. All the while my free hand stiffens with cold. The Telling Stone pulses against my skin like a second heartbeat. I keep it pressed to my hip, concealing it, for such a powerful charm would sell at a grand price, and there are those who wouldn't think twice about stealing it for their own gain. We skirt a wagon, two men on horseback, and a young girl selling wreaths of oon berry to keep away evil. I think to warn them of the mysting nearby, but I've done so before to ill effect. The townsfolk murmur about me, I know, even more so because my warnings have always come to naught. Never has a mysting outright attacked Fendell. The thieves who creep about in the night are usually human, and although a dead traveler is occasionally found in the road, most would sigh and say it is the consequence of venturing so close to the wildwood after dark.

The road whittles back down to a footpath, and then to a trail of trodden weeds.

The knuckles of my left hand ache, but now that we're away from the crowd, I sense the mysting clearly. "Deep in the wildwood," I whisper, though I do not think anyone else is close enough to overhear me. Closing my eyes, I turn my thoughts from the rhythm of my father's steps to the cadence of the Telling Stone's pulse. I grit my teeth as another shudder courses through my body, then open my eyes. "A gobler."

"Gobler?" Papa repeats. "Here?"

I nod and release the stone, though warmth is slow to return to my hand—the silver chain of the bracelet conducts the stone's chill across my wrist. Goblers do not frequent our part of the country. They are not suited for the wildwood, preferring colder lands with plenty of water. But I know it is a gobler the stone has sensed, and never in my years of wearing it has it led me astray. More likely than not, this creature will vanish into the wood like so many before it, never crossing my path.

But the day a person becomes complacent with mystings is the day her safety is forfeit.

I quicken my feet, seeking the refuge of our home, which is not clustered in safety with the rest of the town. Ours is a robust house, built by my father during a time of peace in Amaranda. It's constructed of the sturdiest trees from the wildwood and is a little larger than most of the residences in town. At the time of its construction, my father made good coin and possessed all his faculties.

To understand my father's sacrifice, why he risked so much for a simple stone, one need only look to the horror in which I came into this world.

My mother, Elefie Rydar, was a beautiful woman, or so I am told. I have her eyes and hair, though I've heard she was much taller, with a strong jaw, while I inherited the heart-shaped face of my paternal grandmother. She was a silversmith's daughter, and my father a swordsman for Lord Eris. They fell in love quickly and wed, and my father purchased this land on the border of Fendell, green and fertile as all earth is near the wildwood.

My mother loved the forest. It is easy to love, even with the whispers of mystings weaving through the trees. For one with knowledge, a mysting is no more harmful than a snake or a bear; if you take precautions and avoid them, you can live in relative peace. But even the cautious can fall to the sting of venom or stumble upon a mother and her cub. Thus was the story of my mother.

They were grinlers. They lack speech and common understanding, but their deficiencies in intelligence are made up for in ferocity. Small, feral creatures, they reach between knee and hip height, with wild, matted manes that encompass their entire bodies. Their thin limbs end in humanlike hands that sport long, terrible claws, and their rounded snouts bear short tusks, or possibly thick fangs. They travel in packs like wolves, but any similarity ends there. I would prefer wolves to grinlers. Wolves are more merciful.

My paternal grandmother lived only a few miles away until she died some seven years ago, and my mother went to visit her, cutting through the wildwood. I don't know why the grinlers came so close to the forest's edge. They're drawn to the smell of blood, so perhaps my mother had injured herself. It was not her monthly time, for she was eight months pregnant. But the grinlers found her, and despite wielding the silver knife my father had gifted her, they overtook her.

My father must have known in his gut, or perhaps they had traveled together and gotten separated—he's never been able to clarify, due either to grief or to the missing parts of his mind. He fought the beasts off, but was too late to rescue my partially eaten mother. You see, grinlers do not wait for their prey to die before feasting.

Her life was gone, but her belly moved, and so by the bloodied hands of my father did I emerge into life, barely large enough to survive on my own. I have never sought details of that part of the story. My imagination is enough. So are the imaginations of the townsfolk, for they have numerous versions of this tale, all of which end in my father's mind breaking in sorrow.

He was sorrowful. He still is. But that is not what broke him.

When the king heard rumors of a mysting army, my father was recruited to his side. The war was brief, a short sequence of battles in which my father fought valiantly, or so his medals testify. He heard of the Telling Stone—from whom, I am not sure—and dared to venture into the monster realm to retrieve it. I imagine his grief emboldened him, as did his fear for me, for he succeeded in stealing the stone that now hangs from my wrist. For that, I name him a hero. For me, he gave up much. Too much.

Mankind cannot linger in the monster realm, just as mystings cannot abide here long. Our worlds are too different, and they reject those who don't belong. My father stayed too many hours in the monster realm, and in exchange, it claimed the sharper bits of his mind. And so he retired here with the Telling Stone, learned to grow mushrooms, and the rest of our lives have been uneventful.

I consider this as we step over the curls of oon berry that surround our log home like a fence, though the plants grow only a foot high. Mystings cannot cross oon berry without great suffering. All the mystings I know of, at least, and I know of many.

Yet worry over the gobler rankles me as I help my father get comfortable in a chair by the hearth. They are predators, as nearly all mystings are, and would not traipse the wildwood without a sure purpose to be there. I pinch the icy Telling Stone in my fingers, not liking how close the mysting is. But it seems to be wandering, so perhaps it is simply lost.

I set the mostly empty basket in the kitchen and walk down the hall to my room. It is simply furnished, with a narrow bed, an old bookshelf, a nightstand, and the rocking chair my mother would have nursed me in. On the shelf is a small collection of books, one of which is written in my grandmother's hand. Her mysting journal, in which she recorded all her knowledge and theories about the nether creatures that lurk in the wildwood. Another, larger volume is written in my own script—a tome in which I transcribed all my grandmother's notes and sketches, sandwiched between my own. Theories I've learned from townsfolk, passing travelers, ramblings, or my father's half-forgotten stories. Some of the notes are pure speculation garnered from studying footprints or the like in the wildwood. Once, and only once, I used the Telling Stone to track down a rooter for my research, and thus I have an accurate sketch. I've never tried the tactic to spy on any other species. I value my life too much.

I've attempted to share this knowledge, just as I've shared the warnings of the Telling Stone, but it's earned me nothing but strange looks in town. Needless to say, I've learned to keep my findings private.

I would desperately love to leave Fendell, to attend the king's college, or even a lesser school, where I could earn credibility as a writer or a researcher. Where I could establish a background that would demand others listen to my theories or, better yet, allow me to publish them. Yet my education as a girl was not prestigious, and there aren't enough mushrooms in Amaranda to afford the cost. Those impediments aside, I am a woman, and most advanced schools would never look at me twice, even if I were privately educated and rich. Fear of leaving Papa on his own pins me here as well, for it would take effort greater than I possess to convince him to leave this house. To leave my mother's grave site.

Pushing the thoughts from my mind, I look through my half-filled book for the page on goblers and study the lightly sketched picture of one, the charcoal lines half-worn from rubbing against its sister page. Chubby things, with too much flesh gathered beneath their wide, rounded heads. I've never seen one with my own eyes, and I don't care to change that fact.

I read my grandmother's notes. Though they're in my hand, they flow through my mind in her voice. *Goblers are vengeful monsters who mark their prey with a simple touch. If one fails to destroy it, the mark guarantees others will hunt it down. They dislike pokeweed, tusk nettle, and red salt; all of the listed will help to nullify a gobler mark.*

Shuddering, I press my fingertip to the list. Pokeweed is a desert plant, but tusk nettle grows in my garden, and there are several stones of red salt in the cellar. I set the book back on the shelf, stoke the fire in the hearth, and set a kettle over the flames to ready some tea for my father.

"Where are you going?" he asks when I pull on my gardening gloves. My left hand is stiff with the Telling Stone's bite, but I dare not take off the bracelet.

"To harvest some tusk nettle. To secure the house. I opened the window so you'll hear me."

He grabs the armrests of his chair, as though ready to stand, but lets out a great sigh and relaxes back. "Quickly, Enna."

Promising swiftness with a nod, I step outside, scanning the wildwood as is my habit. Its secrets are cocooned beneath sun-warmed trees and the flitting shadows of flapping bird wings. Were I better able to defend myself, or perhaps had I academic funding for a team of armed men, I could walk deep into that forest and study its darkest workings. How beneficial would it be to mankind to know how to turn back a fevered pack of grinlers? To close a portal made from within the realm of monsters? Or, even, to communicate with mystings forbidden the gift of speech?

I glance back to the house, to the open window. To my father. Perhaps I'll take those risks someday. But not today. Today, I guard against a gobler.

My mysting garden is small—a grave-sized plot I dug into the earth outside the kitchen when I was thirteen and had newly inherited Grandmother's journal. Half of the plants within its fenced perimeter were harvested from the wildwood; the rest I gathered as bulb or seed from local farmers and the town apothecary. Oon berry and lavender are plentiful in these parts; the blue thistle cost me dearly.

I step through the gate and lift my skirt—dark gray and perhaps a little uncomely, but the desire to draw attention has never been mine, and simple lines are the easiest to sew. I seek out the cluster of tusk nettle and kneel in the soil beside it. Tusk nettle is a weed and would overcome the entire garden if left untended, so I'm glad for the excuse to cut back its broad, spindly leaves. I gather a basketful, pull a few weeds springing up by the topis root, and make my way to the cellar.

Our cellar is large, expanded by my now-deceased paternal grandfather after Papa gave up his sword. Great shelves fill the majority of it, reaching from floor to ceiling, sporting bits of dead log, moss, lichen, and composted soil. We grow four varieties of mushroom. The fungi button up from the beds, catching the light as I descend the ladder.

The narrow space not occupied by mushrooms holds our food stores, meager preparations for next winter, dried herbs, vegetables pickled and pickling. A shelf at the end contains a collection of wood and stones, many taken from my grandmother's home. Among them is a large chunk of red salt, which looks like rough, pink crystal. It weighs down my arm and crushes the tusk nettle in my basket. I'm a little out of breath when I ascend the ladder.

When tusk nettle leaves and salt fill the windows and line the doorways of the house, I walk the perimeter of our property to be sure the oon berry guard has not been split, then weave together a few stems where the shrubs are thinning. Returning inside, I warm my left hand by the fire and make my father's tea.

"No worries now," I say, though the Telling Stone persists in its chill. I eye the sheathed sword atop the mantel—its worn hilt, the depiction of a great stag in the center of the scabbard. Straightening, I brush dust from its length with my fingers. "I'll make us some stew," I offer, and wipe my fingers on my dress.

I prepare lunch, sweep the kitchen, and tend to the daily chores. All the while, the Telling Stone hangs cold from my wrist. As the sun makes its descent, I lock the windows and doors, then hide away by the laundry and clutch the stone between both palms. I don't know the language of sorcery—it is very old and no longer regarded with the esteem it once was—but somehow the stone speaks to me, filling my thoughts with its shadowy knowledge. A gobler, and it's close. Closer than before.

But we will be safe. I've taken all the precautions, and mystings don't like trouble. It's easier to prey upon an unsuspecting stranger than a fortified house, and we are not so very far from town. There's no reason my father and I should be on this creature's agenda.

Still, I double-check the nettle leaves and salt before settling into a cold and restless sleep.

It is the clamoring of the larger salt crystals hitting the floor that stirs me from half-lidded slumber. My left arm is frozen. I can barely move my elbow, my shoulder aches, and my fingers are curved into claws. The gobler is near. Very near.

Shallow breaths burn my throat. I throw off my blanket and search for the silver dagger tucked beneath the mattress—the very same one my mother once carried. It did not save her, yet I clutch it in my one warm hand.

Creaking boards sound in the living room. The stone whispers that they do not bend under the weight of my father. But if it's the gobler, how did it get in? Why? No mysting could be so desperate.

Thankful the fire in the front room still burns, I slip from my room, inching along the hallway. My hands shake with both fear and the ice emanating from my bracelet.

Peeking into the living area, I see a thick form blocking part of the glowing hearth. Shorter than myself, and much wider. The dying flames highlight thick rolls of blubber around neck and wrists. It's almost humanoid in that it has a head, two arms, and two legs, but the rest is pure monster. The gobler turns, searching, its large eyes shifting back and forth, its cavernous nostrils flaring. Wide gray lips roll above a nearly nonexistent chin. Burns and bluish blood mar its skin from where it encountered my wards.

Its dark fist-sized eyes land on me and widen. As I lift my dagger, it launches.

My scream echoes through the house.

The beast is too nimble for its size, and it plows into me, knocking air from my lungs as we collide with the hallway wall. My fingers tighten on the hilt of my blade, but the mysting presses against my right shoulder, and I can't bring my arm around to stab it. A desperate cry rips from my throat.

Yet the gobler's focus is not on my face. It grabs my frozen arm with stubby fingers, and I feel an unnatural heat from its touch—a heat that might be painful, were my skin not so permeated with cold. Lifting my appendage, it eyes the bracelet on my wrist and the deep, blood-red stone hanging from it.

I hear a swoosh of movement through air, and the gobler's horrible face tightens before going lax. Its fingers loosen. The mysting slides down me like a drunken lover until its fetid fat puddles on the floor.

Looking up, I realize for the first time how hard I'm breathing, how angrily my blood pumps. My father stands behind me in his nightclothes, his hair mussed, his own breathing labored. He holds his sword in both hands, and down its blade runs bluish blood.

He brings the sword around, his muscles remembering their training, and stabs the gobler again for good measure. The mysting doesn't even flinch. The first blow had been true.

Tears escape my eyes as I leap over the body and run into my father's arms. He keeps the sword in one hand and embraces me with the other. Weeping into his collar, I bless this moment of clarity and swiftness.

Yet though my left arm begins to warm, the Telling Stone quivers, warning of other dangers lurking behind the veil of the wildwood.

CHAPTER 2

*It is painful for mystings to cross oon berry. Weaving a circle
of the thorny plants around your home will act as a proficient
safeguard.*

The gobler left a mark. An incomplete handprint mars the flesh of my
left forearm, a deep gray that is almost black. It doesn't hurt, and the
skin feels no different to the touch, but the mark is undeniable. I've
no idea how long it will last, but per the warning in my grandmother's
notes, I soak a cloth in red salt dissolved in water and wrap my arm,
hindering the magic that would call other goblers to me. Between my
precaution and the fact that goblers do not frequent the wildwood, I
hope I'll be safe.

I add a footnote to the entry concerning goblers, then turn to a
clean page to sketch the mark. Once I've finished, I measure the mark
and jot down the numbers.

Grandmother's notes did not indicate whether the gobler mark
would fade. Part of me is hopeful the salt soak will banish it. Another,
foolish, part of me hopes it will not, for no one could doubt my credibility with such evidence to show. Closing my book, I let my mind
wander for just a moment, imagining the volume in my hands as a true

published work, studied by scholars. All of whom would believe my research, for I'd have garnered a reputation at a fine college . . . then I blink the fancy away and set my thoughts to the household.

I suppose it is fortunate that I prefer prudent dresses, all of which are long sleeved.

My father is confused in the morning, and I carefully explain to him what happened the night before, so as not to overexcite or concern him. He accepts this with clarity and, after cleaning his blade and returning it to its place on the mantel, builds a litter out of rope and wood planks and hauls the gobler's body back into the wildwood. What he does with it, I'm not sure. Perhaps he will leave it for wolves, or for grinlers.

My left arm is no longer ice, but the stone was cold when I awoke, and has gotten progressively colder. Another mysting is near. Never have I sensed two so close together. Clutching the Telling Stone in my fist, I step outside and walk toward the wildwood, kneading the stone, urging it to tell me what approaches.

After some time, it does. A gobler.

A shiver of my own dances across my shoulders, and I rest my hand over the mark left by the first gobler. Surely it is a coincidence, unless my grandmother was mistaken about the red salt. Or perhaps this new creature does not sense the mark, and is merely looking for its predecessor. I thought goblers were loners, but my knowledge of them comes solely from my grandmother. Folk around here have little experience with their kind. All I know is that the stone grows colder, the gobler closer.

I head back to the house, into the thin protection of herbs and salts. The first gobler had been interested in my Telling Stone. There are many charms and baubles that whisper of the nearness of mystings. Why mine is of any particular consequence is beyond me, and there is nothing in my grandmother's writings to answer my unspoken questions.

The first thing I do is gather new cloth and, after stripping away its thorns, sew tusk nettle into it as best I can.

I pull up my sleeve and study the murky print on my arm. Rub my thumb over it, as though it could be wiped away. The salt has faded its edges, but otherwise it remains unchanged.

I'm so absorbed in the mark that I don't hear my father approach, only startle when he takes my hand in his to study the mark himself. He twists it this way and that, his forehead wrinkling. I can see the war inside the mind, old knowledge battering against the fog left by the monster realm. How dearly I wish I could look into his eyes and piece together his memories for him. To have him be whole, and to see the monster realm for myself, for despite my fascination, I would never dare go there to study it.

His hand slides down to the Telling Stone, and he frowns at the temperature. "Another comes?"

I soak the new cloth in salt water. "Gobler."

He helps me wrap my arm. "If they are after you, that mark will help them find us again." He rubs his temples. I wonder if my grandmother's entry on goblers came from my father's knowledge of the monster realm. Masking my thoughts and fears, I take my father by the elbow and lead him to his chair.

"Does he want the stone?" I ask, crouching by his side. "He seemed to want the stone."

My father shakes his head, but in disagreement or confusion, I can't tell.

I grasp his hand. Recently cleaned, even the nails scrubbed. I mull over my words and tamp down the anxiety in my chest. "I can get rid of it." The stone is a treasure and a shield, but it is not worth the danger of safeguarding.

"No."

"There are other means of—"

He turns his hand about and ensnares my fingers. His eyes lock on to mine. "You have lived longer than she did now." He means my mother. "Because of that stone. And I lost . . ." His eyes glaze. "What did I lose, Elefie?"

"Enna, Papa."

He lets go of my hand and breathes deeply through his nose. "Enna. I sacrificed . . . so you wouldn't . . ."

Standing, I rest a hand on his shoulder. "It's all right. I understand." The talisman is a rare one, stolen from the very realm it's designed to protect against. There are many types of Telling charms, but none so accurate as this one. I palm the stone's coldness, wondering why a mysting would batter itself against my wards to obtain it, when in all my twenty years, it has attracted little attention from my neighbors, and none from the other realm. Surely the gobler was after something else entirely, and the stone had merely caught its eye.

My gaze drifts up from the stone to the silver bracelet encircling my wrist. The circle. Sketches copied from my grandmother's journal spin through my mind.

A summoning . . .

"There are other mystings, Papa," I say, tasting each word before letting it pass my lips. I step around the chair to face him. "Intelligent mystings, less . . . harmful ones, who might prey on a beast like the gobler. Force it and any others to leave."

His expression closes. "They're all demons. Evil."

"But they can be bargained with." My own grandmother once hired a rooter—a docile, forest-dwelling mysting—to grow the great tree wall that surrounds her house to this day. As good a protection from predators as any, although I do not know what it asked of my grandmother in exchange, just that they made a bargain. No mysting knows the word *charity*.

Not all human dealings with mystings have been entirely hostile. I suspect it was a mysting who warned the king twenty years ago about a possible war between realms, and a mysting who first spoke to my father of the Telling Stone around my wrist. But for every mysting who's willing to cooperate, there are five others who will eat the flesh off your bones, if you but give them the chance.

It would be safer, perhaps, to hire a swordsman, someone with more wit about him than my father. But this is Fendell. There are no sell-swords here, and there's no time to request one to come from afar, even if we had the money.

A sore lump that bears my mother's name rises in my throat, but I swallow it down. I will not become like her. Nor will I let my father meet her fate. We will not sit in this house and wait for another gobler to attack us.

"We will leave, then."

My father looks up at me. "Leave? Is it market day?"

The conversation is slipping from him. "Papa, there is a gobler on its way. If you will not let me give up the Telling Stone or hire a creature to protect us, then we must leave."

My father's hands grip the armrests of his chair. "Elefie's grave . . ."

His eyes are moist, so I back down in silence, excusing myself to my room. My mother's grave is not the only one out there. My father's parents are also buried on our land. My father will not leave them unless absolutely necessary. One reason of many why even the closest college, in Caisgard, is beyond my reach. My father is not so addled as to be unable to care for himself, but I would not leave him. Not for anything.

And so I need to find another way.

Thumbing through my notes, I find what I need. I linger on the page depicting a summoning ring, first drawn in charcoal to copy my grandmother's hand, and later outlined in ink. An eight-pointed star made of two overlapping squares, each point touching an encompassing circle. A summoning circle can be made with a number of things, but some substances provide stronger magic than others. Blood, for instance, is a strong summoner. Especially human blood.

Cringing, I close the book. It rests in my lap for a long time, my fingers drumming against its worn cover. Long enough for the shadows to shift in my room. I think, ponder, until I've no thoughts but one.

The Telling Stone has grown nearly as cold as it was last evening. The gobler is coming.

In the kitchen, I grab a basket, putting into it a cask three-quarters full of oil, flint and steel, my silver dagger, and all the coin I can find. In my father's room, I retrieve my mother's gold-link necklace and two of Papa's war medals. My mother's wedding ring stays in its safe place in the top drawer of my father's old dresser. Papa may not notice these other valuables missing, but he would notice the ring's absence.

Putting a towel over the items, I make a plate of bread and cheese for my father and hand it to him. "Here you are. I'll go collect the milk from the Lovesses."

He cocks a brow at me. "The milk . . . ? Our collection day is tomorrow, is it not?"

I'm surprised he remembers. It seems almost cruel to take the small victory from him, but I say, "No, no, it's today. You just asked me to fetch it." Guilt worms between my breasts, but my resolve to live, and keep my father alive, is stronger.

"Oh. Yes. Thank you, Enna. The stone?"

Drawing my arm back, I let the dangling stone slip beneath my sleeve. I grit my teeth against a shiver. "Warm. I'll return soon."

He nods, and I escape.

Though the wildwood is a strong emerging ground for mystings, it is a beautiful place, and I know its border well. Despite the chill running up my arm, I clutch the Telling Stone in my aching hand, waiting for it to warn me of more otherworldly creatures. For now, there is only the gobler.

I trek into the wildwood, heading southeast, away from the town and, hopefully, from any of the townsfolk. First, because I theorize the less intelligent—and possibly more violent—mystings will not port into the wildwood so close to human civilization. Any mysting is a danger to a human, yes, but a group of armed humans is a danger to any mysting. The location may scare away a mysting who would kill me on sight, such as a grinler. Second, if I were seen conversing with mystings, my neighbors would ostracize my father and me for good, no matter how wanted our mushrooms are. There are some lines that simply cannot be crossed. Third, I do not wish to draw unwanted attention to any of the townsfolk—although this is a risk I willingly take, no one else should have to suffer for it.

I find a relatively flat, clear space between wild trees. After securing a stick, I carefully trace a circle in the dirt, stamping it out and starting again when the line doesn't curve right. Within it, I draw the eight-pointed star. I trace over the lines, deepening them, before carefully pouring enough oil into the shallow trenches to fill the entire symbol. I will offer no blood to the monster realm, but I will trade them fire.

I work the flint and steel over an old seedpod until it catches, then light the summoning circle aflame. The smoke burns my sinuses, and I have to shut my eyes against the light. But the fire is short lived, and soon a smoldering star stares up at me, dark and angry and *empty*.

Pressing a hand to my chest to calm my heart, I step back as far as the witnessing trees will allow me and snatch up my basket. I draw my dagger immediately. The moment I see even a partial mysting that wants meat more than discussion, I'll strike.

For a moment, I think my spell did not work, and I study the ashy lines to determine why. But as the tiny embers of grass and clover blacken, a glint of pale-blue light suffuses the marks. The chill in my Telling Stone deepens until it burns. Gasping, I pull my sleeve beneath my bracelet. The sensation of being watched by someone else sends a tingle across my scalp.

Twisting around, I see him leaning against the trunk of a great oak, a wicked grin bright beneath blazing, yellow eyes.

CHAPTER 3

Red salt will keep away rodyns, goblers, hepters, and any plant-eating mysting.

I stumble back until my heel breaks the ash of the summoning circle. My mind fails to categorize this mysting; had his likeness appeared in the pages of my grandmother's journal, I'm sure I would have remembered. My mind takes notes even as I struggle not to panic. Another new discovery! I must memorize everything.

He is humanoid, with the face and body of a man, but his eyes are too bright, and I've never beheld a human man, woman, or child with anything resembling their fierce yellow color. He has a strong yet slender jaw and a sturdy nose and brow. Pale red hair hangs over his shoulder in a loose tail. A flowing, angular tunic, or perhaps a wrapped cloak, covers his shoulders, but exposes his left side and the subtle musculature beneath his peachy, too-human skin. Strange pants made of layered leather—*not* bovine leather—and studs cover his legs. He wears no shoes over feet that resemble the hooves of a horse, and a wicked tail writhes behind him, the asymmetrical, pointed end of which looks sharper than the dagger in my hand.

But what stands out the most about this creature is not the make of his clothes or the unnatural brilliance of his eyes. Not even the equine shape of his unshod feet. It is the great horn that protrudes from the center of his forehead, steep and pointing nearly skyward, made of bone or coral or . . . I cannot name its tightly spiraled substance, but it looks like the horn of fabled unicorns, straight and strong and ending in a deadly point. Though the mysting is of normal height for a man, his terrible horn must be three feet long, giving him the visage of a giant.

"Wh-What are you?" I manage, trying to find my wits, for *I* must strike the bargain, and I cannot appear cowardly.

The mysting raises a red-tinted eyebrow and glances over his shoulder. He tilts his head to the side, and I watch the menacing horn shift with him. "You can see me?" His voice is a man's voice, with the slightest edge of a growl.

"Of course I can see you. I summoned you." *Possible invisibility.* I'll theorize later why my summoning has thwarted such a spell.

He laughs and sets his hands on his hips. "I only came to see who was foolish enough to build a summoning circle in the wildwood." His grin fades, and he studies me anew—my chin-length hair, my mother's blue eyes, my plain dress and shoes. "You should not be able to see me."

I twist my wrist to hide my bracelet. "Well, I do, and I wish to strike a deal."

He smirks. His canines are slightly pronounced, and the tip of one touches his lower lip. "And what benefit could interest me in making deals with mortals?"

"To sate your curiosity, apparently."

He cocks that eyebrow again, and the corrupt smile looms on his lips. There have been so few smiles in my home since my grandmother's passing, and seeing such a bold one aimed toward me is unsettling. "Hmmmmm, perhaps. You're no witch or mysting hunter, girl. What purpose do you have for dabbling with the star? I could kill you, and only the trees would hear your screams."

I clench my hands into fists, the Telling Stone at the center of the left, and step away from the summoning circle, willing myself to look taller than I am. "We are not so deep into the wildwood."

"Do your screams carry far?" His eyes glint. He thinks himself clever. "I'm more suited to placing one man's wallet in another's pocket or dousing a wedding gown in pig's blood. If that's what you want, I'm listening."

A trickster, then. I've half a page dedicated to them in my book. But it's unlikely a mysting built as he is, with so deadly a horn, is satisfied with mere teasing. "I have summoned you"—I force my voice to be level—"and you have come. You will help me."

My left hand is behind me, and on impulse, I reach back to pull my sleeve over the icy Telling Stone. My fingers tingle against its bite. I wonder if it's trying to warn me, or if I'm merely squeezing it too tightly. The mysting's brows draw together.

"Tell me your name," I try. "What you are."

"Maekallus," he answers, and his brow rises, almost like he's surprised he answered. "You don't know my kind, yet you want to barter with me? I'm a narval."

A narval! There *is* an entry for his kind in my book, copied from my grandmother's journal, but there is no picture to accompany it. It's a short entry, and I stretch my memory to recall what it says.

He steps forward, and it takes the full strength of my resolve to resist stepping back. He's a head taller than I am. I glance to the horn.

"What, exactly, do you want?" he asks.

I suck in a deep breath. "There is a gobler near my home."

"This *is* the wildwood, is it not?"

"Its companion attacked my house last night." I leave out its interest in the stone, which pulses cold into my hand, and the fact that it also attacked me. "I don't know why, but it ignored my wards, and I fear the other will strike soon. You'll find it in the wildwood, north." I point.

"A gobler, in these parts?"

"Were I lying, I would do better." I squeeze the stone.

His smirk returns. "All right, mortal. I'll make you a deal. I'll find this gobler for you, eliminate it, but I want something in return."

The moment of truth. The fingers of my right hand graze the silver dagger. "I have gold."

Maekallus snorts. "Oh no, I don't want gold. If you dare to take me as your champion, I will have a kiss."

The demand startles me enough that my basket slips down my arm, yet his words trigger my memory, and I recall with sudden clarity what my grandmother first penned on that aging page: *Beware the narvals, formed from the spilled blood of bastards. They feed upon souls, and will steal one with a willing kiss.*

"No." I plant my feet. "I am no witch, but I am no fool. I will not give you my soul for this simple protection."

He laughs. "Your soul? I asked only for a kiss."

"You suppose me naive."

"It will not take your soul," he says, and the Telling Stone shivers. To warn me against the approaching gobler, or this narval's charm? I cannot expect him to be wooed by my beauty, for while I've never thought myself ugly, I am not so fair as to inspire interest in the men of my town. Even if I were, I doubt a mysting, even a humanoid one, would desire someone so prim. As I consider, Maekallus confirms my first thought by saying, "It doesn't have to be *your* kiss, mortal."

I squeeze the chilly stone of my bracelet until my arm aches. "I will give you gold. Two medallions, one now, and one after the deed is done. And more if this gobler has further companions."

My hand tingles, and Maekallus bows his head. "As you wish."

I'm shocked to hear the words from his mouth, but I dare not wait for him to change his mind. Releasing the stone, I reach into the basket for my father's war medals.

"Give me your hand," he says, and reaches his own forward. "There is a sense of ceremony about these things." His tone is so lighthearted, like we're old chums exchanging pleasantries.

I hesitate. Draw the dagger from the basket and settle it in my cold grip. Maekallus laughs at this, but I ignore the patronizing sound. I extend my right hand.

He grasps it, and a sharp pain tears through my palm. I gasp and wrench away. A three-inch slash opens the skin of my palm from below my little finger to the base of my thumb. Blood seeps from its lips. My teeth cage a protest, but I see a similar cut on Maekallus's hand. His blood, too, is red.

"So it is sealed. I'll find your gobler, and with that, I'll find you." He tips his head toward my bleeding hand and slips backward between the trees. When I shift to see him depart, my eyes find only the depth of the wood.

I inspect my hand, frowning at its injury. The towel from my basket becomes its bandage, and I notice that, though Maekallus never reached for it, one of my father's medals is missing.

I stomp out the summoning ring with my feet, all the while pressing the towel into my hand, hoping the wound will not need to be stitched. When that is finished, I escape the space between trees and head home.

A sudden spike of frost shoots up my left arm, and I stumble. Finding my footing, I swing the stone into my hand and squeeze. I sense the gobler, and his nearness, but . . . no, it's different now.

The Telling Stone does not warn me of one gobler, but two.

CHAPTER 4

Some of the intelligent species of mysting are tricksters—
these are creatures more interested in toying with mortals
than feasting upon them. However, do not let that fact
convince you they are docile, for often a trickster will claim
something far more valuable than flesh.

Maekallus waits in the wildwood, crouched in a thick cluster of trees—the kind that refuse to part for any blade. He doesn't usually skulk about human forests. It amuses him more to sneak into mortals' taverns. Humans are such fun pawns when they're drunk. Day or night, they never see him, but the darkness tends to bring out the best players. Drunkards, lovers, thrill seekers. Nothing in the Deep is as fun as twisting the tedious lives of mankind.

Few humans tread this magicked place, especially at night. There are several places where the film separating the mortal world and the Deep grows thin, making it easier to cross from one to the other. The wildwood is one of those places, though Maekallus does not frequent it often. There are far more exotic places to see, far more willing people to devour.

He glances at the clotting cut along his palm. Mere gold, and only a couple of tokens at that. Why had he agreed? There isn't anything alluring about the human who'd engaged him. Well, that isn't entirely true. She was decent to look at, young, quick to think. Her soul would have been vivid. Perhaps its vigor would last longer than others' had. Perhaps he'd get to savor the addiction of human emotion for more than a few hours.

But to devour her requires a kiss, and one willingly given. Not simple tokens. Yet he made the bargain just the same—its mark stings the length of his palm. Maekallus doesn't consider himself noble, but a deal is a deal. He will hunt and slaughter this gobler quickly, then find better prey.

It has to be quick. The strain of the mortal realm already makes his skin itch.

The sky promises twilight, and so Maekallus slinks from the trees and ventures a little closer to the west edge of the wildwood. A gobler. He snorts. Fat, slow things, dull as river stones. Stupid creatures to be frightened of. Perhaps the gold tokens were a good deal after all.

The slash on his hand pulses with the power of the bargain, and through it he senses the location of the gobler the human woman had had in mind when she formed the pact. He will feel that pulse until he completes his promise. He treks, waiting for the ground to smooth. Comes around a boulder and hears the faint growl of a wolf drinking from a shallow brook. He pauses and glares at the beast. It sticks its tail between its legs and dashes away.

The predators of the mortal realm are so docile. No wonder humans lack the means to fight off the most pathetic of his kind. It's nice to play the predator. He isn't always in a position to do so. The Deep is home to creatures far more terrible than narvals and goblers.

A little farther along, the terrain levels. Bending forward, Maekallus takes off at a run, his obsidian-hard hooves pounding against the earth, wind stirring about his ears and shoulders. His tail whips back and curls up for balance, its deadly blade poised to strike.

His hand burns where the spell slices the skin. He makes a fist, relishing the sting. Too long without a soul, and even petty bargains are worth it for the vigor of the mark.

The blue, ashy light of twilight descends, blackening the trees. Good hunting, for Maekallus's eyes are keen in the dark. Close now. He can smell the blubbery *ka'pig*. He slows, reorients himself, and stalks through the brush. Not far from the border. The gobler certainly seems to have intentions with the humans tonight. Odd; their tastes usually run more aquatic.

The trees spread apart, forming an oblong glade. The pudgy shadow of the gobler is not difficult to find.

"Far from home," Maekallus chides as he steps into the glade. The gobler turns around, its large eyes bulging in the emerging starlight. Reaching to his forehead, Maekallus grips the base of his horn and pulls. A glimmer of light dances across his vision, and the horn comes loose from his forehead. His body quickly reorients its balance, and he hefts the horn as though it were a great sword. The separation is easier in the Deep than on the mortal plane. Here, the detachment hurts, and he will not be able to keep the magic going long. Fortunately, this will only take a moment.

The gobler sneers and draws a gleaming hook from beneath its folds of fat. "Do not meddle, narval," it says in the tongue of the Deep, its words garbled and heavy. The sounds of a choking bonehound.

"But I've been paid to." Maekallus lunges forward, jabbing his horn at the gobler's massive gut. The gobler swerves and grabs the "blade" with his silly hook, diverting it. But Maekallus is faster. He yanks the horn free and stabs again. The point pierces flesh easily, puncturing fat like it's no more than air. It slides deep into the gobler's chest until it stabs through the heart and hits spine. The gobler coughs and shakes as its bluish blood waters the forest floor. Maekallus jerks the horn free.

The gobler falls sideways. The horn gleams, burning off the blood, sending the stench of it across the glade. Maekallus wrinkles his nose.

With a squeeze of his fingers, the horn vanishes from his hand and returns to his forehead.

He winces and looks down at his palm, at the blood there. Not the gobler's—his, oozing from the cut that had sealed his bargain with the mortal woman. He flexes and relaxes his fingers. The gobler is dead. Why does the mark linger?

He senses a tug through the magic. The bargain pulls him toward his quarry. Still alive? Close, very close. Maekallus turns—

—just as a knife sticks him in the heart.

His breath whooshes out of him, and he keels forward as a gobler—a *second* gobler, the one the wound on his hand screams for him to defeat—wrenches his blade free and steps back, out of reach of Maekallus's horn. A thin thread of red light travels in the blade's wake. Maekallus sees it's a vuldor tusk, not forged metal. Realizing what it means, his insides turn brittle as shed snake skin.

"No!" he rasps, reaching forward, but that narrow light saps his strength. His elbow hits the ground. Still he reaches. Not that. *Anything but—*

Too late. The gobler plunges the tusk knife into the soil of the earth, and Maekallus feels a crippling *tug* deep inside him.

"Rot where you betrayed us," the gobler says with heavy, scratchy words. He spits on Maekallus's shoulder and flees deeper into the wildwood.

The telling pulse in Maekallus's hand vanishes with him.

CHAPTER 5

*Rabbit's ear, a thick variety of grass, will stave off infection
caused by magicked creatures or bespelled items.*

I lay my blankets by the hearth after my father retires for the night.
The fire burns bright, heating the house beyond what is comfortable.
I do not open any windows. I do not sleep. I write in my book all the
knowledge I gleaned from my meeting with Maekallus. Once that is
done, I lie down, clutching the hilt of my mother's silver dagger with
my right hand, while my left squeezes the Telling Stone until the stone
grows so cold I could not open my fingers if I wanted to.

I don't notice when the stone begins to warm, only that it has.
Sometime in the early morning, when the sun shines at the horizon, I
drop the stone and rub my knuckles, coaxing the muscles in my fingers
to soften. Both threats are gone. Maekallus kept the bargain.

I pick up my bedding and return it to my mattress, falling asleep
instantly atop it. The sun is full and bright when I wake to my father's
footsteps retreating from my room. I imagine he's checked on me several
times. I rarely sleep in so late.

After I dress and comb my hair, I feel the Telling Stone. Cool to
the touch. I focus on it, closing my eyes as I do so. It's Maekallus's presence that keeps the stone from warming entirely. He is either a ways off

or docile, if the stone's reaction is so mild. Yet those yellow eyes could never be described as docile. I immediately assume the first reason.

I returned all my borrowed things from my trek into the wildwood save my father's remaining medallion—the rest of the mysting's payment. With the gold in my pocket, I walk the perimeter of the house, searching the green spaces between old, tall trees. A fawn peeks out near me, and turns away just as quickly. The Telling Stone doesn't change.

Needing to busy myself to stave off uncertainty, I join my father in the cellar and tend the mushrooms. They grow with little fuss, but it benefits none of us if a poisonous breed gets into the mix, or if ripe mushrooms go unpicked and wrinkle on the log.

I do not work for long before a sharp pain dances across my palm. I excuse myself back to the house to treat the cut on my hand. Peeling back the bandage, I frown at the mark. I do not know how mysting bargains work, but the cut has not healed in the slightest. At least there is no sign of infection. I wash it, apply a thick layer of salve—in which I include rabbit's ear, in case the wound is magical—and bandage it anew. My father has not noticed the bandaging; if he does, I'll tell him I scraped my palm on the nail that sticks out of the ladder to the cellar. The one I've known to avoid all my life, but Papa will accept the lie. Even so, I dislike spinning another tale to fool him.

Days pass. I wait for the narval to collect his payment, but he doesn't come. No mysting can stay in the mortal realm for longer than a few days, but my Telling Stone neither warms nor cools.

My hand doesn't heal.

My father slips back into his easy routine, the stress of the first gobler incident forgotten, or at least buried. I try to make a new salve for my hand with lavender and tapis root. It staves off infection, but the cut doesn't so much as crust. I finally show it to my father, for he knows the basics of battlefield wounds. I give him the story of the nail, seasoned with truth—I say I injured my hand days ago, yet it has not healed. His brow pulls taut as he stitches my hand after liberally applying expensive thorrow herb, the seeds of which had been purchased from the apothecary in town. Despite the numbing medicine, the stitches smart. I try to bear them gratefully.

The fine thread holds the cut closed, but the wound does not heal. It grows more tender with each passing hour. Redder and darker. Two days later, with my father's medallion weighing my pocket, I venture back into the wildwood to close the bargain for myself. I do not go far before I hear footsteps coming my way. My Telling Stone remains unchanged. Regardless, I breathe a sigh of relief when it's another human who emerges between the trees.

"Tennith," I say, my start leaving me breathless. A thin beam of sunlight spills through the canopy and dances off his light hair. He's wearing leathers instead of his usual plain clothes, and four rabbits hang over his shoulder, back feet bound by rope. "You startled me."

He smiles, reminding me again of how handsome he is. The leathers hug his person far better than his loose farming clothes, highlighting the broadness of his shoulders. I have to remind myself not to stare.

"Enna, pleased to see you. What brings you into the wildwood?"

"I've traps of my own." I indicate the rabbits.

"I never thought you for a hunter. But . . . of course, it makes sense."

I shrug, though my father is more than capable of sending an arrow into the heart of a boar or deer. That is, if he doesn't first get lost. What we don't get from traps set close to the wildwood edge, we purchase from the town.

He eyes me a moment too long, but before I can think of something to fill the quiet space, he says, "If you're ever in need, I can—"

"Tennith, you're kind." And he is, and were my father and I in better repute, perhaps I would wear a comelier dress and try to catch his eye at fair time. I've dabbled with the fancy, but dreaming can hurt a heart, as Grandmother would always say. "I assure you we are well. There are only two of us to feed."

"Yes but . . . please remember the offer. Would you like escort?"

"Thank you, but no. Only one left to check."

Though his eyes linger on my empty hands, he nods and moves toward the town. I watch him go until the thickness of trees hide any evidence of his presence. Squeezing the Telling Stone, I walk deeper into the forest, focusing on the cool presence of a narval.

The stone doesn't lead me to the place where I burned a summoning circle into the forest floor, but away from it, northward, where I had last sensed the goblers. I tread carefully, scanning the trees, especially where they grow thick and force me from a direct path. A cool prickle warns of a mysting miles off. It vanishes minutes later. I cross a hunting trail and avoid tall grass for fear of traps, step over a brook, and climb up a short, rocky incline. The Telling Stone's temperature doesn't falter, and I wonder at it. Is Maekallus moving away from me at the same pace I'm moving toward him? The stone has previously acted in this manner with rooters, which are docile. And Maekallus is no such thing.

I reach an oval-shaped glade, where oak and aspen part. What I see instead makes me gasp. A grotesque creature is slumped near the center of the clearing, skin blackened and bubbling, though I can still make out arms and legs . . . and a long, stony horn patched with charcoal.

I press my hand against a trunk to keep myself upright. He smells of compost and something foul, something otherworldly. A thin tendril of light, like a glowing red spiderweb, leads from the black mass to the earth, disappearing amid grass and clover.

My voice is a near whisper. "Maekallus?"

The body shifts, head lifting to look at me. His face is patched with black, and a blackened bubble moves across his neck like boiling tar. His eyes are vivid and yellow, but one is heavy, the lid swollen. I see for the first time his cloak beside him, rent and smeared with black ooze.

"You," he says, the word heavy, venomous, and rasping. "You . . . are the bane of . . ."

He doesn't finish the sentence, for a wet cough erupts from his throat. He tries to stand, but his hooved foot slips in its own muck, and he falls to his knees.

I take a step forward, staying well out of his reach. "What's happened to you?"

He glares at me. "Your cursed realm . . ."

He doesn't have to complete the sentence. I need only look at him to know my realm is eating him alive. My lips part in surprise. This is why the stone's temperature has remained unchanged. Maekallus has been in the mortal realm this whole time.

"I have your payment here!" I pull the medallion from my pocket. "Good graces, Maekallus! It's not worth any coin to stay here!"

Maekallus laughs—at least, I believe it's a laugh. It's a wet, cruel sound, sticky and terrible. "You think . . . I suffer for you?" Another laugh. "Stupid mortal. I've been bound here by your quarry. Two . . . I killed the wrong . . ." He takes a deep, wheezing breath. "Did you not know? . . . The bargain is not . . . complete."

I stare at him, then at my bandaged hand. Carefully, I pull back the wrapping to look at the stitched cut, wiping off drops of fresh blood seeping from my father's handiwork. A dark ooze has begun to bleed through the bandage, not unlike what consumes Maekallus. I cringe and swallow, my stomach uneasy. "This? This is why it hasn't healed?" Behind him, I notice blue ink in the wild grass and realize it's gobler blood. Its body is nowhere to be seen.

The mysting shifts to face me. "It will not heal . . . The deal is not done." He pauses for a long moment, long enough that I think he won't speak again, but he does. "You will suffer more slowly than I do, but you will suffer."

"What do you mean?" I ask, cradling my sore hand to my chest. "And what did you mean about being bound here?"

"Can't . . . leave." He gestures weakly to the thread of light, beholding it as a thief would his executioner. Holding my breath, I inch closer.

Again staying out of his reach, I touch the light. My fingers pass right through it. I try to grab it, to break it, but it's no more tangible than sunlight.

"How do I break it?" I straighten, step back.

He snorts, coughs. "Find the gobler . . . kill it. Soon. If I die . . ."

He hacks, and black sludge hits the ground in front of him.

I cringe. "If you die, what?" I clench my wounded hand. "What will happen to the deal? To me?"

He hesitates. "You'll die, too."

My blood runs cold, and I back away from the monster, pulse quickening. "You lie."

I think I see him smirk through the bubbling goop. "You might lose that hand first, but our fates are bound."

I pull my cut hand away as though I could shield it. "I-I made no such bargain."

"The magic . . . is no . . . respecter of . . . mortals." He lifts his head as though it weighs as much as an anvil. "But . . . perhaps . . ."

He wheezes.

"Perhaps what?" I beg. My hand stings, and I unclench my fingers. Blood has worked its way under my nails, and tar stains the bandage.

His bright eyes glimmer. "A kiss . . . may free me . . . and there-fore . . . you."

"You are a liar." I wrap the bandage around my hand too tightly, my movements shaky. "Narvals are soul eaters."

What is a soul if not an extension of the heart? Grandmother had once said to me. To lose one's soul is to lose what makes one human. It's no better than death.

I spit on the ground and, in my head, curse my grandmother for not speaking of mysting bargains in her book. Curse myself for thinking I had a solution. Curse my father for venturing into their world, for if he had never stolen the Telling Stone, the goblers would not have come looking for it.

I retreat into the forest until I find a sizable stick. Gritting my teeth against the pain in my hand, I hack through weeds until I've drawn a large circle on the forest floor, beside Maekallus. I get very close to him, but he does not lash out, only bubbles and moans and suffers. I carve the eight-pointed star across grass and clover.

"Descend." I bark the command at him. The circle won't require sacrifice if he's merely returning home. His blood and body are made of the monster realm.

He laughs. "It will not . . . work."

"Try it, you putrid oaf!"

He glares at me, but concedes. He topples over, straining to roll onto the circle. He lies on his back, staring up at the sky. He does not descend. The circle and its star remain dull, lifeless.

Cursing again, I take my silver dagger and stab it into the earth where the gleaming thread disappears and dig, dig, dig. But the thread burrows deeper and deeper. I slash at it with the blade; the silver passes through harmlessly.

"One kiss won't . . . steal your soul."

I glare at Maekallus. A bubble travels under the flesh of his arm, darkening the skin in its wake. Pity stabs through my gut. This is no way for any creature, even a mysting, to die.

He rolls, just enough to look at me. "A myth . . . Just one . . . will not steal . . . your soul."

My left hand grabs the cool Telling Stone. I wish it would warn me if the narval is lying, but it only whispers that he is here. That he is weak. "Then what is the point?"

"Do not . . . ask me to . . . explain the magic . . . of our worlds."

I feel a pinch on my scalp, and only then do I realize I've grabbed my own hair, fistfuls of it. I feel light headed, and the smell—gods above, the smell. I can't think straight. My heart pumps as though I've run the length of the wildwood. My legs feel like thick tree roots spiraling into the ground. My lungs are iron, and each breath struggles to fill them. The stinging cut on my hand bleeds and burns with the promise, *You're next.*

I struggle for words, for composure. "When."

Maekallus groans against his unseen torturer.

"When!" I rip my hands free, taking a few strands with them. "When will it kill us?"

"Don't . . . know . . ."

"A wild guess will do!"

He stares at me even as his heavy eye finally swells shut, weeping black tears. "Perhaps . . . a day."

I look up at the sun, so cheery, so uncaring. Only a day . . . Thoughts push themselves against my eyes, but I can't think all of them. I can barely breathe.

I turn from the glade and run back through the wildwood, seeking escape until my legs can carry me no farther.

CHAPTER 6

Intelligent mystings may be willing to work for hire for mortals, and are bound to their promises by reciprocal laceration. Be wary of making such deals, for the price paid may amount to more than originally bargained for.

I do not lose myself in the wildwood. I know it too well and have been taught too much caution for that.

I collapse at the foot of an evergreen, dried needles like old bones poking through my skirt and into my knees. I inhale the hearty scent of pine for a long time, until the back of my hair burns from the touch of the sun and my wrists ache from holding myself up in this cradle made of forest. I lean against the evergreen's trunk and force myself to my feet. Heat ignites in my right palm. I look at it only to discover I've bled through my bandages. In this, at least, I know Maekallus was truthful—if he does not heal, neither will the cut on my hand.

Is there any truth to the rest?

I cradle my injured hand and stumble away from the tree, picking through foliage and undergrowth toward my home. My grandmother's writings warn me away from narvals, as does my own common sense. Yet if Maekallus's death equates my own, then what do I risk by giving him what he wants?

Besides, although I have no heart for mystings, a sliver of me chafes that his cruel suffering is my fault. Had I not summoned him, had I not insisted on this bargain, he would not be . . . *melting* in the wildwood, bound to the mortal realm with, seemingly, no chance of escape.

I touch my lips, my true inexperience pulsing at my fingertips. My mother married my father when she was but eighteen. I, at twenty, have never so much as kissed a man. To think that my first kiss could be with a *mysting*, let alone *this* mysting, tears apart my very soul . . . I shiver despite the warmth of summer.

I clear the wildwood and see my home, ringed with oon berry, ahead. My father is outside, beating a rug, and spots me. He waves one arm. He may wonder where I've been, or think he's merely mistaken the time. I can never be sure.

Time. I have so very little. And what if Maekallus's guess was generous? What if he—we—have less than a full turn of the sun?

I wipe away a tear with the heel of my hand. I should not cry. My mother never wept, or so my relatives have told me. I've strived to be as strong as she was, yet another tear escapes, and another. I slow my pace so my father will not see, then slip around him and into the house.

My hand aches. I clean the wound again—several stitches have popped free, revealing black corruption mingling with blood. I bite my tongue to keep from gagging and use the rest of the thorrow herb to numb the sting. I try not to imagine that black ooze consuming my arm, my chest, bubbling and popping and—

I rush to the washbasin, but not quickly enough. Falling to my knees, I vomit onto the kitchen floor.

I try to apply my thoughts elsewhere, but it's of no use. I burn dinner, leaving my father to eat bread and cheese for his evening meal. I don't eat anything. My stomach has twisted too tightly. My pulse hasn't settled. The Telling Stone hangs useless at my wrist. At least, though Maekallus failed to seal the bargain we made, the gobler hasn't come back. At least there is that.

As the sun begins to set, I look out the kitchen window toward the three graves at the back of our property. Their stones are small, and oon berry and lavender cluster like weeds over them, protecting them from the worst kinds of mysting. My father has already lost his wife and his parents. I imagine him plunging his shovel into the ground a fourth time to dig a resting place for me. Me, whom he gave up so much to protect.

I weep.

So this is it. I've two options: kiss Maekallus or leave him to die. The outcome of either choice is unsure.

Let Maekallus die, and die with him.

Let Maekallus die, and hope I live.

Kiss Maekallus and save him, but lose my soul.

Kiss Maekallus and save him, and myself.

It's a chance, albeit one that requires me to trust that the narval being devoured in the wildwood will not devour *me*.

But before I do that, I must do something else. Whether I live or die, I want one good memory to cling to. And so after I settle my father by the fire, I sneak out the kitchen door and venture toward town, my path lit orange by the sunset. It feels strange to walk this way without a basket on my arm, for I never go into town unless driven by need, and that need is always to sell and to buy. Empty handed save for a lantern, I feel awkward. I notice the people around me more, and even if they don't glance my way, my mind tricks me into feeling their stares. My pulse echoes against my hand. I force myself forward. I will not cow from this, though I've never in my life been so bold about anything.

By the time I reach the Loviss farm, I'm sweating, so I slow down and let the descending twilight cool me. I light my lantern and check my pockets for tapis root, just in case my stone chills. But the Telling Stone remains only cool, a reminder of Maekallus's distant presence.

My belly flutters when I reach the farmhouse, like my body is stuffed with grass clippings stirred by the wind. I keep moving onward. Reach the door and knock. If I die tonight, and if I keep my memories in the world beyond, I will regret not doing this. Tennith can turn me away, certainly. But at least I will have tried.

Fate pities me, for it is he who answers the door. Changed out of his riding leathers into mud-stained breeches and a loose linen shirt tucked snugly at the waist. The laces of his collar are done up tightly and modestly. Light from the hearth makes his hair look the deepest shade of gold.

He does not hide the surprise from his blue eyes, or from his voice. "Enna? It's almost dark—has something happened?"

"Who is it?" calls his mother. I'm grateful when he doesn't answer.

"Nothing is amiss," I whisper, embarrassed to know his family is so near. "But . . . I must speak with you, if you'll grant me a moment. Alone."

His brow furrows ever so slightly, but he nods, then calls back into the house to say a chicken is loose. He lies so easily. I wonder if an escaped animal is commonplace, or if he's needed reason to leave home at night before. Perhaps his wits are simply quicker than I give him credit for.

I don't linger on the subject. He closes the door. "This way," he says, and steps past me. I smell earth and lavender on his clothes as he passes. I extinguish my lantern, preferring to lose any looming humiliation to the shadows.

He brings me past the house, around to the barn. It's locked up for the night. I hear the shifting of cattle and a few bleating sheep within. Twilight fills the air with hues of violet and indigo. He stops by the side of the barn, and I linger near him, somehow able to feel the heat radiating from him.

"Enna . . ." His voice is soft. "What's happened? Your father?"

I manage the smallest smile. "Did you not believe me when I said nothing is amiss?" It *was* a lie, but I cannot trust the truth of my peril to Tennith. I dare not even confide in my own father. Not where a mysting is concerned.

He returns the smile, though the night begins to blue his features. "I thought perhaps you were sparing the family. Being private."

"I suppose I was."

His head tilts slightly as he studies me, and I'm grateful for the dark. "Did you find your rabbit? I assume it was a rabbit snare you set."

"Alas, Tennith, I have little time, and I can't spend it chatting about my ventures in the wildwood." I try to make my tone light, but Tennith instantly sobers. I steel myself, but there's no way around this. No flowery words that will give me what I want without asking for it. I'm afraid I must be blunt, and my heart pounds in the anticipation of it.

I take a deep breath. "I was hoping you would kiss me."

Tennith straightens against the barn door. "What?"

"I spoke clearly. Please don't make me repeat myself." My neck and face burn like I've fallen headfirst into embers. "And please . . . don't ask me to explain. I'm hoping you'll see this as, well, a simple request. You may, of course, turn it down. I will harbor no grudges toward you if you do."

A single soft chuckle escapes his lips, and he runs a hand back through his hair. "Huh. I just . . . I'm surprised, is all."

"Is it so surprising?"

He drops his hand. Focuses on my eyes. "Perhaps not so surprising."

I roll my lips together. Clasp my lantern before me. Try not to fidget. Wait.

Tennith steps away from the barn door, closing the distance between us with a single stride. His fingers come up beneath my hair, and the warmth of them shoots shivers down my shoulders and back.

My clammy hands grip the lantern tighter. Thoughts without meaning or purpose sing through my mind.

He tilts his head and presses his lips to mine. I stop breathing, savoring the feel of my first kiss. It's warmer than I expected. His lips are a little rough, but his movements are gentle, as are his fingertips at the nape of my neck.

It lasts a moment, then another, before he pulls away. I breathe again, filled with the scents of earth and lavender. The world looks a little darker; twilight has slipped into night, and I can barely make out his face anymore. But perhaps that's for the better.

"Enna—"

"Thank you," I say, a little breathy. He begins to speak, but I talk over him. "Please don't ask me to explain. Not now."

He closes his mouth and acquiesces.

His kiss lingering on my lips, I light my lantern and walk away. There's nothing more to be said. I only hope that Tennith understands.

Stars begin peeking through the shade of night as I make my way into the wildwood.

No one ventures through the wildwood at night. I am no exception. Or, I was.

I've herbs in my pockets, and after I ensure I'm not followed, I chant little spells my grandmother taught me as I pass between trees that, in the darkness, have grown into looming giants, their branches like claws and their leaves hundreds of teeth. I clutch my Telling Stone in my left hand, waiting for it to turn cold. It chills twice, once for a freblon and again for a rooter. I quicken my step. They are miles off, but I track them in the back of my mind, ever wary. I hear a sizzle, and then another, as blood from the cut on my hand seeps through the bandage and drips onto the hot glass of the lantern. From that alone, I know Maekallus is still alive, but barely.

If he dies, will my death creep upon me as his corruption has, or will I fall to the earth suddenly, my life fizzling away like these drops of blood? Will I be denied entrance into Shava, the world of spirits, if I die by the magic of mystings?

I would not know the way to his glade if not for the stone. I smell that putrid scent as I near. The light of the lantern spills onto him, a mass of tar and waste, bubbling and writhing. He looks up, hair matted to his skin, one heavy yellow eye taking me in.

The red light binding him glows through the darkness my lantern does not reach. I turn slowly, holding my lantern high, ensuring there is no one else in this part of the wood. *No one* can witness what I'm about to do. I'd only give fodder to the rumors that I'm a witch, though name-calling is the least of my fears.

When I'm certain we're alone, I whisper, "Maekallus," though my voice sounds loud in the forest. Even the crickets and nightfowl fear to go near him, driven away by the wrongness of his misery. He does not answer, but a heavy, struggling breath passes from him. The mound of his back and arms shifts up and down, straining for air.

I'm strangely calm as I approach him. Perhaps my body has expended all the nervous energy it can hold, and it can spare no more. Perhaps Tennith's kiss has calmed my soul. Perhaps, unknowingly, I've finally resigned myself to my fate, whatever it may be.

I set the lantern down on matted grass three paces from the mysting. I clench my fists, and blood squelches from my right. Avoiding the ashen horn, I kneel before him. His wary, pained eye watches me. It's a morbid sight, and I hold my breath against the smell.

I push my fists onto the ground for balance. Count to three once, then again, before leaning in and pressing my lips to the sludge smearing his. It is cold, it is vile, it is nothing until something shatters deep within me and claws upward like spiders.

It wrenches loose, tearing free from my body, and I gasp as it escapes.

CHAPTER 7

Rooters are generally docile mystings. They are intelligent, enjoy solitude, and prefer dwelling in a mortal forest over anything else.

Maekallus chokes as the soul fills him, evaporating every lesion and boil from his skin, spinning away the bloody slurry as though it had never been. Swelling vanishes, pain fades, and hunger quenches. He rasps as crisp, clean air fills his stinging lungs. Relief stronger than any his soulless body can feel on its own winds cool circles under his skin.

The soul's vigor—its emotions, its power, its *life*—dances inside him, a newly lit flame, bright and real and . . . incomplete?

Maekallus blinks, coming to himself. Looks at the trodden but clean grass underneath his fingers. His skin, unmarked and clear. He pushes himself onto his knees, his back popping like freshly kindled firewood. He rolls his neck, flexes his fists and arms. Yes, the vigor is unmistakable, but it feels . . . different. His eyes shoot to the trembling mortal foolish enough to save him. Her blue eyes look back at him, pained and deep and very much alive. They lack the dullness and complacency of a mortal whose soul had been devoured.

She solidifies the assessment when she croaks, "What did . . . you do to me?"

Maekallus is up on his hooves in an instant, cloaked by the thickness of night. He presses a hand to his chest, where the soul burns—and where the gobler's binding tugs him earthward. Still the thread holds him to this realm. The feeding—can he call it a feeding if it's incomplete?—has not broken that.

He curses, but his attention steals back to the girl.

This has never happened before. Somehow . . . yes. Somehow, he only absorbed *part* of her soul. He stares at her, trying to figure it out, all while his limbs flood with energy, aching to stretch and leap. Her soul invigorates him, even if it's only a piece.

He steps back, then forward, holding her gaze, trying to decipher it. What makes her different? Was this, perhaps, why the goblers had come for her? Had they sensed she's special?

She pulls her gaze away first, focusing on a bloodied bandage around her hand, where the deal had been struck. She tugs off the gauze and holds her hand to the light. It reflects off a thin, smooth scar. Had the bargain been fulfilled, there would be no mark at all. But this . . . this exchange had healed it, for now. Maekallus looks at his own hand. His own matching scar.

He licks his teeth and flicks his tail, considering. He can break the bargain, of course. Free the mortal. But then she'll have no further reason to help him. He'll die and descend into nothingness, but not before going mad by this cage of trees . . . gods below, he's *still bound to this cage.*

Even if he refuses to release the mortal from their deal, no consequences will come to her should he die. Yet his survival depends on this woman—this strange woman—believing otherwise.

He breathes deeply, savoring the vitality, the *feeling*, inside him. "What are you?" he asks.

Her eyes look back to him, one shadowed by night, one lit by the lantern. "What do you mean?"

"You're different from other mortals," he says, crouching so he can see the rest of her soul through her eyes. Humans have such telling eyes. "What are you?"

Her fine brows cross. "I am what you call me! What have you done to me, mysting?" Her gaze falls to the narrow web of red light projecting from his chest. "Why is it not broken?"

Maekallus growls. "I don't know. I don't know how to break it, without killing the gobler. And I cannot kill the gobler because even *if* I could leave this forsaken glade, I wouldn't know where to find him. Not until he resurfaces in this realm." And close by, else Maekallus might be unable to decipher the tug of the bargain. Perhaps if he can get the blood of a mystium . . . but that is just as unlikely as finding the *ga'goning* bastard who'd bound him here. The only binding spells he knows are the ones that seal promises between mortals and his own kin.

The woman clutches her breast, breathing deeply. He can almost sense her pain through the partial soul's vigor. How strange.

"What is your name?" he asks.

"Perhaps if you answer my question, Maekallus, I'll be tempted to continue answering yours."

He grins. Fiery, for a mortal. "Part of your soul lives within me."

Her head snaps up, eyes brighter than the lantern. "What? But you said—"

"I said I wasn't sure what would happen." He stands to his full height. A lie. A partial one, at least. He hadn't known *this* would happen, but he can steal the soul of any mortal with a willing kiss, whether or not he wants it—though he always does. To feel the way humans do, with their cluster of ever-changing emotions and vitality, even for the few hours it lasts . . . yes, he always wants it.

Humans attribute their emotions and their ability to experience them to their hearts, but hearts are simple flesh, just like all the body's organs. It's the soul that hosts those sensations, and the soul alone.

She takes several deep breaths before speaking again. "But you are healed . . . and so am I." She grabs the lantern and struggles to stand. The light from the tiny flame swings through the glade, making the trees' shadows lean and bend.

"For now." He studies the binding, passing his hand through its red shimmer. "For now."

CHAPTER 8

The best song for keeping away mystings is "The Widow's Lullaby": Bai sharam, sharam, on whi. Bai sharam on whi, repeated over and over. I theorize that it is not the words that stave off evil, but the rhythm in which they're said.

"My name is Enna."

The words hurt as they come up my throat. I feel as though the narval reached his hand down it, up to his elbow, and grabbed something from deep inside me. I'm raw and sore and so very tired. I struggle to keep my eyes open, despite the revelation that Maekallus hosts a piece of my soul.

A *piece of my soul.* What does it mean? I squeeze the Telling Stone for comfort and focus on keeping the lantern steady.

"Enna."

I look up at him, at his yellow eyes and calculating stare. The moment I kissed him, all the tar, all the rot vanished as though it had never been. The way he looks, the way he stands, is entirely predator, as though I'm an injured boar and he doesn't know if I'll fall or summon the strength to strike one last time. He seems almost as surprised at our predicament as I am. At least there is some tiny comfort in that.

He snorts. "Mortals have such simple names."

"Then you can start calling me by my simple name and stop calling me 'mortal.' Or 'girl,' or 'woman.'" I falter, and the light of the lantern swings. "I feel . . . ill." And Papa must have discovered my absence, unless he fell asleep in his chair. I pray that he has. I should not leave him for so long, besides. "I must go."

"The binding still holds."

"I know. I'll come back tomorrow." I can't think like this. I don't even know if I can walk all the way home, but I know better than to sleep in the wildwood. "You'll have to suffer until I'm back."

He steps forward, his body tense, tail twitching. "I cannot stay here." He looks at the surrounding wood as though it's ready to come alive. What does a mysting have to fear from the wildwood?

"You'll have to." I eye him, the shadows hugging his shirtless body, masked by the night. He'll last at least a few days. He did before, he can do it again. And maybe . . . maybe the piece of myself that lives within him will make him last a little longer.

I can feel it, somehow. My heart aches for its return.

I don't offer him any more goodbye than that. I press my hand against a tree, then another, picking my way out of the wildwood. Trying to listen to the forest beyond my own labored breathing. I think I fall asleep on my feet a few times as I trek toward home under the light of the moon, praying and chanting verse to keep evils away.

I don't even remember arriving home, but when I awake, that is where I am.

The hurt is less in the morning, as is the fatigue, but they're both present, as though it's the end of the day and not the start of it. So is the nagging sensation that something is missing, like I've forgotten something, yet I can't pinpoint what it could be.

The Telling Stone is cool where it touches my wrist, reminding me that Maekallus is near, while promising that other mystings are not.

I wash my face, comb my hair, and change into my favorite dress. Sage green with a high neck and long sleeves trimmed with homemade lace. I trace the mark the gobler left before wrapping it with more salt and tusk nettle. I help my father with breakfast, chatting with him as though I hadn't kissed a mysting in the wildwood last night, giving up part of my soul. As if I hadn't offered myself to Tennith Lovess just before. I wonder what Tennith thinks of me, then realize it doesn't matter.

What does matter is the scar on my hand, smooth and slightly pink. Healed, for now. There's a bit of a stitch embedded at the base of it, and I pull it free with my teeth.

My father goes down to work with the mushrooms and some hides he'd hung earlier. I don't make an excuse to leave. If he's busy, I'm free, so I take my basket and fill it with my silver dagger, breakfast leftovers, some bread, and my book, more for the purpose of taking notes than from the hope of finding an easy answer. Flint and steel and a candle, just in case. Then out to my garden for lavender, rabbit's ear, oon berry, tusk nettle, blue thistle, aster leaf, and tapis root. I harvest all of it before venturing back into the wildwood.

I don't see Maekallus at first, only his cloak hanging high in a tree. But he isn't hard to find, even if he did wish to hide. The string of red light remains rooted in the earth, and it points to the heavy branches of a tree.

The Telling Stone throbs as I stare at it, and curiosity drives me to unhook the clasp of my bracelet and let it slide from my wrist into my basket. The light vanishes. When I touch the Telling Stone, it reappears. I feel a sliver of relief, knowing that my secret is unlikely to be discovered by passersby. Fortunately, there will be few in this area, only hunters, and unless they have a charm like mine, they will not see the binding spell. According to the narval, they're unlikely to see him, either.

After securing the bracelet, I walk toward the spot where the spell skewers the ground and set down my basket. "Are you trying to hide?" I ask.

"I'm *exploring*," his voice replies, and it has almost a metallic ring to it, like a heavy bell swaying in the breeze. He falls to the earth in a blur, graceful and swift, landing on two hooves, his other hand skimming the dirt. His reddish hair falls over his shoulder, tied with a long piece of grass. The binding spell shifts with his movements as he comes near, menacing horn leading the way, tail swishing behind him . . . and maybe it's a trick of the light, but the asymmetrical end of that tail no longer looks sharp as a blade. I wonder if I should modify my sketch.

"My cage is complete." Maekallus doesn't look at me, but into the wildwood, toward the town. A stupid part of me marks the spectacle of his half-naked indecency, now much more notable in the daylight. His shoulders are just as broad and well sculpted as Tennith's. His waist is narrow. A body that, by the standards of my world, hasn't seen a bottle of mead or many lazy days.

But that tail twitches, driving the foolish thoughts away. I grab the silver dagger and let my basket drop to the earth.

The sound brings his attention back to me. He smirks like I've told a good joke. "You mean to kill me? Even if you had the skill, you'd be authoring your own—"

"Oh be quiet." The words are hard, and I let them be. "We must be allies in this."

I crouch next to the spot where his glowing leash pierces the earth.

Maekallus snorts as I try again to cut it with the silver dagger. "You've tried that."

I pause long enough to glare at him. "Do you want my help or not?"

He hesitates, then folds his arms. The light of the binding gleams right through them. He consents with a small nod, but in his eyes I see desperation. I imagine a creature of his make is not used to being trapped, especially in a place that threatens to destroy his very being.

I dig, trying to cut the string where it anchors to earth. Dig deeper, try again. Each time my dagger, though made of silver, does nothing. My father's sword is enchanted against mystings. Would its edge do any better?

Needless to say, the earth is ruining the soft metal of my mother's dagger. I stand, brush off my skirt, and try to cut the glowing strand again. Step along its length, closer to Maekallus, and swipe out with the blade. Again and again, until I reach him. He's taller than I remember, but perhaps that's because I last saw him as a bubbling heap of refuse.

"It will stretch about thirty paces in any given direction," Maekallus says. His tone isn't friendly, but it lacks malice. "Pierces through stone and tree. Unaffected by blood. At least hart blood."

I pause on my way back to my basket. "Hart blood?" I scan the clearing. "Where . . . ?"

He glances up to the tree. I see a smear of blood on two of its branches; the rest is hidden by foliage.

I sigh and drop the dagger into the basket. "At least you'll be fed. I trust you eat food."

He snorts. "What other reason have we to come here? The selection is far better. You know little of us."

I wait for him to say, *We prefer souls,* but he doesn't. Wise of him. "What do I eat? For how many meals? And do tell me my favorite leisure activities, Maekallus."

He cocks his head.

I snatch lavender and tusk nettle from the basket. "You don't know all there is to know about humankind, either." I approach him, leaves in hand. His face wrinkles, and he steps back. "Let's see if we can break this spell so that we won't have to learn, hm? Put this in your mouth."

He cringes at the lavender. "It smells terrible."

At least my herbs still affect him. "Good. I grow these to keep away your kind. Perhaps they can break the spell your kind created. Open your mouth."

He doesn't, but opens his hand—his perfectly human hand. I put a sprig of lavender in it, and he immediately drops it, hissing through his teeth.

"Vile," he spits.

"Better than tar."

Growling deep in his throat, he takes the tusk nettle from my hand and puts it in his mouth. I watch the binding light as he chews, hoping it will fizzle or darken, but it holds strong, and soon Maekallus gags and spits the nettle out. I hope the thorns caught in his gums.

I pick up the lavender. "Again."

That herb makes him dry heave, with no effect on the spell. None of the herbs work. They all pass through the light just as the dagger did, and even when I bunch them up around the hole I made trying to dig the spell up, there is no alteration whatsoever.

I kneel by my basket, one hand pressed to the ground as I steady my breathing. My efforts have exhausted me, more so than they normally would. My chest aches for its missing soul. I pull free my heavy book and turn to the next blank page, where I diagram the binding spell and recount my failed attempts to break it.

Maekallus regards me silently. Something about his gaze infuriates me, and once I've recorded my thoughts, I unleash myself on him.

"You knew you'd take my soul. From the beginning you did, before the binding. You tried to barter it from me."

"Only a piece." He looks me over. I tug my sleeve over my bracelet.

"Only a piece! What if you'd taken my leg? It's *only a piece* of my body!"

He steps toward me—the press of his footsteps equine, the pace of them human. His horn hovers high like the ax of an executioner.

"Would you hate me for surviving? You're narrow minded, Enna. You mortals pity the songbird clutched in the fox's jaws, yet you possess no remorse for the kit whose fur hangs around your neck?"

I force myself to stand, to be less small. "Do you see fur on me?"

"You would don it." His yellow eyes narrow.

I take a few breaths. "You're very cunning in your speech, I'll cede that."

"I've had a long time to improve it."

"How long?"

He hesitates. Turns toward the deepest part of the wildwood. For a moment, his eyes lose focus. "I'm not sure."

Despite my desperation, my uncertainty, and my hate, his answer intrigues me. What is Maekallus, to not know his own age?

I eye my tome. *Formed from the spilled blood of bastards.* Human bastards, of course. Where the human ends and the magic begins, I haven't a clue, and I imagine Maekallus doesn't, either.

"Then tell me," I say, turning back to my growing entry on narvals, "how long do your kind live?"

He glances down at my book and frowns. "Until something kills us."

Constitutionally immortal? I write. But I am tired, and Maekallus is ornery, so I close my notes and set the breakfast leftovers and bread on the ground. Straighten and lift my basket. "Eat this if the hart isn't enough. I'm going to get a sword and see if that helps. I'll return."

He bids me no farewell.

My father's sword is heavier than it looks.

I knew this, of course, but I have not tried to heft it for several years, and it reminds me of its weight as I carry it, wrapped in linen, through the wildwood. I want to be swift. Even with his faulty mind, my father will notice his sword gone. Before leaving, I wrote down a list of chores that need to be done and things that need fixing (which I may have broken myself for this purpose) to keep his eye away from the mantel. So long as he doesn't misplace the list, I should be successful in my ruse.

I'm exhausted when I reach the clearing. Again, too exhausted for the effort I've expended. Something is wrong with me, and I know precisely what. If I let myself focus on it, if I wait for my breath to calm so I can listen with something other than my ears, I can hear that sliver of my soul burning inside the mysting with the great horn. I try to beckon it back to me, silently, but it doesn't heed the call.

I note that the food I left is still there, save the fried pork. *Solely carnivorous? More study needed.*

"And this will work when the dagger didn't?" Maekallus asks, but the remark only has an edge of cynicism. He's curious, and he looms close when I set the scabbard against the earth and, with both hands and some effort, pull the blade free.

He instantly steps back. "Ah. Clever Enna."

The blade is carved with runes and flecked with silver—a sword forged for the battling of mystings. Specifically, for that brief war two decades ago. Hefting the blade, I swing it through the gleaming thread—only for it to pass through, just as the dagger did.

I don't give up. There are half a dozen runes on this blade. I cut through the binding spell, or try to, six times—each time aligning the cut with a different rune on the sword. Alas, this blade has no effect, and I'm soon wheezing from the effort.

Planting the sword's tip in the soil, I lean against it, trying to summon more energy.

"Cut it out of me."

I look up at his words. "What?"

"Cut it out of *me*," he repeats, and points to the center of his chest, just below his heart, where the red line of light pierces him.

I straighten. Blood rushes from me so quickly I sway on my feet. "You're joking."

"I heal faster than a human." His tail flicks. "Try cutting it out of me."

My stomach squeezes. "If you die, I'll go with you."

"I won't die from this. Even so, I'd risk it. So should you." He shakes his head, as though the trees surrounding us whisper to him. "I can't stay here. I'll do anything."

Though I tote about my mother's dagger, I've never actually stabbed a living thing before. I've flayed, and I've butchered . . . but the thought of pushing this heavy sword through a body where blood readily flows, feeling the resistance of flesh . . .

I press the back of my hand to my mouth and try not to retch.

Maekallus emits a sound somewhere between a sigh and a groan and grabs the hilt of the sword, picking my fingers from it. The humanness of his touch is unnerving, and it strikes me that he feels warmer than I remember.

He looks over the workmanship and turns the blade about. "Unwieldly. But there's not enough silver to kill me." His arms are just long enough to point the blade at his chest.

I realize with cold mortification that he's actually going to attempt to cut it out, and I turn away, covering my ears. My imagination, however, betrays me, and I see it all in my mind's eye—the gaping wound, the blood—

My hand stings, and I lower it enough to look at the cut. The scar has reopened.

A *thud* of the sword hitting the grass pulls my attention behind me.

Maekallus sucks in a shaky breath. "That . . . didn't work."

Bile climbs up my throat at the sight of the deep wound, like a mouth, staring at me from his chest. It bleeds readily from torn muscle. All the while, the thread of the binding shines through it.

Maekallus drops to one knee, and I come to myself, urgency pushing past my revulsion. I look around and spot his cloak hanging from its branch. My strength returned, I grab it and run to Maekallus, pressing the fabric against the wound.

He coughs, and a thin line of blood dribbles down from the corner of his mouth.

"Oh gods in heaven," I mumble, gathering the fabric and pushing.

He winces, and suddenly his weight presses against me, knocking me to my knees as I try to hold him up while keeping the cloak in place. He mutters, "Not . . . healing as fast . . . as I thought."

My stinging palm openly bleeds against its bandaging, reacting to Maekallus's self-inflicted wound.

"Lie down," I urge him, and help him onto his back. Looking around the clearing, I search for any witnesses, but we are alone. I lift the cloak just a bit to look at the wound. Blood bubbles up, and I press down with both my hands.

I focus on my own breathing to keep my thoughts clear. "How long does it take you to heal, normally?"

"Not . . . long," he wheezes, but the sound is not as bad as when he was a sludgy mess, so perhaps there's hope. "Even here . . . faster, in the Deep. The immortal waters are swift . . ."

I've never heard of "immortal waters," but I assume the "Deep" is his name for the monster realm. Were I not staunching the flow of blood from a very large and stupid wound, I would hasten to write down the information in my book. "Perhaps the binding spell is preventing you from healing."

"Obviously."

I push harder against the wound, and he cringes. "But there is something," I go on, "for I think a normal man would be dead by now. Or closer to it."

He manages to grin. I stare at it a moment, surprised. How can he grin when his chest has been cut open?

I should probably inspect the wound, but I don't want to disturb any clotting, if mystings clot. "I need to go home, get some supplies." The thought of the journey fatigues my body, but the sting in my hand reminds me of worse fates.

"A soul . . . will help."

"I will not kiss you."

"Doesn't have to be yours."

"And you think I'd lure some unsuspecting person here for you to feast on?" I shift my hands slightly and increase the pressure, almost enjoying the grimace the pressure elicits.

"For your own well-being? Yes."

"No. And even if I did, I'd make it the ugliest, oldest man I could find."

Maekallus frowns, winces.

I sigh. "Perhaps I can catch a hare—"

He coughs. "Do I look like a hare to you?" When I don't answer, he explains, "We . . . consume human souls . . . because we're of human make."

The blood of bastards. "Here." I take his hand and put it atop the cloak. "I'm going to get supplies. I'll move quickly."

"See that you do."

I leave my father's sword in the clearing—if anything will slow me down, it's that, and the blade is smeared with mysting blood, which may result in questions I can't honestly answer. Papa is not home when I arrive, or he's in the cellar. I collect whatever I can and drag my weary body back to the glade, wrapping my own bleeding hand as I go.

Maekallus is where I left him. "Has anyone seen you?" I ask.

"If they did"—he wheezes—"they failed to introduce themselves."

I drop my basket of supplies at his shoulder and ready a bottle of antiseptic, a jar of salve, and my father's thread and needle. I've never stitched skin before, but having recently watched my father do so, I have some confidence that I can manage.

Though this wound is more serious than a surface cut.

Except it's not quite as bad as I recall—perhaps Maekallus *is* healing. Either way, it's a terrible sight, illuminated by that blasted spell. I pour on antiseptic, and Maekallus seizes like I've dropped a cannonball on his gut. New blood spurts from the wound.

"Lie *down!*" I push his shoulders back. "Gods, it will help you heal faster!" Or perhaps I'm wrong. What little knowledge I have about healing is specific to humans. Although it won't help him to say so. If my own life weren't inextricably tied to his, I might jump at the chance to learn more of mysting physiology.

Maekallus lies down, but his limbs remain taut and strained, and vile-sounding words from what I assume to be the tongue of monsters sputter from his lips. I'm somewhere outside myself when I stitch him closed and smear on green-tinted salve. The sun is beginning to set, and a well-trained part of my mind reminds me that it's not safe to be in the wildwood after dark.

If only I'd avoided it entirely.

He sits up of his own accord, and I press gauze to the wound—I'll need to buy more after this—and wrap it. I have to get very close to him to do this, and loop my arms around his chest. He watches me as I do, silent. Perhaps, were he a man, this moment might possess a flare of intimacy. But he is not, and so it doesn't.

I tuck the end of the bandage in. My hands and fingers are stained red. Blood coagulates under my nails. My bandage is wet, but I don't know if it's from my blood or his.

I am a sight, and so I wait until the sun barely peeks above the horizon to return home, all the while clutching the Telling Stone in my hand, my book under my arm, and my father's sword to my chest. The stone whispers of mystings at the perimeter of its reach, but none come searching for me.

Perhaps the greatest deterrent to them is the blood of their own.

CHAPTER 9

Grinlers are carnivorous pack hunters. Despite their small size and lack of speech, they are quick on their feet and manage to communicate hunting plans through grunts, snorts, and body language.

This is wrong. It isn't fading.

Maekallus sits between the thick roots of an oak, his back pressed against the trunk, his hands touching the bandage wrapped around his middle. The wound hurts more than it should. Too slow to heal. But that isn't what bothers him.

It's the fire. The feeling. The *soul.*

Not even a soul. A *sliver* of a soul. But it continues to swirl inside him, every bit as alive as when he first consumed it.

It isn't right. When he takes a soul, it burns inside him for a few hours, then fades into nothing. Dead weight. A too-big breath of hot air. Once he returns to the monster realm, his body digests it, and that is that. But more than a *day* has passed since Enna parted with this fragment of herself.

A soul's vigor never lasts so long. Not for anyone.

His mind tries to piece it together. Is this slice of soul alive because the rest of it still lives inside its original host? Is it affected by the gobler's damnable spell? Whatever it is, the bits and pieces of human feeling, that bizarre inner awareness they have, live within him. Perhaps that is what makes his chest hurt.

Or perhaps that is why, when a splotch of black begins to form on his shoulder, Maekallus feels a tendril of fear.

CHAPTER 10

Some mystings cannot be killed by standard metal-worked
weapons. All, however, are susceptible to sharpened silver.

The cut on my hand is worse in the morning. There's no trace of black
in it, but the skin around the fissure is red and sore. I wrap it best I can
before I set off for the wildwood. I have little hope when I wander to
Maekallus's glade. Although I skimmed both my and my grandmother's
notes late into the night, I found nothing that might save us.

He leans against the base of a tree, nestled between two thick roots,
his eyes closed. It surprises me how peaceful he looks, almost as much
as it surprises me that he's asleep. I don't know what I expected. I never
put much thought to the question of whether or not mystings slept. I'll
note it in my book later.

I let myself stare at him, the way I never would were he able to witness it, all while trying to look away from the blots of blood staining
his bandages. He does not know his age, but physically he looks to be
in his mid to late twenties. If I put my bias aside, I can admit that his
is a handsome face. A different one—no one in Fendell looks quite like
he does, and I've never met a man or woman with red hair. His pants,
layered like armor, are dirty and speckled with blood. The hem skims
the top of his hoof feet. I wonder, beneath his clothes, how much of

him is equine. His knees, bent slightly in rest, look entirely human. Somewhere between ankle and knee, he changes, then.

I wonder again at my grandmother's words, *the blood of bastards*, as I near. I notice that his breathing is not smooth, like there's phlegm in his lungs. I don't get much closer before he opens his eyes, and their vivid canary-colored irises remind me of what he is.

My wound throbs. "You haven't healed."

He shifts. Something pops loud enough for me to hear. "This world . . . this spell. It's weakened me."

Even his voice has lost strength.

I roll my lips together and approach him, kneeling down by his knees. I don't ask permission—it seems strange to be polite to a mysting—and gently pull at the edge of his bandage to peek at the wound inside. The poultice I applied has kept the scabs from sticking to the bandage, and a lot of the injury has clotted over. Good.

What is not good is the black ooze seeping between the stitches—the infection of the mortal realm.

And the smell. I pull back, and press the bandage back down. "The corruption didn't happen this quickly last time, did it?"

He shrugs. "Last time I didn't have an open wound on my chest."

"Don't talk like it was my doing." I pick up a different poultice from my basket, but instinctively I know it will do no good. The mystical parts of Maekallus have kept him alive where a mortal would have died, but nothing monster or man will save him from destruction if he cannot descend to his own realm.

At least, nothing I possess.

I massage my fingers, thinking. "I'm going to go into the village. See what I can find there, unless there's more you're not telling me."

He scoffs. "Unless you have a sorcerer on hand who can find the gobler, I fear we're at an impasse."

I don't, of course. Sorcery is a dying craft, thanks to growing laws regarding mystings. Sorcery is enormously the conjuring and brewing of magical ingredients, many of which stem from the monster realm. Even if sorcery were still a viable profession, a sorcerer would never waste his talents on a wayward place like Fendell.

Maekallus perks up. "You could lure the gobler here. With whatever he wanted the first time. What did he want?"

I lean away from him, touching my forearm through my sleeve, seeing the black mark there in my mind. "I don't know."

He narrows his eyes. He clearly doesn't believe me. "The only way I know for certain to break the spell is to obtain the knife he used to make it, or to kill him. If three of their kind have come here for the same purpose, they're bound to come again." He groans and leans back against the tree.

I stand slowly, pondering his words. I feel a shiver and, where Maekallus can't see, grasp the Telling Stone in my hand. But the stone is only cool; the chill is all my own.

Come again. Would they come again? And why do they want *this*?

Is there more my father hasn't told me? Perhaps he never knew the true significance of the stone, or the knowledge may have been relegated to the misty part of his mind.

I force saliva down my tight throat. "Tell me about the gobler's knife."

"You won't find one in a human—"

"Tell me about the knife." I grab my book and a charcoal pencil from my basket.

Maekallus grumbles deep in his throat. "It's made from the tusk of a vuldor."

I've never encountered the term. "What is that?" My tone betrays my eagerness.

His lip curls up. At least he can find humor in our sick predicament. Is it because he is a trickster? I look away from the smirk. "A beast of the Deep, what else? Shoulder-heavy mutt with three eyes and great tusks." He points his index fingers skyward and holds them over his lower canines to illustrate. "The gobler used a knife made of that tusk, hollowed out to hold mystium blood. At least, I think that's how it works."

I pause in drawing my rendition of a vuldor. "A mystium?"

"A mortal-mysting mix."

I shift away from him. "A child? Such a thing isn't possible."

"Not common." He watches me as though my revulsion amuses him, and I have the urge to slap him. Then I see a dark patch on his shoulder, and I lose the courage. "But possible. If the female is mortal."

I imagine a mysting—every horrid picture in Grandmother's journal rushes through my head—emerging into this realm under the cover of night and finding some unsuspecting maiden, taking her someplace where no one could hear her screams . . .

I turn away, trying to blink away the visage. Could such a thing have happened to me, when I ventured into the wildwood and drew a summoning ring without so much as an escort? *How foolish I've been.*

I write down the information, pondering what it could mean. Could I interview a mystium? But to find one I'd have to do a great deal of surveying, and most would think me mad for the very idea, especially if I claimed to have heard it straight from the mouth of a mysting. I sigh to myself. Only an affiliation with a college could give me the credibility and resources I'd need.

I turn the book about and show him my vuldor. "Like this?"

He eyes the picture, brows drawn together. "Hardly helpful."

"It's helpful to me."

Maekallus frowns. Hesitates. Watches me like *I* am the object of study. "Its head is wide"—he spaces his hands about a foot apart—"and flat. Their feet have three toes."

I smear charcoal with my thumb and adjust my depiction. He doesn't correct the stance, which has the vuldor on all fours, so I assume I got that much right. I truly hope none of these vuldors ever find their way across the threshold. Glancing up, I see the bandage around

Maekallus's chest. Black has begun to vein out from its edges. Further questioning will have to wait.

I set my notes aside. "Do you have the medallion I gave you?"

His eyes narrow until he almost scowls at me. "Why does it matter?"

"I'm going to get supplies. Bandages, if nothing else. I'll need money." I avoid looking at his face and hold out my hand. There are several seconds of stale silence between us. Finally, he shifts his hand, and the medallion appears between his first and second fingers like he's a parlor magician. I take it, snatch my basket, and tromp from the glade. I walk quickly, and the exercise forces stress out of my shoulders, making me focus more on my heavy breathing than vuldors and the creation of "mystiums." Were all such half-bred children begotten by violence? There are many humanoid species of mysting, some my kind could even find attractive. Could such a coupling come from want or desire?

My cheeks burn at the thought, and I cast it aside. Of course such a thing is impossible. Mystings are incapable of tender feelings. They don't have souls.

I walk farther, past the food market, silversmith, baker, wainwright. The sun makes me too warm in my high-collared dress, and weariness pulls at me again. I reach the apothecary at the end of the way and slow, staring at the mortar and pestle engraved on the sign overhanging the door. I have not been to this place in a long time—the last time was over a year ago, when I needed a starter for the nettle in my mysting garden. People here have a tendency to gossip. The apothecary is a flunked scholar of the supernatural, come to Fendell after his botched study in Wellsgard, the capital. I once asked him too many questions about mystings and the monster realm, and needless to say, word spread of my eccentricity. But if anyone in town has a strange cure for my unspeakable predicament, it is Lunus Mather. That's worth the risk.

The hinges of the door creak loudly enough to hurt my ears when I enter. The metal has never seen oil, and I wonder if it's intentional. Lunus is in the back room, and I hear glass break before he parts a half curtain and peeks out at me. Many of the shelves in the main room are empty save for common things. What Lunus considers valuable is kept in the back.

He is of an age with my father, but the years have not treated his body well. A slight hunch presses against his back. Frown wrinkles drag at his forehead and mouth, and a swollen wart nests against the side of his large, hooked nose. He is terribly pale, perhaps because his musky shop always has its curtains drawn.

"Oh, it's you," he says, like I'm a great disappointment. I would think a merchant of any kind would be happy to host a customer of any make. "Bulbs? Seeds? I probably don't have it."

"I'm looking for something strong to counter mysting spells."

"Did your little herb garden die, Rydar?" he guffaws, calling me by my surname. "Or did Daddy think they were weeds?"

I swallow a sharp retort. My Telling Stone rubs against the side of my hand, and I palm it, seeking strength. "I have coin. Do you want it or not?" *Please want it.*

He considers me. "I've many things against mystings. You'll need to be specific."

"Mysting *spells*. I need something to nullify their handiwork."

He raises an eyebrow. "And what sort of mysting has been visiting you long enough to cast a spell?"

He's already sowing his seeds of rumor—*witch*—and it's an effort to keep disdain from leaking into my expression.

"It's a matter of study." I'm holding the Telling Stone so tightly the clasp that connects it to the bracelet pinches my hand. "Do you have anything of use?"

He taps his spindly fingers on one of his shelves. "I might know of something. Somewhere."

I bite the inside of my cheek. I don't have time for this. I truly *do not have time*, as my aching hand reminds me. I squeeze the stone hard enough that my fist tingles around it. "Tell me, Lunus. Something to affect a spell cast by mysting magic. Anything."

He straightens as though suddenly interested in me. I don't think I've ever seen him stand so tall, and it gives me a fright. However, for one reason or another, my directness coerces an answer out of him. "I've nothing of the sort here, but in Caisgard there's a great library, the largest one in this quarter of Amaranda. Once belonged to the Duke of Sands, but the family turned it public some fifty years ago. Perhaps you'll find what you need there."

I release the stone and rub my hand. Caisgard is the closest city to us, some three hours away on horseback. I wonder if this library is affiliated with the college there. I've only been to Caisgard twice in my life, both times with my paternal grandparents. The second time, my grandfather took me to meet with a professor, and it ended disastrously. The man had looked me in the eye and insisted women had no place at the college.

I shake the memory from my head. The largest library I've ever visited is the single shelf of books in the apothecary's shop, so the thought of the greatest library in our quarter of the kingdom sends a thrill across my back. Even for just a day, it would be . . . nice . . . to dive into literature, to feed this hunger always gaping in the back of my mind. Of course, I won't have the time to explore to my heart's content—I'll need to limit my research to my immediate predicament.

"Thank you."

He eyes me, but doesn't ask for payment, so I turn from the shop and step back into the sunlight.

I mull over my options. I cannot take my father with me—he will need too much tending, and I must focus on the task at hand. But I will need to offer him a convincing excuse for going there alone. I could tell him the truth about everything . . . yet I can't predict his reaction. Nor can I trust him to keep secrets, and I direly need Maekallus to remain a secret, else Fendell will hunt me as though I were a mysting myself. Perhaps I can convince him I need more herbs for the garden, something strong to be used against goblers. If I put enough emotion into it, maybe I can persuade—

"Enna?"

I pause, noting that I've nearly stepped off the cobbled path, and look up to see Tennith with one of his brothers. My thoughts leave me for a moment, flying away like dandelion seeds. Tennith says something to his brother, who nods and continues up the path, leaving us alone.

I can still feel the pressure of Tennith's lips on mine, the smell of his clothes—

"You look concerned," he says, approaching me. He's had a day of hard labor; dirt and sweat stain his homespun shirt. He reaches out and touches my arm.

My thoughts piece themselves back together, and before I realize what I'm saying, the first one tumbles from my mouth. "I'm going to Caisgard."

His hand drops. "Caisgard? What for?"

I hesitate, but I cannot think of a good lie, or a good enough reason *to* lie. "There's a library there I wish to visit. I keep an herb garden of sorts. Protection against the wilds. I think there's much more I can do, but I need to research it first."

He looks impressed. "I didn't know you could read."

I didn't realize he could not.

He considers for a moment, chewing on his bottom lip, which only makes me think again of the side of his barn and the dark of night. Uninvited, Maekallus rises in my thoughts, oozing and wheezing. I rub my eyes with my fingers and smudge the image until it's indecipherable.

"Do you . . . want an escort?"

I drop my hands. I had not expected such an offer. The word *no* weighs my tongue, but I hold it there, considering. I cannot take my father. But I, a single woman, should not travel to Caisgard alone.

"Truly?" The word is almost a whisper.

Tennith leans on one foot. "Harvest isn't ready yet, and Pa has mentioned wanting a new milking cow. They have good stock in Caisgard. I think it can be arranged for next week."

"No, it must be tomorrow," I blurt. And yet . . . even if we leave on the morrow and return the same night, it might be too late. Even now, the wound on my hand throbs, the bandage growing bloody. I keep it pressed into my side to hide the black tendrils reaching toward my fingers.

I press my lips together. There's a slim chance this will work, but it's a chance nonetheless. I *must* go.

"Is it so urgent?" asks Tennith.

I run my thumbnail along the smoothness of the Telling Stone. "I'm afraid so."

He rubs his chin. "Then I will speak to my father this afternoon. I don't foresee him needing the wagon. Though if you can ride horseback, it would be better."

I bounce on my toes with elation. "Yes, I can ride. Tennith, thank you."

He smiles at me. His smile is different from Maekallus's. Kinder, yet . . . plainer, in a way. An expected smile. "Let's plan for an hour after dawn?"

I thank him again, and hurry on my way. I have to prepare. I have to convince my father—

I have to kiss Maekallus.

My steps slow. The mortal realm hasn't devoured him yet, but it will, and this time the blight is spreading more quickly. I don't know how long he will last, I only know I need to buy myself as much time as possible.

Only a piece, I remind myself. *It should only be a* piece, *right?*

Distracted, I purchase bandages, food for the journey, thread. Return home and speak to my father in a soothing voice, massaging the stone between my fingers as I tell him of Caisgard and Tennith, of how he needs to stay and protect the house. It takes a little persuading, but not nearly as much as I expected. Perhaps he senses the need I have for this. Perhaps he is more perceptive than I give him credit for. And he will be safe, for a day. He is forgetful, but he is not incapable. He proved as much with the first gobler.

I prepare for the journey, finishing too soon, and cook a hearty dinner for us to enjoy together. While we eat, I try to savor my father's company, listening to the stories he never tires of telling and that I never tire of hearing. I sit with my back to the fire, facing him in his chair, so that he won't notice the bandage on my right hand, only the glistening treasure on my left.

I kiss him goodnight, claiming the need to turn in early for my journey on the morrow, then slip out of the house with my stone, a crown of oon berry, and the silver dagger. Trifles unlikely to offer much protection against my increasingly foolish ventures. The sunset turns from orange to pink to violet. A shiver warns of distant mystings—there's been more activity in these parts than usual—but they're not moving toward me, and the warning soon fades. It takes me longer to reach the clearing this time, for the weariness of my lost soul is compounded by the exertion of the day. I don't rush, though darkness looms, and the wildwood surrounds me. Perhaps I am more a fool than I thought, if these shadowed trees no longer frighten me.

I hear him breathing before I see him. He's moved across the glade, holding on to a low branch of a young birch. His bandage is scarlet. Black pocks his skin like freckles, and I wonder what they feel like. Are they painless, like the mark of the gobler's hand on my arm, or do they burn, like the bite of a newly spent match?

I almost ask him.

"I'm going to a library in the neighboring city." I cross the glade halfway, standing close to where the thin line of light pierces the ground. "There may be books there to aid me. The apothecary seemed to think so, and he once studied the supernatural."

He looks at me, gaze luminescent. "Still trying to use humans to solve a demon's problems?"

"Would you rather I tried nothing? I can frolic around the wildwood as bait for the gobler, but I cannot actually summon it." I touch the mark, wondering if that would be enough, or if it would simply paint me a target for something else. "I must consider other options."

He presses his forehead against the branch. "I'll go mad here."

My shoulders soften. I hug myself against the chill of settling dusk. "I . . . am sorry. Could I undo all of this, I would face the gobler myself."

He laughs like that's a grand joke, and I suppose it is, for I know from experience that I alone am no match for the bulbous breed of mysting. But I meant the words sincerely. I do not enjoy his suffering.

A patch of black expands before my eyes, and I think I hear his wound squelch, but I can't be sure. I clench my teeth, trying to keep my dinner.

"How long?" he asks.

"I don't know. A day, maybe two."

"I . . . *we* might not—"

"I know."

I approach him slowly, my feet heavy. It's different this time. Maekallus is hurt, but he's alert. Far more a man than a writhing ball of tar. The last bits of sunlight glint off his horn. I wish it were darker, like with Tennith. Here, even in the growing shadows of the forest, I feel exposed. Small. Unsure.

I stand before him, less than half a pace between us. He doesn't move, but hunger gleams in his eyes, and I wonder how long a narval can go between soul meals. It must be a while, or they would be more common on the mortal plane. More people would be wandering around without souls. Or perhaps their doctors and families have locked them away in a room somewhere, hidden from society, staring into nothingness and waiting for death to claim them. Fendell is tucked away from large cities, and only small merchant caravans bother to pass through. I've never heard stories to make me believe otherwise.

The cut on my hand twinges. I close my fist around it.

I try not to touch him, but our height difference makes it hard. I stand on my toes, ignoring the quiver of my hands. Maekallus, however, is not so meek. His hand grabs my hip, and with a swift pull, the space between us evaporates. His lips claim mine, and it's as though I'm standing right under the town warning bell, its ceaseless gongs radiating through my bones.

It's nothing like Tennith's kiss. There's desperation in the movement of his lips. They're rough, but in a different way. Tennith was much warmer. Maekallus is like kissing the twilight.

I feel it break inside me, another piece of my soul. It doesn't hurt this time, but instead leaves me with a deep pit of sorrow in a place I didn't know I possessed.

We break apart, and I gasp for air to fill the emptiness. The breath doesn't reach.

. . .

I hear my name.

Again.

Maekallus's hand slaps my cheek.

I startle, take in my surroundings. The glade. The wildwood. Twilight. I stumble back, putting space between myself and the narval.

He studies me. In the dim light, I see the spots of black are gone. His breathing has evened, quieted.

I touch my cheek. "What . . . ?"

"You weren't answering."

I blink. The twilight. I . . . I don't remember. There's a moment of time that merely . . . vanished.

Maekallus tugs at his bandage. Breaks it, without unraveling it. His chest is entirely healed. My soul did that, too.

My soul.

Caisgard.

"I'll leave in the morning." I feel there is more I should say, but my mind can't piece the words together. And I'm tired. So I go.

As promised, Tennith arrives in the morning on a dappled mare, with her sister for me to ride.

Caisgard feels a lifetime away.

CHAPTER 11

A mystium is a crossbreed between a mysting and a
mortal. Incredibly rare, as most mystings and mortals are
not a reproductive match. One can only assume violence to
be involved in their creation.

"We're almost there."

I start at Tennith's voice, though I can't remember where my
thoughts had been, if they'd been anywhere at all. I look up the road
ahead and note the spire of a shrine over the next hill. We're nearly to
Caisgard. I should be excited, yet I find myself tightening my grip on
the mare's reins. For how long had I been . . . aloof?

"Oh, we are."

I focus on the nearing city, trying not to notice how Tennith's gaze
lingers on me and not the road. It's been clear since morning that he
wishes to ask me something. Something, no doubt, pertaining to the
night I approached him and asked him to kiss me. Still, he hasn't said
a word, and I can only assume my own words—*please don't ask me to
explain*—are the reason for his hesitation. I'm grateful. I don't know
what I would say to him.

"I think I know where the library is, but we'll have to ask to make sure when we get inside the gate." He shifts his mare closer to mine. "I'll see you there, then go to the market to look for that milking cow."

"Thank you, so much." I twist the reins in my hands. "This means a great deal to me."

He smiles, though it exposes no teeth. "I'm happy to help, and Frera needs the exercise."

I glance down to my mare. Did he tell me her name before? I can't recall. She is a black beauty with blotches of white. The uneven coloring makes me think of Maekallus, covered in tar, bubbling . . .

I squeeze my eyes shut for a long moment.

"Enna?"

"Just a headache." I try to be gracious. I wish I could say something to lighten this heaviness around us, but my mind is blank.

"Do you need to rest, or—"

"I need to go to the library. Please, don't worry about me. Take your time with the animals. My task will take some searching."

And I am correct.

The Duke of Sands's library is enormous, a castle in and of itself. I'm instantly lost upon passing its heavy doors, although lost in the best way possible—between innumerable shelves stacked with leather-bound books. I see only a few occupants, half of whom are armored guards. I try not to look at them too long. I'm not used to guards, and an irrational part of myself fears they will take one look at me and know my conspiracy with Maekallus.

My thumb strokes the tip of my scar as I wander between the shelves. So many books. Shelves upon shelves upon shelves of them, and I wish to open them all and dive into their words. To imagine, as a student, I could spend day after day among these aging spines, squinting at worn handwriting and building upon my own knowledge, my own theories.

Surely these have not all been cataloged. Such a feat would demand a lifetime of work. I look over titles, hoping to find something that aligns with my present subject of interest. I do not, and though I find myself at the other end of that first cavernous room, I can't remember walking through half of these shelves. It's as though I perused them as the undead.

I shudder and grip my Telling Stone. *Focus, Enna.*

I spy an old man sitting at a table, sorting through newer-looking volumes. Hoping he's the librarian, I approach.

"I'm sorry to trouble you, but I need help finding some books."

Without even glancing at me, he says, "Nothing leaves the library."

"I . . . That's fine. But I'm hoping to read on the supernatural."

Now he lifts his gaze, peering over the small spectacles resting on his nose. I'm used to this kind of look, ill-concealed scorn mingled with feigned disinterest. "They teaching women that nonsense now?"

"If you could point me in the right direction."

The man sighs. "His Highness the duke had a fondness for the occult. His collection is recorded in a book in that corner." He points. "You'll have to thumb through it." His attention falls back to his sorting, so I thank him quietly and head in the indicated direction.

Sure enough, several indexes sit on a high table in the corner. I brush dust off one, only to discover its focus is farming. Frowning, I check the next index, and the next, until I find one the thickness of my thumb that reads *Mystics and the Bizarre.* My broken soul leaps at the find, and I open it at once. There is no guide in the front, so I pore over each page individually. My eyes widen at the sight of so many volumes that could further my own research, none of which can come home with me.

Focus, Enna.

I do. Using paper and charcoal from the sack I brought with me, I write down a few promising titles.

Though the massive library has the semblance of order, it is poorly organized. The books on the supernatural appear to be in three different locations, one of which is up a flight of stone stairs. I try to breathe lightly when I ascend them. I've yet to accustom myself to this lack of energy, but determination fuels my quest. The sooner I free Maekallus, the sooner I'll be back to normal.

I consider this as I run my fingers over aged book spines. The bits of soul living inside him—are they forever gone? Will they return to me once the binding is broken, or will he simply . . . eat them?

Will one of these tomes tell me the secret to getting them back?

What use is a soul when you're dead? I remind myself.

Quiet voices nearby draw my attention, and I find myself pulled toward them, my eyes still on the shelves as I search for what I need. There's a short, round table tucked into a stone nook nearby, and two men sit at it, across from each other. One is remarkably old, his hair and beard stark white, his glasses thick, his back hunched. The other appears to be a few years older than my father. His hair is fashionably coifed, though I've never before seen someone sport the style of facial hair he has. It rings around his mouth, yet his cheeks are clean. He's well fed and wears glasses nearly identical to his companion's.

"It can't be. This finding was in three, remember?" The older man sounds gruff and tired. He pulls out a paper from a scattered stack and shoves it at the younger man. "Wyttens walk on two legs."

Wyttens. I've never heard the term before, but the style of the word instantly screams *mysting*. I write in the back of my mind that, whatever they are, they walk upright, and pray that my hole-filled memory will be able to recall the information later.

The younger man shrugs. "I walk on two legs and could have made that pattern. This is cast from a bog, Runden. Perhaps the other half of his stride fell into a puddle."

"A puddle!" the man named Runden exclaims, then winces at his volume. He mutters to himself and sorts through his papers.

Scholars. My lips form the word, and my pulse picks up.

"I don't think it's the footprints that will help us," the younger man insists, quieter, and I slide around a shelf to hear him better. "It's the meal." He pulls out a bone—No, it's made of plaster. A replica?—and gestures to a long row of teeth marks across it. "Nothing has a maw so wide. The largest wolf can't do this."

"I refuse Addon's theory that it's a reptile."

The younger man snorts. "No gators or the like in the whole area. Of course it's not. This"—he punches a finger down on the paper handed to him earlier—"is supernatural. But it's certainly not a wytten. Just because they have three toes . . ."

He doesn't finish his sentence, and my mind spins with the information. *Three toes.* In my mind's eye, I open up my book of notes. I see every letter, every stroke of pen and charcoal, even the smudge of earth I earned trekking out into the wildwood.

"Vuldor." I'm sure of it. And when both men turn toward me, I realize I'd said the word out loud.

Runden's thick white brows furrow. "Excuse me?"

An apology sits on my tongue, and I back up a step to escape, but stop myself. I know this, don't I? It certainly matches Maekallus's description! "That is, it might belong to a vuldor. They're . . . as far as I know . . . never seen outside the monster realm, but it *does* match. They have wide jaws and three toes on each foot. They walk on all fours, like a dog."

Runden only looks angry at being interrupted. But his friend is astonished. That I, a woman, dared to interject, or that I have such knowledge?

"Nonsense." Runden returns to shuffling his papers.

But his companion asks, "Where did you hear of such a creature?"

My throat tightens. "I . . . cannot reveal my source."

Runden snorts. Even I know research is useless without a valid source.

I bow my head in apology and turn to leave, but the younger scholar says, "Could you draw one?"

I look back to him. Pull my sleeve over my bracelet. "I can try."

The man fumbles for a clean sheet of paper—it's very fine, which means it's very expensive—and turns it toward me. He has a sharpened pencil at the ready.

Eyeing Runden, I crouch at the table, moving closer to the younger scholar so as not to block the lamplight, and do a loose sketch of a vuldor, just as I had in my notes. I'm sure it's not perfect, but Maekallus had seemed to think it accurate enough. When I'm finished, I write, *Vuldor,* below it—admittedly, if only to prove that I can write and I'm educated—and step back. The scholar picks up the paper and examines it, adjusting his glasses as he does so. Runden continues to ignore me.

"Fascinating. What did you say your name was?"

"Enna." Excitement twirls in my chest. A real scholar is asking my name! He is impressed by my knowledge! "Enna Rydar, sir."

"Call me Jerred." He extends his hand. I grip it firmly, hoping to impress. Hoping he doesn't notice the reddening scar across my palm. "You're local?"

"A day's ride away." *A day,* I remember. I have only hours to find the information Maekallus and I so desperately need. Bother! Why am I presented such an opportunity to talk to well-studied men when I cannot take it? I feel my heart flake and crumble, like mud dried too quickly beneath the summer sun.

"And you cannot tell us more?" Jerred presses. He means my source, most likely. And I cannot tell *anyone* about him.

Swallowing a sob of frustration, I say, "I'm sorry. I have research of my own to do and only a short time to do it. But . . . good luck, with your studies."

I duck away, hurrying to the shadows between the shelves. I can't give Jerred, or even Runden, opportunity to respond, for they'll draw me into the fantasy of their academia and I'll never accomplish my task. I need not remind myself that my soul and my life are more important than my study.

Once I'm away, I take several breaths to reorient myself and begin scanning the shelves again. Force myself to concentrate.

Fate grants me mercy, for I find the first book on my list quickly and pluck it from its shelf.

I read for a long time. Long enough for the guard shift to change. My mind grows fuzzy, but I shake myself, forcing attention. I may only have today to search for an answer, but as I look at book after book and return to the index again and again, I fear that no amount of time will be sufficient, merely because the knowledge I seek is not to be found in the Duke of Sands's library.

There is little on mystings as a whole; my grandmother's journal is more precise than these volumes written by scholars. I've learned a great deal about herbs I now desire to plant in my garden, as well as various theories on the creation of the realms and what many call the "War That Almost Was" between the people of Amaranda and a horde from the monster realm—the very war my father fought in twenty years ago. But nothing mentions binding spells, or goblers, narvals, or even mystiums. Nothing mentions antidotes. None of these authors have traveled into the monster realm, and none, I believe, have ever seen a mysting with their own eyes. All the more reason to, someday, publish my own useful findings.

I do discover a scrying spell in a skinny book, its pages filled with tight, nearly illegible script. I jot it down, though I would need something of the person or being I want to find to activate it, and I've nothing of the gobler who bound Maekallus to his demise, and me alongside him. I'm near tears, a headache pulsing down my neck, when a hand grabs my shoulder.

I gasp and jump from my chair, a book on forest phenomena dropping from my lap to the floor.

"Easy, Enna." Tennith pulls back his hand. He frowns. "You don't look well."

"I . . ." I realize I've not eaten, though I have dried fish and bread in my sack. Glancing out the window, I determine it must be the end of the afternoon—time to set off, if we want to reach Fendell before the dark swallows us.

I pick up the book on the floor, tempted to rip out its useless pages. Even if I could neglect my father and convince Tennith to stay another day, I don't think it would be fruitful, and then there would be the gossip. Curse this world, for how it runs on rumor! All I have is the scrying spell folded in my pocket.

"I forgot to eat." At least I can be honest about that. "I can do so as we ride. Did you find your cow?"

He nods. "A fine young lady with eyes like sunstones. Got a decent price on her, too. But she's not fast, so we'll need to set out . . . Are you sure you're well?"

"Yes, quite," I lie. I leave my books on my chair to be sorted later. "Let's go. I—"

I wince and hold up my hand. The very center of the scar has opened, the cut thin as baby hair and short as my pinky nail, but the musty library air makes it sting.

"That's a nasty scar." Tennith reaches for it, but stops himself. "Where'd you get it?"

I pull my hand away from his line of sight. "A while back, playing with one of my father's swords."

"Your father was a swordsman?"

It surprises me that Tennith doesn't know this, given the stories spun about us, but I suppose only the oldest in Fendell would, and the best things about people always get forgotten beneath the worst.

"He was." There is pride in my voice, and I'm not ashamed of it. "One of the best."

Yes, my father. A man who has trekked where no scholar has gone: to the monster realm. Somewhere in the recesses of his broken mind, he *must* know more than what's recorded at that library.

I return home at dusk and bid Tennith a chillier goodbye than I wish to give him, but I cannot welcome conversation about the other evening. Not now.

My father paces the living room when I arrive. "Enna, didn't you say you were hunting new wood in the forest? You've been gone so long—"

"I went to Caisgard, Papa." I place my good hand on his forearm, the Telling Stone dangling from my wrist, cool and complacent. "Tennith escorted me, so I could go to the library."

His forehead wrinkles, then relaxes. "Oh. That's right."

"Sit down, Papa. I'll make you some tea."

"I've no mind to sit."

"Then do it so I can talk to you. Please."

He eyes me. I must look frightened, or determined, for his features soften and he drops into his old chair by the fire. I add a quarter log to the dwindling flames and kneel before him. Unclasping the bracelet from my hand, I place it in his palms, then put my hands on top.

"I need you to tell me what you know about mystings and their magic, Papa. I've done something foolish and I"—my voice chokes, but I clear it and speak strongly—"need your help."

"My girl, what have you done? Oh no, you must never take this off. Never take it off, and never show another." He busies himself refastening it to my wrist. If he notices its lack of warmth, he doesn't say so.

"If a woman were to make a bargain with a mysting, like Grandmother did," I say as he sets the clasp, "and the mysting failed to fulfill the bargain—"

"Foolish to bargain with mystings." His eyes grow distant. "Oh, Elefie."

"Papa."

He looks at me.

"If this bargain bound the woman to the demon, and a new spell bound that demon to the mortal realm, what should she do?"

My father shakes his head. "Mystings can't stay in our world, sweet Enna. It will kill them if they do. They must go back below."

"I know, Papa. But if this mysting dies, so will the woman."

He watches my face.

"They're bound together, and she can't break the spell keeping him here. She can postpone fate, but it costs pieces of her soul. Pieces she might not get back."

"The Telling Stone protects you."

I shake my head and drop my hands. "Only when I heed its warnings."

"Have you done something, Enna? Has Mother been pestering you about the wildwood again?"

"Grandmother is dead these seven years, Papa."

"Oh." He gazes into the fire, expression slack, for a long moment. "Oh, yes. I buried her."

"Yes."

"Is that where my sword went? To break a binding?"

I straighten. "Yes, Papa. But it didn't work. A thread of light holds the mysting to the earth, and it cannot be cut by knife. Or even by the sword. There must be a way. Do you know a spell I could use?"

He draws with his fingers in the air, and speaks as though in the middle of a story. "And you draw an *X* in the center of the summoning circle, stand at its very center, and murmur, *'Kardish wer en apt li mon.'* That's how you get into the realm of monsters. But don't stay too long. If the mystings don't kill you, the realm will."

My father has never before told me how he entered the monster realm nearly two decades before; I never imagined it would be different from a mysting's descent circle. I marvel at his words, watch him draw the circle in the air. Repeat the enchantment over and over until I can barely hear or think anything else. Memorize it. I fish in my pocket for a charcoal nub and scrawl the words phonetically on the wooden floor. I must write them down, for my father may never repeat himself as long as he lives.

He drops his hands and sighs. "These questions are best left to your grandmother. You'll have to ask her in the morning, after the chores are done."

Clutching the Telling Stone, I blink tears from my eyes. "Yes, Papa. I will."

CHAPTER 12

It seems that a mysting can tolerate the atmosphere of the
mortal realm for three to eight days, perhaps depending on
~~his~~ its specific composition and endurance.

What if she doesn't return?

Maekallus paces the length of his chain of light, though this time
more from—what, anxiety?—than boredom.

Anxiety? Is he feeling *anxiety?*

He pauses and grabs the sides of his head as though he can rip the
unpleasant sensation out. He's felt it before, of course. Anxiety, fear.
Not often—he has little to fear in the mortal realm—and never for
long. But even those sour emotions are more exciting than the lack of
them. They are *alive*.

And yet, this is different. These feelings don't ebb or wane. He can't
just . . . ignore them, like he used to. Nor can he pop into the Deep
and digest them, for only in the world beneath does he have the ability
to do so.

He lowers his hands and stares at the light of the binding as though
seeing it for the first time.

His head throbs, and for a moment he's somewhere else, inside a
building made of old wood, a counter stretching before him. Anxious.

He's feeling *so anxious*, because they are coming, and they won't take no for an answer—

He groans and shakes his head hard enough to hurt, and the strange vision dissipates. He paces faster, trying to burn off the plague of feeling. Maybe, if he moves quick enough within the gobler's cage, the mortal realm will struggle to keep up with him.

A thorn pierces his hoof near the south edge of the glade. Cursing, Maekallus bends to see it better in the moonlight.

A thorn.

In his hoof?

He grabs the obstruction with his thumb and forefinger and pulls it free. It's shaped like a skinny arrowhead. He doesn't know what plant it hails from.

He does know that his hooves are too hard to be bothered by thorns.

He looks down. They appear the same, but . . . leaning his weight from one to the other, he notices they're . . . softer. Softer? Changed. Just like his tail.

Anxiety flares again. He turns about and runs several paces before the binding pulls him up short, yanking and throwing him onto his back. He pulls at the thread until his chest aches, making him remember the biting sensation of the sword point digging into his muscles.

"Enna!" The shout echoes between the trees. Prey and predators, what if she doesn't *come back*? The cut on his hand points him in her direction, but it has barely changed over the last day, and it won't tell him how far . . .

A new feeling stabs the anxious one, something spiny, hot yet cold. It twists, and he rubs at it, raking his humanlike nails over the skin of his chest. He doesn't know this one. Or maybe he's experienced it once, eaten it, and forgotten.

But he wants Enna back. With news of this library, with another stupid mortal trick to try, or just to *be* there. To keep him from going insane. To keep the black fire away.

What if she knows? What if she's learned she'll survive, just short a couple of fractions of a soul, if she leaves him to die alone?

The pieces of her soul writhe inside him. He lunges at a tree, his horn piercing easily into its hard flesh. He rips it out, savoring the tugging ache on his skull.

He flings himself at the tree again, and again, and again, until chips of wood surround him. Exhausted, he falls onto the splintery bed and descends into a restless, too-human sleep.

CHAPTER 13

*Aster leaf, which many aquatic mystings are allergic to, is
also good for the lungs.*

My hands tremble as I prepare breakfast in the morning, a simple meal
of boiled wheat. I'm not entirely sure why they tremble, only that too
many things trouble me.

I must face a mysting.

I must tell Maekallus that I failed us.

I'm missing part of my soul.

Papa sleeps late, and when he comes into the kitchen, he says,
"Enna, when we spoke last night . . . that cut on your hand. Surely . . .
but you are your grandmother's granddaughter."

I school my face before turning around and setting the breakfast
bowls on our tiny table. "What are you going on about?"

"You made a deal with a mysting, didn't you? And now you'll
perish—"

I smile. "Papa, I think you were dreaming. I have this, remember?"
I hold up the Telling Stone.

His brows touch as he considers. "But you said . . . and the cut on
your hand . . ."

I wear a thin bandage around my palm again. The scar has split farther open beneath it. "The nail on the ladder, remember?"

"But when—"

"Just yesterday. Don't worry yourself and come eat. Don't we go to the market today?"

My father looks from me to the bowl, then back to me. His brow relaxes, and he sits down. "We're to the market today, aren't we?"

"Yes, Papa. I'll help you gather the mushrooms after we eat." I think of Tennith, of his kind words as we traveled. He never remarked when my thoughts went blank, and I'm sure it happened more than once. He gained some courage to speak to me as we returned to Fendell, but I changed the subject to the weariness of his milk cow, and so he ultimately didn't ask me anything.

I let myself briefly wonder what he would have asked, had I let him. *Why did you want me to kiss you?* is the most obvious. *What are we?* is another. I don't know if Tennith would ever want to court me—I'm hardly the first choice of his family—yet he didn't complain when I asked him to kiss me.

I would hope to be filled with laughter and excitement at the prospect of Tennith Lovess taking an interest in me. Me, a woman who has always planned to live her days a spinster, gaining the attention of the most handsome young man in town. I know how I *should* feel—there are songs about great loves and great heartbreaks. They must be true, for even twenty years after my mother's death, my father mourns her. Yet the thought of Tennith fills me with neither elation nor sorrow. I can think only of the monster realm, of Maekallus, and of Shava, the world beyond. At least, I hope Shava would still welcome me, should I die from this venture.

Perhaps the highs and lows of emotion, of love, are not meant for me.

I collect mushrooms and walk with Papa into town. Tennith's mother is the one manning their booth, and she frowns at me the entire time we make our exchange. We buy our necessities—and more bandages—before returning home. I tell my father I forgot the cabbages for tonight's stew, and then load up my basket with oil, flint and steel, a leg of mutton purchased in town, my silver dagger, my notes, a pair of Papa's old slacks, and a water canteen. In the wildwood, I pick up a sizable branch to use as a walking stick. I move slowly to preserve my waning strength, most of which was eaten up by the trip into town. My father did not notice the way I leaned on him. At least, I don't think he did.

It's noon by the time I near the glade. Before I even reach the flat space between the trees, Maekallus's voice says behind me, "You returned."

I jump, nearly spilling my basket. My hand goes to my heart. Soul or not, it beats wildly from the scare. Maekallus grins at this. I don't think he smiled the last time I came.

I try not to notice the spots of black dotting the side of his neck and his left hand.

"Of course I came back." I pass him and move into the glade, searching for others, but we're alone. "But I'm afraid the library had nothing of use, except maybe this."

I find the spell and hold it out to him. He takes it, looks at it sideways, and hands it back. "I can't read mortal script. Tell me what it says."

"Please," I add.

He cocks an eyebrow.

I sigh. "It's a scrying spell. A spell of finding. But it will only work if we have something of the gobler's. I don't suppose you grabbed anything off him before he vanished?"

Maekallus wipes a hand down his face. "No."

I sigh again. "Then I'll just hold on to it. Here." I place the canteen, mutton, and slacks on the ground. "I don't know how hungry you get, or how thirsty, but I brought these. And the slacks should fit well enough. What you're wearing is filthy."

He eyes the offerings like I'm trying to poison him. After a moment, he says, "What are you trying to gain, Enna?"

"What do you mean?"

"What are you trying to accomplish here? I won't die if I don't eat mortal meat; the fractions of your soul will sustain me."

"Are you not hungry?"

He mulls over that. "As you said, I don't fully understand your kind. What trick are you playing?"

I sigh. "It's no trick. Merely a kindness." I grab the clean slacks and hold them out. "You don't need to accept."

He eyes my hand, the bandage around it. Hesitant, he accepts the clothing.

And begins stripping right there.

I immediately turn my head away, a flush running up the back of my neck. I don't grasp the reason for it—he's only a mysting. But a humanoid one. More human than monster, even if he lacks propriety.

The old, leathery pants fall on a path of clover beside me. Distracting myself, I reach for the flint, steel, and oil in my basket. I say, "There's one more thing I want to try. A descent circle. My father told me about it, and there's little to lose in trying."

"Your father's descended to the Deep?"

There's interest behind the question, and I know at once I shouldn't have asked. When I believe it's safe, I turn to meet his eyes. The slacks are loose on him and ride low. My ears warm. From the misplaced information, nothing more.

"He knows how to." But Maekallus's yellow stare makes my skin burn.

He strides over, human and equine, and crouches in front of me. "Tell me what you are."

"I'm a mortal."

"Then what is it you have?" he insists. "Why did the goblers want you? Why does your soul break off in pieces?" He pauses. "And why does your father know what a descent circle is?"

"You know what it is?" A question to avoid the questions.

He frowns, stands. "For a mysting. I'm not sure if it works for humans."

I stand as well, my stick in hand, and draw a circle just as I had that first time in the wood—an eight-pointed star made of two overlying squares, surrounded by a circle. I add an *X* to it, the points of the lines just exiting the circle's boundary.

"Hmm." Maekallus's only response.

"Might as well try it. I'll light it—"

"Blood is a better offering."

"—and you'll stand in the middle and try to descend. Even if the binding spell doesn't actually *break*, if you can get inside the monster realm, you won't have to worry . . ."

I trail off, watching as a spot of black appears on his bicep and widens like a drop of ink against parchment. Maekallus follows my gaze and frowns, scratching at it.

"Don't—"

He glances at me.

I swallow. "Touch it. It . . . might make it worse."

He drops his hand. Instead of arguing with me about my latest pitiful attempt to break the gobler's spell, he simply says, "Light it."

I wonder if he's growing used to me, or if he's merely desperate and tired, like I am.

I spread the oil over the lines and light it, backing away in time to avoid the brunt of the smoke. When the flames die down, Maekallus walks to the center of the *X*, careful not to break the lines.

For a moment, the circle shimmers blue.

He takes in a deep breath through his nose, loud enough for me to hear over the sizzling of forest grass. "There's power coming through."

He closes his eyes, tail flicking. I clasp my hands over my breast, praying to whoever and whatever will listen. *Please, please help him.*

Us. Help us.

But the light doesn't return. Maekallus opens his eyes. I don't need to ask; the disappointment is evident in the slouching of his body.

I try, "Perhaps blood—"

"I don't think so." He remains in the circle, studying it. Perhaps looking for mistakes. "A little more power might seep through, but this is not the answer."

"You don't know—"

"When you douse an oil fire with water and the fire spreads, do you try again with *more* water, Enna?"

I pause, wondering not only at his question, but at the way he says my name. It's different, somehow. "I suppose I'll trust you on this one."

His expression perks.

"Does my trust surprise you? We're bound in this, Maekallus."

He doesn't answer, only steps out of the circle and walks to the edge of the glade, looking out into the forest. I wait for him to . . . I don't know. Do or say anything, but he doesn't. I lick my lips and try, "Are you hungry?"

He turns enough to eye the lamb. It's such a human gesture, made more so by his human expression. My mind wanders to the growing page on narvals in my book.

"Maekallus."

His gaze meets mine.

"Did you ever consider that, maybe, you *are* the bastard?"

He turns toward me and folds his arms. "I've been called many things."

"No, I mean . . . your birth. Your creation. The lore is that narvals form from the blood of bastards. But what if your origins were human? What if . . ."—I hardly dare to say it—"you were once human?"

He almost doesn't react. Almost. His body remains motionless, arms folded, brow lax. But I see it in his eyes: a spark, a loathing, a hope. Somehow, all at once. He looks away, back to the forest, for a long moment before he says, "Do humans suffer boredom?"

The question takes me aback. "Pardon?"

He drops his arms, but forms a fist with one hand—one bloodied hand—and hits the trunk of a tree with it. "This realm is driving me half mad. I'd almost rather it consume me."

I laugh.

I don't know why. It isn't funny. It's rather pathetic, really. But I laugh, because our demises shine on the horizon, and Maekallus complains that the situation is *too dull*.

I suppose it would be, trapped in the same spot of forest for days on end.

But I laugh anyway. It feels so strange, so foreign, so good, and I realize I can't remember the last time I laughed.

Maekallus growls.

"I'm sorry." I hold myself, placing my hand over my ribs. "I'm sorry. It just . . . I . . ." I don't have an explanation. Despite the laughter, I'm saddened by the realization that I've gone so long without it.

I can tell by the scrunched look on the narval's face that he doesn't understand me. It's no use explaining.

I cross toward him, purposefully scuffing the descent circle as I go—I don't want any unfortunate hunter or lost child to drop into the monster realm, should they wander this way. I unwrap my hand as I do so, tearing free a length of bandage that is still clean. I didn't think to bring extra bandages with me today. I won't make that mistake again.

I reach him and move his bloody fist from the tree. Coax his fingers open—are they warmer?—and examine the cut that mirrors mine. No mystic corruption yet, only a bit of debris at the heel. I brush it off and bandage the wound.

"Does yours not bleed?" he asks, low and petulant.

"I have more of this at home." I tie a small knot at the back of his hand. Look up at him. I didn't realize how close I'd gotten. Close enough to kiss.

But the blackness has only begun to spot him, and I wish to keep as much of my soul with me as I can. I turn away. Glimpse the descent circle.

"Maekallus," I say, quieter, "you say you can't descend, but could we coax the gobler to ascend? He was in this very glade. Is there some sort of . . . trace, we could use? Mystical . . . residue?"

Maekallus snorts at my lack of knowledge, but he studies the circle as well. "I don't . . . perhaps. I don't know the methods of goblers. But he will return, or his like will." He shifts his gaze to me. "As for bait . . . reckon they want whatever it is you're hiding."

His words shoot through me like lightning. I step back from the trees, away from his aura.

He looks me up and down, as though searching for my secret. "But where will you get the blood to summon him, Enna? What human would you dare to torture?"

"Not human," I whisper. I clear my throat. "Not human. But I can find a young boar or a hare in the wildwood. Perhaps one will trespass here, and you can collect the blood in that canteen."

He smiles—a wicked grin that at once reminds me of what he is. "Oh, Enna. The animals here have learned not to pass by. Or haven't you heard the silence?"

I stiffen, hold my breath. Listen. I never noticed it before, the lack of birdsong, the absence of buzzing and chirping of myriad insects. When did the creatures of my realm abandon this place?

The silence is a reprimand. *He is a mysting. A* mysting, *Enna.*

As though I need the reminder.

Grabbing my basket with my uninjured hand, I turn it away, concealing the Telling Stone. "I'll find something. I'll be back as soon as I can."

"Truly?" A smirk, not one of humor, tugs on his mouth, showing a pronounced canine. It isn't so much animalistic as it is roguish. I chide myself for staring. "Even in the dead of night?"

I hold his gaze. "That depends. Are you frightful enough to scare away the demons who linger in this wood, or only the birds and the flies?"

He raises an eyebrow, and I feel as though he's almost congratulating me. I leave, taking my basket with me. Back to the house. Slow, so as not to tire. As for blood, I will set snares, but they can take days to catch prey, and I dare not wait days. My soul aches at the thought of it. I wish not to waste money in the market for something I can hunt myself, but I'm poor with a bow and arrow, and if I ask my father to help me, he'll wonder where the meat has gone. In the end, I'd rather be penniless and alive than dead and soulless.

As I step over a brook and navigate an unseen path becoming increasingly familiar to me, I ponder on the exchange with Maekallus. *What if he was human once, Grandmother?* I think, wishing she were here to answer my questions. *He's of human make, isn't he?*

The thoughts turn on me. *And what does it matter? What would I think of him if he was human?*

My chest hurts. From the walk. I slow my pace even more and clutch the Telling Stone.

When I arrive at my home too soon, I realize I missed a piece of my journey—my mind blanked again. Yet one thought burns strong.

I must find that gobler.

CHAPTER 14

The only thing that can break the binding spell made by a
vuldor-tusk knife is the knife itself, the death of its wielder,
or the blood of a mystium.

There is a hierarchy of animals in the wildwood. Insects and crawling
things are at the bottom, followed by mice and birds. Then there are
larger animals, like harts, and more vicious ones, such as boars. Wildcats
and wolves dominate unclaimed land, but more often than not forfeit
it to humans, who ultimately surrender to mystings.

I do not understand the magic that loops my world and the monster realm together, and every question I have seems to beget ten more.
I will not use human blood to awaken the summoning circle, even at
the peril of my own life, but do the unseen mystics prefer fowl over
fawn, or hart over hare? Will the circle heed my desire to find a specific
mysting, or will it merely let out whatever is closest, as it seems to have
done with Maekallus? Something even more dangerous . . .

I do my best given the circumstances. In the evening, when the
sun begins to paint the sky, I trek again through the wildwood with my
basket in hand. I have to stop once to rest, for the unplucked pheasant I
carry with me is heavy, and I am weary. I stop on a hunting trail carved
with the intent to avoid mystings and listen to the distant whispers of

the stone. When I arrive at the glade, Maekallus is waiting for me—I see him standing between the trees at the very end of his leash, his yellow eyes brighter than the rest of the forest, his arms folded across his bare chest. I pretend not to see the black spot growing like a bruise on the side of his jaw, or the one that darkens his ear, or the dozen others that were not there this morning. His magnificent horn is pure, as is his right hand. I know the latter, for when I arrive, he reaches for my basket and takes the load from my arms, silently leading the way back into the glade. I pause for a moment, surprised. A simple action, yes, but Maekallus has never done anything to aid me. I wonder if he's grown so desperate that even kindness is beginning to eat away at him.

He's already drawn the summoning circle. The circle I drew earlier has been stamped out, and the new one etches the northernmost part of the clearing. Maekallus sets my basket down several strides away from it and picks up the pheasant by its neck. He examines it, then glances to me.

"What? We can always try again with a larger animal."

He smirks and lifts his tail to slice open the fowl, only to notice—remember?—that it's lost its sharp edge. His frown confirms my own observation. I lift my silver dagger from the basket and offer it to him, hilt first. He takes it and beheads the pheasant.

I accept the bloodied knife back. "Do you think it will work?"

"No." At least he's honest. "But I hope it does."

I cock my head slightly to the left. His words pull on me. Maybe because they don't feel like the words of a mysting. "Do you hope often?"

The question causes him to hesitate in the grisly work of painting the summoning circle with the pheasant's lifeblood. He looks at me like I've said something profound, and it's a gaze that makes my skin ripple with gooseflesh, though the summer evening is warm.

He straightens, the point of his horn slicing through a low-hanging leaf on a nearby oak. "I don't . . . think I have."

And it strikes me suddenly, like a snowstorm in the late spring, and I don't know why I didn't consider it before.

What happens to a mysting if he receives a soul?

Maekallus has only a partial soul. *My* soul. I can feel it inside him as though I'm peering into a faded mirror, where I can only make out shapes and nothing more substantial. But it lives inside him. He hasn't eaten it. He did promise, though it remains to be seen whether I can trust his word. Could it be the fragments of my soul that cause him to hope?

Our eyes are locked for too long. He turns away first, focusing on the task at hand. I hug myself and soothe the chill bumps beneath my long sleeves. Turning to my basket, I retrieve my notes, open to a fresh page, and write, *The Question of Souls,* across the top of it. I needn't worry about Maekallus looking over my shoulder, since he has already confessed his inability to read mortal script.

I write, *What does one call a mysting with a soul? Do they exist?*

What would one call a human with only part of a soul? And how large is each portion? How many times can my own soul be divided before there is nothing left?

Oddly, the old saying of my grandmother's springs to mind. I'm not sure how pertinent it is, so I write it in small letters in the bottom corner of the page. *What is a soul if not an extension of the heart?*

My heart beats inside me still. Granted, Grandmother more than likely meant it metaphorically.

I don't dwell on the philosophy of it long, for soon the summoning circle is soaked crimson. I close my book. The moment Maekallus completes the eight-pointed star, the circle flashes pale blue.

"I don't suppose you brought a weapon for me?" he asks.

I eye the dagger beside me. I hadn't considered it. I offer the silver weapon to him, but he shakes his head and points to the wood behind me as he backs away from the circle. "Best to hide."

I hesitate, eyeing the edge of the glade. Snatching my basket, I rise and dart behind an old pine, clutching the dagger in my hand. My mind itches to experience whatever it is that's about to happen. To document it. To *know* it. Maekallus grips the base of his horn and pulls on it for some reason. He tries twice more, pulling harder each time, until frustration paints his face red—or perhaps that's the light of the setting sun. He backs away, out of my line of sight.

I crouch behind the tree, peering around its rough bark just enough to watch the circle.

For a long moment, nothing happens. Without woodland creatures to occupy this space, it is utterly silent. My gooseflesh returns. My Telling Stone turns bitterly cold beneath my fingers, and it speaks of so many mystings I can't decipher a single one.

The circle glows again, and I cringe as a grinler emerges—the very kind of mysting that slaughtered my mother, uncaring for the life inside her belly. It's a foul creature with a round, furry body and pointed tusks jutting from the bottom half of its jaw. The teeth in between are sharp as sickles, as are its long claws.

Grinlers travel in packs, but this one comes alone. It's only in the glade a second before the circle flashes again and a mysting I've never beheld pushes through—a long, serpentine being. Several holes line either side of its head—ears?—and I hold my breath in macabre fascination, fearing it will hear me.

The grinler grunts, and the serpent rasps something foreign in response. Terror overpowers captivation as my imagination fills in their words. *Who made this circle? Where are they? Are you hungry? I smell mortal flesh.*

And then my eyes dart to the binding spell, the red bit of light that points directly to where Maekallus is hiding. I've grown so used to the ethereal magic I'd forgotten it was there. Surely these creatures can see it.

A chill consumes my body. My hand is glass around the Telling Stone. I feel my mind starting to blank, and I dig my nails into the pine tree to keep from slipping under. The cut on my hand warms as new blood seeps from it.

Another mysting ascends, then another. The fourth is a freblon, a humanoid mysting only hip high, just taller than the grinler. Its face is mutated and ugly, half man and half bovine. Its human arms end in bearlike hands. It's naked, though thick fur curls about its thighs and genitalia.

As one, the mystings notice the beam—only the width of a hair, but to me it looks like a beacon—and turn toward Maekallus's hiding spot.

I can't hold my breath anymore. I try to let it seep out slowly, but my lungs are desperate for air. The serpent's head snaps toward me.

Then I hear a sickening crunch, followed by a wet moan.

I force my shivering body to move so I can look out again. Maekallus jerks a sharpened stick from the body of the freblon. The grinler snarls and leaps. One of the creatures, the third to emerge, runs off into the forest, swift as a swallow. Maekallus grabs the hair at the back of the grinler's head as the smaller mysting sinks its nasty teeth into his arm. My right hand stings with the sensation.

The serpent moves to strike—*gods, anyone, help him!*—and misses. Maekallus throws the grinler hard into a trunk, then stabs the serpent in the back of its head with his makeshift spear. Its tail touches the summoning circle. Its death, or perhaps Maekallus, activates the thing, and in a flash of blue, the serpent is gone.

Maekallus's hoof slices through the spell, and the circle becomes dull, nothing more than a broken, bloody drawing on the ground.

Blood runs down his arm as he stalks to the grinler. He watches it for several long seconds before turning away. I know it's dead. Not only because of Maekallus, but because the icy pain in my hand is receding, enough so that I can force my fingers open and let the stone drop from my palm. For now, the stone whispers only of the runaway mysting, who continues to distance itself from the glade, and Maekallus.

I'm shaking. I try to calm myself, but I cannot. I rub warmth back into my left hand, though it hurts my right to do so.

"Enna. There are no more."

I keep massaging my fingers. Mutter a verse for protection against the supernatural.

"Enna."

He's standing at my tree. Reaches past my right hand—perhaps because of the newly bloodied bandage—and grabs my left. He pulls me to my feet with shocking strength, and releases me just as quickly.

"You're freezing. I've never felt a living thing so cold."

I pull my sleeve up over the bracelet. "I was . . . There were so many . . . I . . . You killed them. Thank you. But that one . . ."

Maekallus snorted. "Beuhgers are cowards. She won't be back."

Beuhger. So that was the word the Telling Stone murmured. I wonder what makes the mysting a she, but keep the question to myself. Maekallus studies the broken summoning circle, his red-tinted brows drawn, his tail writhing like a cat's. A splotch of corruption blooms between his shoulder blades.

"Those mystings were close," he says, "very close, to come up so quickly. The more that press against a portal, the harder it is to cross over."

The statement reminds me of something similar my father said once, when I asked him about the War That Almost Was. "It's difficult for large numbers on either side to cross over at once, and neither side can keep an occupying force. It's what makes a war between realms so unfeasible."

Maekallus nods. "There was someone who didn't think so once."

The words send new tremors across my shoulders. "Who?"

But Maekallus doesn't hear me, or chooses not to. He's watching the circle. I touch my Telling Stone, but there's no danger. The beuhger must have descended elsewhere.

I eye the thin rivers of blood drying in the crook of his elbow. Coming to myself, I rush to the basket for the bandages I brought. I wet a cloth with water from a canteen and hurry to Maekallus's side.

He grabs my forearm before I can administer to him. Holds me tightly, pulls me close. For a moment I think he intends to kiss me again, to relieve the disease spotting him, but instead he says, "It's like they wanted to come here." His voice is low, his eyes searching. "The same place the gobler was. Why?"

The Telling Stone dangles from my free hand. I hold very still, not wanting to draw attention to it. "I don't know," I whisper.

Maekallus frowns and releases me. I hesitate. He says nothing, so I dab his arm with the cloth. He twitches.

"Sorry." The word is pathetic on my lips.

"I've been attacked by grinlers before. It didn't used to hurt. Not like this."

I lighten my touch near the wound itself. It's mostly stopped bleeding, but a freckle of corruption burgeons between two of the teeth marks. Maekallus winces, as though he feels it. And maybe he does. "The . . . soul?" I ask.

"I don't know. I don't understand any of this." He looks at the thread of the binding spell, the ever-unmoving leash stemming from the center of his chest. He wipes his hand over his face. "I'm going mad."

"You seem sane enough to me." I press gauze to the wound. Maekallus eyes me like I've said something insolent. I manage to shrug. "If it makes you feel better."

He growls. I wrap his arm.

"The gobler didn't come." An obvious observation, but I feel it needs to be said.

"No."

"What next?"

He shakes his head. A piece of hair spills from the tail holding it. Without thinking, I brush it back.

Our eyes meet again. His yellow, demonic eyes. I almost forget the horn is there.

He looks at my lips.

My chest aches in remembrance of the lost pieces of my soul. I step away from him. My handiwork is finished.

The sun is beginning its set, but I can't leave. Not yet. Not before I've put this experience to page. I pull my basket free from its hiding place behind the pine and grab my book. Open it to the new section on souls, turn the page. "Beuhgers. Tell me about them."

He eyes my book. "Beuhgers can't help us."

I shake my head. "I want to know about them. I've never seen them documented. Never heard their name uttered in story." Unless they had a second name. "How did you know that one was female?" I begin a sketch, trying to remember the creature's appearance. I pause long enough to write, *Cowardly,* beside it. "What is their range of height? Are they docile? Do you know their diet, their intelligence, their—"

My book zooms out from beneath me, causing my charcoal to scrape a hard line down the open page. I protest as Maekallus lifts it up to his face, flipping through the pictures.

"What is *this*?" he asks.

I leap to my feet. "You'll get blood on it. Give it back."

He flips another page.

"Give it back."

My skin tingles at my own boldness. Maekallus looks at me with a questioning gaze, but hands the book back, upside down. I pull a bit of my sleeve over my thumb and use it to blot out as much of that charcoal line as I can.

When I'm nearly finished, I say, "I like to study. To learn more about your kind."

He snorts. "Beuhgers are *not* my kind."

I pause, glance at him. "You sound like you don't like them."

"They're dumb-witted carrion eaters. No one likes them."

A grin works its way across my mouth—I can't hide it, despite how I try. Maekallus looks at me like I'm a madwoman. Perhaps I am.

I set my notes against the grass and write down, *Unintelligent carrion eaters.* I return to my sketch, only to realize I'm having trouble seeing the lines. I glance over my shoulder, past the trees, to the rays of the setting sun.

A long breath escapes me. It's edged with the residual anxiety from the arrival of so many mystings in this glade. "It's getting dark. I need to return."

He growls again.

Closing my book, I glance to the red thread stretching between Maekallus and the ground. Feel the sting in my palm. "I'll . . . think of something. I don't know what, but I'll think of something." I stand. "I'll set you free, Maekallus. Both of us."

His jaw clenches at the sentiment. Perhaps he doesn't believe me. He doesn't meet my eyes.

I gather my things and walk a different way back—straight west to leave the wildwood as quickly as possible, then south toward home. I clutch the Telling Stone the entire time, half expecting the escaped beuhger to return. Maekallus must have spoken truth, however, because I never get the slightest shiver of cold. Wherever the creatures are, they're far away.

And so is the gobler.

CHAPTER 15

While grinlers hunt in packs, they attack their prey one at a time. This may be to prevent the prey from escaping, should it evade a strike. More study is needed.

While I've studied mystings from afar for several years now, I'm not sure what entertains them. But I try to imagine what I'd want to do if chained in a confined space for days, weeks, with nothing to pass the time. I would climb trees, or burn circles in the weed-clotted earth, or maybe weave crowns of leaves or flowers. Carve my name into a tree, perhaps. But I would grow restless, and I am a simple woman who leads a simple life. When Mackallus tells me he's going mad, I believe him.

After I tend my mysting garden, I pack a meal for him, hoping Papa won't notice the shortage of food in the cupboards. Meat is expensive, but Maekallus seems to prefer it. He is, after all, a predator. Then I gather some string for cat's cradle, a few books from my meager shelf, and my father's strategy game, fell the king. He has not played it in some years. He taught me the rules, more or less, but kept forgetting his strategy, and after so many losses, his interest in the board and its cherrywood pieces waned. I bring my usual supplies, including bandages, and belt the dagger at my waist.

Once my father is cared for and occupied, I venture into the wildwood. The sun is well out, so I head into the forest straightway. I suppose if I run into anyone who cares about my destination, I could tell them I'm visiting my grandmother. While the gossip mill delights in stories about my immediate family—my mother's passing, my father's mind, my infatuation with the wildwood—few even knew of my grandmother's existence, let alone her passing. She and my grandfather were incredibly self-sufficient, and when they did need supplies, they went to the market in Crake, not Fendell.

I try to ignore the ache in my right hand, which has already begun to bleed tar again, and enjoy the beauty of the wildwood. Its trees are tall and ancient, and the summer sun against the canopy bathes everything in warm green light. Gnats sparkle over a decaying log. Crickets chirp with the rising heat. The shadow of a bird crosses my path, and the call of a jay pierces the symphony of insect and fowl.

I take a break near one of the wildwood's slender brooks, one that will dry up before winter comes. Sitting on a short stone, I look into that water and breathe deeply, feeling the emptiness within me and trying not to dwell on what I've lost. On whether I'll ever get it back. Then I put my feet under me, brush off my gray dress, and continue on my way, tucking a bit of dark hair behind my ear as I go. I pick my way over root and rock, grass and clover, admiring the fiery orange of some wildflowers.

I am some ways into the wildwood when my stone turns cold.

I halt, my heart riotous, my thoughts rushing to the mystings from the night before. I grab a crown of oon berry from my basket and settle it over my head. My dress is washed in lavender. I fear it will not be enough.

I hurry toward the clearing, knowing I'll never make it before I'm overtaken, and grab my Telling Stone and my dagger in slick hands. The stone is cold, so very cold, and it whispers the word I fear most.

Grinlers.

The irony of my ready lie strikes me enough to bring tears. Visiting my grandmother. My mother had been doing that very thing, with this very knife, when grinlers tore her apart. How utterly foolish I have become, to have treated the wildwood so casually.

I run.

The Telling Stone chills to the point where I must drop it or have a hole burned through my hand. I stumble on something, but don't fall, and keep running. If I can just get to Maekallus. If I can just make it to the glade—

I hear them. It is not just the grunts and snorts once described to me by my grandmother, but a mad giggle, high pitched and half-swallowed. The quick, brushing steps of their feet startle two quail from a nearby thicket. The grinlers are closing in. Oh gods above, I can *smell* them. Subtle and sour, like decaying mushrooms.

Tears stream down my face. "Help!" I cry through my burning throat. Anyone. A hunter, Tennith, even a pack of wolves. The furry creatures appear between the trees, and I stop short, digging my toes into mud. I turn, but there are more charging toward me from behind, giggling and snorting, their marble eyes blazing with hunger, their clawed hands raised.

I will die just like she did.

Tears fall from my chin, and I lift my dagger in my bleeding, shaking hand. "Maekallus," I whisper, my throat tight.

Help me.

The cut on Maekallus's hand burns fiercely enough that he loses his grip on the branch and falls back to the earth, knocking his horn on the way down. Pain shoots up his tailbone and across his forehead. Cursing, he examines the bandage Enna tied around his palm, which is now mottled and sore from the black bruising of the mortal realm. Blood seeps through the gauze, two drops rolling down the curve of his wrist.

Within him, the fragments of her soul whirl, panicked.

He stands, ignoring the cut on his hand as he presses it against his chest.

And then a tugging, stronger even than that of the binding spell, jerks him south. He knows that feeling. It's the same compulsion he felt upon first meeting Enna. It's why he'd answered when she asked his name. Why he stupidly accepted those two gold medallions in exchange for killing the gobler.

This same force had been used to control Maekallus twenty years ago, in the War That Almost Was.

The urge is strong, and without thinking, he charges toward the south edge of the glade, then past it, to the binding spell's limit.

The soul swirls. The urge *pulls*.

He takes another step. Then another.

The binding spell, still bright and implanted in his chest, doesn't pull back. He would laugh, but the *need* propels him forward until he is running with his head down and horn pointed forward, deep into forest he doesn't recognize, the uneven floor biting his softening hooves. Blood whips from the soaked bandage on his hand. Black corruption seeps over his hip, his abdomen.

He runs, not understanding how, but knowing it is her.

The grinlers are more intelligent than I ever gave them credit for. It's no wonder my mother couldn't escape them.

There are a dozen of them. They've surrounded me, blocking every escape—assuming I possessed the ability to outrun them. The beasts march forward like trained soldiers, leading with the left foot, holding out their razor-edged hands, creating an impenetrable fence. A few cringe at the oon berry, or maybe the lavender. No worry. They'll start at my feet, discard my clothes, and save my head for last. They'll eat me alive, too hungry to wait for my death, too monstrous to give me a swift end.

They hardly notice my silver dagger, even when I swipe toward them. I drop my basket and hold the blade with both hands. Point it at one, and then another. Maybe I can kill one before the others take me down. They'll leap all at once, I'm sure of it, and . . . and . . .

I'm sorry, Papa.

I've never been so cold. I'm shaking all over. I pick one grinler, one that giggles louder than the rest, and point the dagger for the narrow, furry space between its eyes. I will . . . I will focus on that one, even when the others sink their teeth into my skin and chew through my muscle. Even when their bodies blind me—

I'm wrong—they don't all strike at once. One attacks before the rest, vaulting over the space between us. My courage fails me. The knife drops to the ground, and so do I, arms over my head.

Just before the grinler strikes, a blur knocks it aside, sending it flying beyond the pack. I know instantly, even before I see the horn or the yellow eyes.

Maekallus.

Maekallus.

Maekallus.

He is swift, though weaponless. He grabs a grinler by its upper arm, lifts it, and slams it into another as a third jumps onto his back and rips into his blackening flesh with its claws. I cry out. The mystings have focused on him, save for one, which charges me.

I scream and fumble for my dagger. *Help me!*

And he is there, grabbing the demon by the head and twisting it until the cracking of its spine echoes against the silent trees. Two grinlers brutalize his back. One clings to his leg. Blood rivers down the side of his neck. Three more strike. He knocks one away, but the other two grab his arms. He cries out when one sinks its teeth into the blackened pit of his elbow, sending a splatter of blood across my face.

I'm frozen. So cold. So . . .

They're going to kill him. Gods above, they're going to kill him.

Every fiber of my broken soul screams at them to die, to leave, to *stop*.

A wave of ice washes through me, the lancing of a thousand needles, the sensation rushing outward from my left wrist—up my arm and down to the tips of my fingers.

The grinlers stop. Claws, teeth, the maddening giggles. They fall away from Maekallus, dripping with his blood. Ignoring their dead companions, and me, they look around for a moment, as though blind, and then rush off into the wildwood until the Telling Stone warms once again.

Maekallus drops to his knees, blood glistening against peach-and-black skin. A bubble of corruption rolls across his ribs, deflating near his shoulder.

My voice. Where is my voice? The Telling Stone has warmed, yet I tremble as if just pulled from the broken ice of a pond.

The red line of the binding spell shimmers through the carnage, pointing back toward the glade.

"M-Maekallus?"

His breath is wet and raspy. He looks up at me, blood flowing from his hairline over one of his eyes. His cheek turns black beneath it. "How?"

I reach out and touch the dark spot, then wipe the blood off his eyebrow with my thumb. "I'm sorry," I whisper, new tears tracing the paths of the old. "You saved me. How? How are you here?"

He starts to shake his head, then winces. Hot blood pours from a deep gash on his shoulder. So many gashes. A network of them across his back. Blood and tar patter in droplets against the forest floor.

He reaches out a hand—the one with the bargain's seal on it, the bandage torn—and grasps my left wrist. Weakly hauls it up to his eyes. The Telling Stone dangles from its silver chain.

For a moment, the pain contorting his features lifts. "This," he croaks, eyes wide. His yellow gaze shifts to me. "You never . . . needed me . . . if you had this."

He tenses and drops both his head and my wrist, groaning. Black pours from his wounds. He starts to collapse, but I grab him, hooking one arm beneath his shoulder. His blood seeps through my sleeve.

I turn his face and kiss him.

His blood is metallic, just like human blood. I taste it on my lips. He doesn't respond, but he doesn't need to. I feel the break inside me. It makes me weep all the more as it passes from me to him, ethereal and unseen.

Maekallus jerks back, breath rushing into him. He gasps, coughs.

Blood patterns his skin in honeycombs, but the lesions close, and every last speck of blackness vanishes.

It's the last thing I see before shadow swallows the wildwood.

CHAPTER 16

*One can summon a mysting by drawing a ring on the earth
and, within the ring, an eight-pointed star formed by two
overlapping squares. Each corner of the star must touch the
outer ring. A sacrifice must be made to activate it. Blood is
the surest means of stimulation, but fire will also work.*

I open my eyes to Maekallus's face framed by the sun-laced canopy of
the wildwood. His yellow eyes dart back and forth, studying me. I blink
several times and try to sit up. An encompassing headache introduces
itself.

His hand on my back helps me until I'm upright. Blood crusts on
my sleeve. Crusting already?

I blacked out. For several minutes, at least.

"Enna?" he asks.

It takes me a moment to comprehend. I see my surroundings. I'm
in the wildwood, but I cannot remember how I came to be here. A
grinler with a broken neck lies some paces away. A grinler? I stare at it.
For a long time. Maekallus repeats my name.

I look back at him, at the thread of light wrapping around the
right side of his chest and beaming back toward the glade. That's when
it strikes me.

He's not in the glade.

He's here. Where the grinlers attacked. The memory seeps into my mind like molasses. I wait until it's all there before speaking.

"How are you here?" My voice is raspy. There's water in my basket, but I don't reach for it.

His eyes drop to my wrist. There's no point in dissembling, not anymore. I lift it and take the cool Telling Stone in my other hand, turning it about, letting its smooth surface catch filtered sunlight.

"That's what they wanted." It's a statement, not a question. The goblers, he means.

I nod. "I don't know why. It's just a Telling charm."

His eyes narrow. "That's no charm."

I clutch the stone in my fist, hiding it from him. "It is. That's how I knew about the gobler. It turns cold when mystings are nearby."

He takes my wrist and pulls until I release the dark rock. He lifts my hand so the stone dangles before my face. "This is Scroud's Will Stone."

My mouth is dry. I try to swallow, to work up some moisture. "Will Stone?" *Scroud?*

He lets me go and leans back. A long breath passes his lips. "It's said to be the petrified heart of the god who first created the mystings."

The words chill me. "But . . . a god cannot—"

"I don't know the lore." He glances down, his horn dangerously close to my forehead. I push the point away; he lifts his head to oblige. "That once belonged to a very powerful mysting lord named Scroud. An orjan."

Orjans are in the notes I copied from my grandmother's journal. Humanoid and intelligent, like a narval, but with bluish skin similar to a gobler's. Two great horns that curve back over the head like a helmet. Tusks similar to a grinler's. The eyes are shaded completely black.

Had my father stolen this Telling—Will—Stone from such a creature?

"What do you mean, a 'Will' Stone?" I press.

He watches me for a moment longer, perhaps trying to discern my genuineness. Then he stands, pushing off the bloody muck beneath him.

His tail is gone.

It once hung over the waist of his pants, but it's vanished, and Maekallus's backside is smooth. I gape at him, choking on words. Should I tell him? How?

Emptiness echoes inside me. My dwindling soul?

"Scroud was powerful *because* of that." Maekallus points to my bracelet. "It bends the will of those around you. He built up an army with it." He cringes. "Even I bowed to its power once."

When I don't answer, he continues, "You've heard of the War That Almost Was. Scroud's first attempt to claim a piece of the mortal realm. Foolish, but none of us could deny him. Not with *that*." He spits the last word. "He wanted my kind for scouts. And we couldn't say no. The second his army grew too numerous and he got distracted, I ran for it. Then your mortals drove him back, and *someone* took his precious amulet away from him. His war barely started before it ended." Then, as an afterthought, he adds, "He's spent the last two decades looking for it. He's held on to some of his recruits. The goblers, for instance. He must be poking holes all over the mortal realm, looking for it."

He regards me with something between disdain and awe. I, of course, was not the one to take it, but surely he is piecing together who did.

I stand, my legs sore, my dress bloody. I wipe my hands clean on the skirt. Beneath my loose bandage, my palm bears a pale scar. "But I . . . I never . . ."

My mouth closes. My mind is slow, but the memories come. Maekallus agreeing to my meager price so easily. The apothecary relinquishing information. Tennith escorting me to Caisgard. My father allowing me to go. Maekallus returning my book so promptly. The grinlers running away, their meal uneaten.

My gaze drops to Maekallus's chest. Had I not, in my heart, called out to him as the grinlers surrounded me?

"I willed you here." The words are but a breath. I broke the limits of his mortal cage.

He touches the spot on his chest where the spell buries into his flesh.

It makes sense. Even with half a mind, my father should not have permitted me to go to Caisgard in the company of an unmarried bachelor. And knowing Maekallus as I do now, I know he never would have consented to help me for mere coin. And he . . . he's seen this stone before. It bent him to another's will then, just as it does now.

Did the stone also compel him to fight so brutally, or did he *want* to defend me?

"Mystings have searched for it for years," he continues. "Somehow that gobler traced it here, and when he didn't come back, his friends came looking. I wonder . . ."

"What?"

He presses his lips together.

"*What*, Maekallus?"

"If they're Scroud's henchman, we're in more trouble than we thought. He might not have the stone anymore, but his influence is . . . substantial."

While I'm somewhat comforted by the use of the word *we*, I shiver. "They've not returned." Besides Maekallus, the only mystings who have witnessed my ownership of the stone are dead.

Maekallus frowns. "No. Not yet." He perks up suddenly and looks at me as though I'm a stranger. Like he's realized something.

I realize it, too. "Maekallus, I could will you back to your realm."

Surprise opens his features. So that hadn't been his thought. What, then?

"Perhaps." A whisper.

I palm the stone. Hold it to my chest. Close my eyes. *Descend, Maekallus. Return to the monster realm. Go. Return. Leave this place.*

Nothing happens.

I open my eyes. "Perhaps we need a circle . . ."

"No," he replies darkly, looking away. "The stone only controls the will of living creatures. It will not work."

"Then how did I will you outside that glade?"

He grumbles. "You willed *me*, not the spell." Wiping a hand down his face, he adds, "It never did affect me, when we were in opposite realms. Scroud usually stayed in the Deep, planning. I could *breathe* in the mortal realm. But if I didn't carry out his commands, I'd feel it the moment I returned."

Which would explain why Scroud couldn't just force the human generals to surrender from the safety of the monster realm. How far did the stone's influence reach? Enough to persuade a small army, but perhaps not enough to also cull a second army into submission. "We could *try*—"

"And we will fail!" he barks.

I teeter back from the power of his anger as though he'd struck me. His eyes blaze. I want nothing more than to be away from that stare.

I'm still holding the Will Stone.

The realization barely registers before Maekallus flies backward from the forest as if shoved by a great gust of wind. His arms and legs shoot out as he sails away, narrowly missing a branch, following the line of the thread connected to him. I gasp and watch him fly away until the trees mask his path.

The stone drops from my fingers. "Maekallus?"

Only a magpie answers back.

I am a coward, for I don't follow Maekallus into the glade.

I gather my things and run back home, until my body is weary and ready to sick up from the exercise. I collapse inside the kitchen. I must have fallen asleep right there on the stonework, for I wake with a crick in my neck, and the side of my face is cold.

I hear the creaking of the cellar doors—Papa coming up from the mushrooms.

Pushing my basket aside, I pick myself up and grab the metal bathing tub, half hobbling as I pull it into my room. I fill it with two pitchers of unwarmed water before stripping off my bloody dress and scrubbing myself until my teeth chatter.

The bracelet hangs from my wrist. I palm the stone. How often have I used this unknowingly? When my father told me about the descent circle, was it because I willed the information out of him? Surely I hadn't willed Tennith to kiss me . . . No, I had been prepared for him to decline. But I may have willed him not to speak to me about it, on the way to and from Caisgard.

Could I not also will the townsfolk to treat us kindly? Force Lunus Mather to give me fair prices? Will animals into waiting snares?

Persuade, with just a thought, a headmaster to permit my acceptance into a college?

For a moment my spirits lift, until something leaden and dark pushes down on them. What would my father think, knowing I'd forced his hand with the supernatural? Or Tennith, or . . . anyone? What must Maekallus think, for surely he must have pieced together what I'd already unknowingly done.

What if someone wielded the stone's power against *me*, bending my will to theirs and forcing me to do what was against my nature?

I almost take the bracelet off. I don't want to affect others in such a horrible, absolute way, especially not my father, who could not have realized the power he had bestowed on me when he first placed the bracelet around my wrist.

But then I think of the grinlers, of the hunger in their eyes, and I leave the bracelet be.

I let myself be normal—as normal as can be—for a little while. I don't wish to see Maekallus. He saved my life, yes, and in turn I saved his. But I need to be with my father right now. I need to be . . . away from Maekallus's revelation and the confusion his presence stirs in me.

My father is happy to have me around. I play fell the king with him, and to my sorrow, I also forget my strategy. Memory just . . . doesn't hold as easily as it should, and the explanation is clear. It's a long game, and it pleases me that Papa wins.

I fear the following day, when we must return to the market, but while my soul is in pieces, my mind is still sharp, and I manage just fine, though I change my usual path to avoid Tennith. I'm not sure what I'd say to him, and my moments of listlessness and blankness have me on edge. Occasionally, pain spikes in that deepness where my soul resides. I can't remember the recipe for my grandmother's meat pie, and I allow my too-tired body more naps than I should. But if I look past all of that, I'm well enough.

My father, however, is not. He starts to cough and look a little pale, so I put him to bed and make him vegetable broth and tea. It revitalizes him for a time, but when he goes to our vegetable garden to pull weeds, he sickens again, and I order him to spend the rest of the day in bed. I try to will him better, but it seems illness is not something that can be coerced.

With my father abed, I'm left to stew in my own thoughts. I wonder about the grinlers and how far the Will Stone's power stretches. Nearly a dozen grinlers heeded my command, but they have limited intelligence. Would such a tactic work on greater mystings, like Maekallus? Like this Scroud? Could I not simply will him and his goblers to leave me be, should they return?

I write all my thoughts into my notes, filling page after page with questions and theories. I had willed Maekallus out of the glade to rescue me. Did he sacrifice himself to help me merely because the stone bid him to do so? Or perhaps he was persuaded by the fact that I am the one keeping him alive. Us alive.

Does it matter, his motivation? Why do I even care?

I wonder if I could will another creature to come to me. The gobler in the wildwood, the one who set the spell on Maekallus. Could I force him to break the spell, or will that interworld barrier prevent it, just as it banned Maekallus from descending to the monster realm?

I try, but the stone does not tingle, nor does it reveal its secrets to my mind. I document all of this in my book.

Papa sleeps late the following day. I make him a hearty meal in hopes of improving his stamina and a tonic of aster leaf, which is good for the lungs. My stone is cooler that morning, warning of the approach of a mysting—a rooter—nearby. I will it away, and the stone warms.

It's the knowledge of its protection that finally gives me the strength to return to the glade, basket in tow.

Maekallus has worn an ovular track in the clearing with his pacing. I remember his claim of impending madness and feel guilty for my absence. The black spots blemishing his skin mark the time I've spent away. Gripping the stone, I try once more to will him back into the monster realm, but the stone does not heed my request.

I drop the stone. "I'm sorry."

He spins about, finding me amid the trees. I can't read his expression. Not quite relieved, not quite angry.

I swallow. "I needed some time to think. I . . . I didn't mean to trap you here." I lift my basket as a peace offering. "I brought you food and books."

He guffaws. "I told you, I can't read mortal writings."

"I'll read them to you. I don't mind." I step into the glade, over the matted grass and packed dirt of his track. I cross almost to where the binding spell pierces the earth, then set my basket down and sit on a patch of orchard grass. It's strange, this absurd predicament I'm in. It's bizarre and morbid and deadly, and yet in this confined space with this impertinent mysting, I feel . . . normal. Not the outcast, not the peculiar woman who lives on the outskirts of town. It's as if here, I am truly myself.

And with that thought, the sudden urge to explain boils up my throat.

I say, "I should tell you—" at the same time Maekallus asks, "Have you been amusing yourself with your newfound power?"

A frown tugs at my lips. "Of course not."

He smirks. "To think of the games you could play with humans— with anyone—with a stone like that."

"Then it is a good thing I possess it, and not you."

He cocks a brow.

I pat the grass next to me. "Sit."

He doesn't move. I wait, and he says, "You can will it."

"Now that I know I have the ability, I will be more careful not to use it. If you do not wish to sit, I will not make you."

He considers this. "I find you odd, Enna."

"Most do." I pat the grass.

He sighs and crosses the glade, sitting beside me. He smells like the forest, like summer and ancient trees. I offer him the food I brought. He takes it, but doesn't eat.

After several seconds of silence, I speak. "My mother was killed by grinlers." I watch the glimmer of the binding spell where it lifts from the earth, stretching toward the mysting beside me. "It happened in the middle of day, just like . . . then. She was pregnant with me. They killed her, and my father cut me out to save me."

I glance to Maekallus. He looks almost . . . sympathetic. But surely no mysting could experience such a sensation. Not toward a mortal.

But what about a mysting with a soul?

"Their attack frightened me, but I suppose it helped us in a way," I continue. "Since now I understand this stone better. If I cannot get you back to your home, at least I can relieve these weeds from your incessant stomping."

His lips quirk into a smile. The expression lights something in me, near the ache of my missing soul.

I look away. It is not attraction. Any such feelings I harbor for Maekallus merely spring from my desire to learn more about his kind, from my yearning for the lost bits of my soul. Yet are they bits? I have no idea how much he's taken, or how much remains inside me.

"Thank you," he says.

I start.

He eyes me.

"You've never once thanked me for anything."

He frowns. Considers.

I turn back to the binding spell. "I'm not sure what to do next. I tried willing the gobler here, but nothing has happened."

Maekallus rubs his jaw. "If I can leave this place," he gestures to the glade, "I have a friend of sorts who frequents the wildwood. Rooters enjoy mortal forests."

Rooters. One of the few generally docile mystings of which I am aware. My grandmother was especially familiar with their kind, which is why I had the courage to track one before. I think of the one I recently sent away. "You're sure he's here?"

"I think I could find him. His name is Attaby. He's more familiar with magic than I am. It might be a ways."

"I . . ."

He glances my way.

"How far? My father isn't well. Not terribly so, but . . ."

"I don't know. Not too far. He frequents the wildwood. I may be able to call to him if we draw another one of those circles. There was . . . some . . . power in it."

I mull over this for a moment. "I could try to will him to us."

Maekallus doesn't hide his frown as his gaze flicks to the stone hanging from my wrist. He's sensitive to it, but I would be, too, had it acted like my prison in the past. "If we can't find him, yes. But believe me, the fewer creatures who know about that thing, the better. Attaby is intelligent. He might be able to figure it out."

I nod. "Then we might need provisions. And to see that my father is well."

"Can it be done today? I don't need to eat. You . . ."

He glances downward. I think he meant to indicate my stomach, but his eyes linger on my breasts. Feeling warm, I cross my arms, and he looks away. "I can leave now." He thumbs a black spot on the back of his hand.

The cut on my hand has opened again. I massage the Will Stone. "Let's go. The worst we'll get is some exercise, right?" *Tennith, stop by the house and check on my father. If this Will Stone can reach you . . . ensure he's provided for.*

The stone tingles against my fingers.

Maekallus stands and offers me his hand, another surprising gesture. I take it, and he lifts me to my feet.

"First, the circle," he says, and draws a star in the soil.

CHAPTER 17

*A vuldor is an unintelligent mysting of canine make that
lives exclusively in the monster realm. That is to say, neither
I nor my source have ever seen its kind on the mortal plane.*

Maekallus stands in the center of a descent circle. Although mystings
don't need a circle to return to the Deep, and the binding spell won't
allow such a circle to work in its intended manner, he's discovered this
rune opens the space between realms just enough to let him suck up a
little power. Before his fight with the grinlers, he hadn't realized how
powerless he's become, how . . . mortalesque. He isn't as fast or as
strong. He can't remove his horn. And gods below, he's lost his tail. It's
as though the growing soul inside him clashes with his immortal body,
and as compromise, his form becomes more and more . . . human.

Maekallus closes his eyes as the circle lights, drawing upon the
energy it emits. He will need the boost to find Attaby.

"But you don't mind if we use the basement. Of course you don't mind."

He rears back. *The man doesn't even bother to offer him a bribe. The
glint in his eye and the knife beneath his coat is enough.*

Maekallus grits his teeth against the strange . . . what, memory? . . .
surfacing in his head.

Enna's voice follows it. *"Maybe, you* are *the bastard?"*

So what if he is? He was made from a human. From the murder of one. Thus his humanoid form. He's always known that. He'd been born a fully formed adult—there *are* no infant mystings. They don't generate the way humans do. He isn't the bastard who died to create him.

So why is it that, somewhere in a dark pit inside him where the pieces of Enna's soul nest, he wants her speculation to be true?

The bit of power snuffs out. Maekallus opens his eyes. Feels the tendrils of energy dancing through his black-mottled fingertips. No. Humans—mortals—are weak. Pathetic. He wants nothing to do with them. He certainly doesn't wish to be one.

"Maekallus?"

He looks up at Enna's voice. The fragmented soul stirs within him. Would it be so terrible, to be like her?

He knows now why he hadn't consumed her inner being with that first kiss; the Will Stone explains as much. He'd realized it after the grinlers' attack, when they stood there in the forest, surrounded by the bodies of the fallen grinlers, Enna covered in his blood. It's simple.

She doesn't *want* to lose her soul, so she wills it to stay.

The magic of his kind pulls, and the stone resists. The conflicting forces reached this strange compromise, just like the way his physical form changes to accommodate the newfound soul within.

Is that the reason why the soul inside him continues to live so fiercely? Because she wills it not to lose its vigor? To stay alive? To possibly, one day, return to her?

Is this newest piece of soul the reason why, when Enna had fallen into deep slumber after healing him, he'd felt panic entirely his own?

He turns from her, focusing on the task at hand. There is a way for mystings to sense one another, if they want to be sensed. Attaby is the type to not have his guard up.

Maekallus pushes the magic out of him, deeper into the forest, away from human civilization. The energy is so thin already; it barely grazes the surface of the wildwood. But just as it burns out, he detects something distinctly rooter. Straight east.

Opening his eyes, he walks out of the circle, letting his hooves—the hooves that now bear five points, similar to toes—scuff the rune as he goes. He gestures in the direction.

"Attaby."

"You're sure?" Enna asks.

"As sure as I can be."

"But if it's not . . ."

He folds his arms and leans his weight onto one leg. "What was it that you bothered me with, over and over? That we should *try?*"

A small smile touches her lips. He tries not to mirror it. "Then we should go, while we've still time. Lead the way."

Maekallus passes out of the glade, to the point where the binding spell prevents him from going any farther. He presses against it; the curse presses back.

Enna takes one step past him, clutching the stone in her hand. He can't fathom it—the Will Stone, all this time, in the hands of a mortal. The rumors that it had been stolen by a human must be true. A human of Enna's acquaintance? This father of hers? Or had it simply traded hands from merchant to merchant, sold as a simple charm of warning? Leave it to humans to peddle away the greatest weapon of his time.

The spell slackens. He takes one step, another. Grins. It's like stretching after a year-long slumber. Like sex after months of solitude.

"Prey and predators," he mumbles, ducking under a tree to avoid catching it with his horn. Thick forests really aren't prime locations for narvals. When he isn't lurking about human cities, he prefers open plains. "I almost feel free."

Enna smiles beside him. "I'm glad."

The gobler's spell, however, begins to tug again.

"You need to actively want my company." He moves to jab her with his tail, only to remember it's been sacrificed to the maw of the mortal realm. Will it return, once he descends? "Otherwise I can't accompany you. Unless you know this part of the wildwood, I would suggest willing me here."

Needless to say, the first time Enna had given up willing him out of his prison, it had not been pleasant. He'd been jerked back to the glen so forcefully it was a wonder he hadn't broken anything.

She doesn't respond.

"Enna?"

She snaps to attention. "Oh, sorry."

The spell relaxes.

He eyes her. She's been . . . leaving the present more and more lately. In response to the thought, the bits of her soul light up like fireflies, pressing against him as if attempting to get closer to her. It's *only* the soul, he tells himself, and it's . . . strange. Maekallus has never *felt* for so long in his entire existence.

The one he can clearly remember, anyway.

Enna begins to prattle. He isn't sure why. Perhaps she doesn't like the silence, or she wants a distraction, or she has some weird human need to share her stories. She talks about growing a mushroom farm— how anyone can eat those things is beyond him—and the different plants in her garden, all of which Maekallus had to put in his mouth during their first attempts to break the gobler's spell. He cringes to remember it. She asks him questions about the beuhger again, then talks about what she knows about goblers, and then prods him for information about the slyser—the large, serpentine mysting who'd come up through the summoning circle—for that ridiculous book of notes of hers. Then she goes on about her grandmother, and how the older woman had once hired a rooter to protect her home. How it was the one true evidence Enna had that a docile mysting *could* exist, though her grandmother had never recorded the rooter's name.

"Maybe it was . . . what did you say his name was, again?"

"Attaby."

"Attaby." She smiles. Such a small, simple thing, but it's strangely beautiful. "It doesn't sound like a mysting name."

"I suppose you're the expert."

She shrugs. "It's just . . . too friendly."

Maekallus picks his way up a sudden, short incline in the forest floor. "Then it's perfect for him."

Enna struggles behind him; he grabs her forearm and hauls her up. She scrapes her knee, but doesn't protest. "Is it?"

"Rooters are doleful little *ka'pigs*. They do well in this realm, frolicking in the meadows and wiping their asses on the doorsteps of humans."

"Maekallus."

"You deny it?"

"No." She takes a second to catch her breath. "It's just . . . I don't think anyone has ever said 'asses' in front of me before."

He shrugs and trudges ahead. Stops so she can catch up. Gods, she's weak. He knows humans aren't usually so weak. It has to be the soul.

She's weak because she's helping you stay alive.

Because you lied to her. Because you're still lying to her.

Maekallus clenches his jaw. Enna stumbles.

"Here." He grasps her forearm and, careful with his horn, stoops over and scoops up her knees with his other arm.

Color returns to her face. "I can walk—"

"Do you want to make it back before dark or not? We'll go faster this way."

Her body tenses with complaint, but as Maekallus picks up speed, winding through the uneven wildwood, she relaxes into his arms. "Just until I catch my breath," she insists.

Gods, she's small. She doesn't look that small, just . . . feels it. Like he could crush her without trying. Like if he drops her, she might not get back up again.

His stomach tightens at the thought of it. He wishes it wouldn't.

It's farther than he anticipated; the mortal realm's sun has crested and begins to fall by the time he senses Attaby.

"He's close." Maekallus searches the wood. A fox darts to the south.

"Put me down." Enna presses a hand to his chest; it ignites something strange in his skin, something that seems at odds with the corruption coursing through his veins. He obliges. She takes a moment to look around, rolling the Will Stone between her fingers. "Are you sure? The stone hasn't chilled."

"Chilled?"

"It gets cold when mystings are nearby."

"It should have been cold this whole time, then." He points to himself.

Enna turns and looks him up and down. He feels her gaze like the winds of the Azhgrada, the desert of the Deep.

"It stays cool for you. It hasn't thought you dangerous since the binding."

That takes him aback. Not *dangerous*? Hadn't he been dangerous to those grinlers? And to the mystings who passed through the portal to the Deep?

He growls deep in his throat. Steps closer to Enna, until the space between them is as narrow as his little finger. Enna tenses. He stoops low, letting the base of his horn press against the highest point of her forehead. His hands slide around her neck—softly, but he can feel her pulse hammering under his thumb. Is it for fear, or something else?

"Does it still think I'm not dangerous?" he murmurs. His nose hovers just above hers. He thinks about the way her lips feel, warm and willing—

"M-Maekallus," she croaks.

Two heavy footfalls sound ahead of them. "Am I interrupting something? Maekallus, I wasn't expecting you. Ah, you're missing a tail."

Maekallus straightens, letting his hands fall from Enna's neck. She backs away instantly, a small squeak escaping her when she beholds Attaby.

He looks as any rooter will—about eight feet tall, with hard, dark skin that resembles the bark of a tree. His head is broad and rectangular, and if he closes his eyes, his face will be nearly indistinguishable from the rest of it. He has long arms and skinny, wood-like legs. Thick, flat fingers on each hand. In a place like the wildwood, a rooter can stand stationary and never be noticed by a mortal.

"It's been a while." Maekallus bends his head in greeting.

"Indeed. You are not one to traipse the wildwood." He studies Enna. "Especially with a mortal. Has this anything to do with your tail?"

Enna glances at her stone, then back at Attaby. She pulls her sleeve over the bracelet.

"In a manner of speaking." Maekallus gestures to the thin stream of light emitting from his chest.

"At least you didn't lose your horn. Narval horns make for excellent sorcery." Attaby moves closer, ungracefully, crushing vegetation underfoot as he goes. He squints at the red light. "Ah, that's a terrible chain to have." He looks to Enna. "And you can't untie it?"

Enna blinks. "I, uh, I'm not the one who bound him here. It was a gobler. I hired Maekallus to eliminate him, and it . . . didn't end well."

She opens her right hand and pulls back the bandaging on it, showing the weeping red cut.

Attaby chortles. "Trouble with a gobler? Really, Maekallus?"

"There were *two* of them," he growls. "The second crept up on me."

"In a forest, no less? Hmm. Follow me. I've a nicer spot to chat." He turns, far too slowly, and stomps back through the forest. It isn't hard to see where he came from. Rooters leave clumsy trails. At least the mellow pace will be good for Enna.

They don't go far. Attaby brings them to another glade, much smaller than Maekallus's cage, the grassy ground littered with leaves green and yellow. Dogwood—Maekallus thinks that's what it's called— springs up in patches around it like the claws of a fergshaw. The rooter has set up a sort of table, a long split log propped up on other logs.

Speaking of sorcery, atop it sits a collection of things: a hare's foot, leaves and needles from various plants, gemstones, ash, a bowl of slop from the River of Blood in the Deep. Enna takes an immediate interest in them, toeing behind Attaby to investigate. No doubt she wishes to sketch the lot in her book.

"And the girl?" Attaby asks, as though they'd been conversing this whole time.

"We're bound by the bargain. She . . . has an ability to break up her soul."

"Truly?" He turns about and looks at Enna, who takes the opportunity to look right back. She doesn't seem afraid. Granted, Attaby is hardly terrifying.

"How do you do it?" the rooter asks.

"Uh"—she glances to Maekallus—"I don't know. It's . . . something I was born with."

Maekallus groans inwardly at the obvious lie, but Attaby accepts it. "Interesting. And you're keeping him alive. But of course, the bargain spell is simply—"

Maekallus clears his throat loudly. Gesturing to Enna, he says, "We'll worry about the bargain. What we need help with is breaking this." He juts a thumb at the binding spell.

"Hmmm." Attaby considers for a moment before walking to Maekallus and grabbing his jaw in his wide, rough fingers, turning his head this way and that. Maekallus resists the urge to knock the rooter away. Like it or not, he *needs* help.

Attaby releases him and looks him over, possibly studying the spots of black growing like mold over his body.

"You're not corrupted," Enna says, drawing the mysting's attention away. "You've obviously been here a long time, but the mortal world doesn't consume you."

The rooter chortles. "Oh, it does indeed, young one. But a dip back into the Deep is all I require to return renewed. It is not hard to linger here if one visits home on occasion. That is why so many of our kind haunt uncultivated places like this wood. The weather here really is more pleasant, as is the food."

"Truly? What is it like in the monster—"

"To the task at hand," Maekallus interrupts. Even as he says it, black oozes out from the slice across his hand, eating up his palm. It stings.

"I've no mystium blood to unbind it," says Attaby. "I'm surprised it lets you come all this way. Binding spells tend to have short leashes."

"Can you break it?"

Attaby frowns. He places his large, woody hand against Maekallus's chest. The thread of red light passes through it.

Then he digs in all four of his jagged fingers, and the tips begin to glow blue.

Attaby is an old mysting, well versed in the workings of both worlds and the sorcery between them. It's why Maekallus sought him out. This time, and the last, though he'd been too late, then.

But Attaby's workings are never pleasant.

Heat like a thousand suns pulses through the rooter's hand, and it takes everything Maekallus has to stay standing. Air storms from their connection. Something beneath Attaby's grip cracks and sizzles. Maekallus's knees give out, but he doesn't fall. The power holds him up.

It pierces him, and he screams.

"*Stop!*" Enna's cry is muffled by the surge of Attaby's power. She grabs the rooter's other arm and tugs, as if she'll ever possess the strength to move him. "You're hurting him!"

The gusts and the light die down, as does the strength holding Maekallus upright. He drops to his knees, palms against the earth.

Enna runs to his side. His chest smokes and smells terrible. "Are you all right?"

He trembles. Grits his teeth to stop it, but his body is repelling the workings of the rooter. It will take a moment.

"Maekallus?" She grabs either side of his face, searching his eyes. Is she going to kiss him, like she did after the grinlers' attack?

He reaches up a hand and grasps her wrist. "It'll leave a mark," he rasps.

"Hmm." Attaby strokes his wide, flat jaw, completely unmoved by Enna's screams or Maekallus's . . . whatever. "Alas, this binding is absolute. It wavered for a moment, but that is all I can do without killing you."

Maekallus looks down. A strange circular burn mars his chest, the skin there gray and waxen. The glimmer of the binding spell beams bright in comparison.

He spits the vilest curse the Deep had taught him.

"Interesting," Attaby says, but when Maekallus lifts his head, he realizes the rooter isn't referring to the spell. His dark eyes shift back and forth between Enna and Maekallus, a flat finger pressed to his mouth.

"Attaby," Maekallus warns. The name scrapes up his throat.

Attaby turns to Enna. "You should know, little mortal, that there's been more activity in this place than usual, closer to the heart of the wood. Magic quakes through the air. Mmm, yes. Mystings all about, sniffing something out. Not all are as tolerant of humans as I am. Or, apparently, as Maekallus is."

Enna stands. "Tolerant? This is *our* world. *We* tolerate *them*."

Attaby shakes his head. "Oh no, no. The strong prey on the weak, it has always been so. The setting is just happenstance."

Enna frowns. Maekallus, biting down on a groan, gets up on one malformed hoof, then the other. Slowly, every muscle in his back pulling and twisting, he stands, albeit hunched over.

"Scroud's minions," Attaby continues. "Something around here he wants. I can't think of another reason for them to brood about in the wildwood, unless it's a grab for resources."

Maekallus licks his teeth. *Scroud.* More mystings in the area. Do they know Enna has the stone? But the gobler who escaped him never made it to her home. Perhaps they have determined to look elsewhere.

"Hmm. May I?" Attaby steps closer to Enna. Places a hand on her shoulder. Maekallus can tell she's trying not to shrink back.

Since when could he read a mortal like this? Since when has he cared to try?

Attaby stoops low, almost leveling his eyes with Enna's. He stares long and hard. "Little mortal, you've just half a soul left. Be careful how you divide it."

Enna's mouth works, forming the word *half*, but the word has no voice. Her smooth skin drains of color, making her dark hair stark against her cheek.

Attaby looks a moment more. "Ah, yes. I've been about these woods many years. I knew your grandmother. Wily woman." He straightens and drops his rough hand before turning to Maekallus. "I'm sorry. A mystium, a tusk, a death. That's how those spells work, as I'm sure you know."

The slivers of soul sink down to his pelvis, cold and desolate.

"I do not think you'll have time for the first," the rooter continues, peering from Maekallus to Enna and back. "Mortals have such slow gestations."

Maekallus rolls his eyes. All the blood returns to Enna's face at once, turning it redder than his hair.

He'd be lying if he says he hadn't thought of it, for one reason or another.

"I'm aware." He grits his teeth against the pain in his chest, stifling the words. "Thank you, for trying."

Attaby pulls his broad head back. "My, my, a narval with manners. You're changing, Maekallus. And I don't just mean the tail."

Enna glances at him. He doesn't meet her eyes.

"Another option gone," she whispers.

Maekallus winces, feeling sore blackness spreading behind his knee, hot and . . . wet. He tries not to cringe. The wet spots are much worse than the dry.

The walk back is slow. The soreness Attaby left through his chest and back is deep and aching. But Enna keeps up with the slow pace. She puts Maekallus's arm around her shoulders as though she can hold him up. By the time they reach the glade, full night has fallen, and stars peek from the sky. Maekallus has to lead the way; Enna's eyes can't pierce the dark like his can.

She moves to her basket, pulling from it a lantern. She makes a few sparks before it lights. "This would be easier if you'd stop injuring yourself."

"Not every injury is intentional."

She stares at the light of the lantern, frowning at it. What is she thinking?

He pounds the heel of his hand against his brow. Why did he *care*?

Changing, the rooter said. This damned soul is reworking the way he looks, the way he thinks. The way he *feels*. Its vigor is as bright as the day he first tasted it.

Is this how he'd felt before? In his past life? Those memories . . .

"I'll come back tomorrow. You'll make it through the night." It's almost a question. "I'll . . . continue willing a wider perimeter for you. So you can move about. But meet me back here in the morning. I don't have the strength to look for you."

Now that he has some semblance of freedom, all he wants to do is sleep. His body is wanting more of that, too, these days. He grunts a response.

"Good night, Maekallus."

And like that, she is gone.

CHAPTER 18

Orjans are humanoid mystings of high intellect. The origin
of their creation is unknown.

"Enna?" Papa calls from his bedroom when the wood in the hallway creaks under my feet.

I snuffed my lantern outside, so it's dark within the house. I poke my head into his room. "Yes, Papa?"

"Where have you been? Are you just getting home?"

My heart aches to hear his worry. "Oh, no, Papa. I've been home since before the sunset. Don't you remember? I just needed to use the outhouse."

I can't make out his features in the dark room, but I can imagine his face crinkling, especially around the eyes, as he tries to remember. I hate lying to my father—he has a hard enough time determining what's real and what's not without my inventions. My struggle with my own weakening memory makes the betrayal that much sharper.

He must accept the falsehood, for he goes on, "Tennith came by while you were away to check on me. Said he wanted to talk to you, but wouldn't say why."

The Will Stone hangs heavy from its chain. Did my unspoken plea make it to him, then? I vow to offer him my utmost gratitude when we next cross paths.

I step into the room and sit on the edge of my father's bed. Feel his forehead. No fever, but his skin is a little too cool for a man who's been bundled in blankets on a warm summer night. "How are you feeling?"

"Tired."

"Such should be expected. Can I get you anything?"

His hand finds mine. His thumb brushes my bandage. "No, my dear. Get some rest. I'm sorry to keep you. That nail, on the ladder?"

"Yes."

"Thought I hammered it in. I'll check in the morning."

"You'll stay in bed." I pull from his grasp and straighten his blankets. "I want you well. I'll take care of the rest."

"Thank you, Elefie."

"Enna, Papa."

"Mmm." He rolls onto his side.

I kiss his head and leave for my own room. Sleep takes me without a fight.

I submerge my hand into the cool water of the bucket, watching stains of red and black diffuse through it. I know Maekallus has worsened over the night, more than usual, for my realm seems to be eating this sliver of myself as well.

I pull my hand out, apply a nearly useless salve, and wrap it again. I managed to rise early and finish the chores, though my soiled clothes are soaking in the washtub. Blood is a tricky thing to clean. Fortunately, most of my dresses are dark and don't show evidence of my adventures in the wildwood. Regardless, I don't like knowing it's there.

I hold my hand to my breast and take a deep breath. Maekallus will need me again today. The words of Attaby ring in my head: *Little mortal, you've just half a soul left. Be careful how you divide it.*

Half a soul. What will I lose today by bestowing another kiss on Maekallus? I must redouble my efforts to break his binding. I'm not ready to die.

And I don't want Maekallus to die, either.

The sentiment lingers in my thoughts as I prepare my basket for another trek through the wildwood. I think of Maekallus carrying me, his arms pocked by corruption, yet still strong and . . . warm. I stroke the wrapping around the unchanged gray mark the gobler left on my forearm. The gobler's hand was so cold. Maekallus's touch warms by the day.

I try to ignore the pressure in my chest as I check on my father.

He's paler than yesterday. His voice rasps, too. I put down my basket and straightway make him more aster leaf tea and soup. I take the pillows and blankets from my bed and make him as comfortable as he can be. He wakes from his dozing and smiles at me.

"I'll get over it," he promises.

"Of course you will. I'm not caring for all those mushrooms myself." I need to tend the oon berry surrounding the house. I may have the Will Stone, but my father does not, and I am not home as much as I should be. If only I'd healed Maekallus last night instead of trying to save a few hours. Then I could have stayed at Papa's side today.

I help my father drink his tea. I won't be gone long. I pray that my body will have the strength it needs to be swift. The cut on my palm throbs in response, soaking the bandage.

I wait until slumber claims my father again, then take a long moment to listen to his breathing before I set out for the glade.

The Will Stone tells me Maekallus has not wandered far. I find him only an eighth of a mile from the clearing where his binding spell is staked. I'm glad—it takes so much of my energy just to make it this far, and I can't spare time waiting for him to return.

He's tucked into a small space between clustered trees, a little rocky to get to, the ground slightly sloped. He leans against an aspen. His breathing is similar to my father's, but heavier, wetter. The mortal realm is working hard on him. His skin is more black than peach, and black streaks through his bound hair. Half his face is darkened with corruption. The muscles of his back are taut. I can only imagine the pain it causes him.

When I speak, it startles him. It is becoming easier and easier to sneak up on Maekallus. I imagine few could scare him, before he met me.

"I brought you some stew," I offer. "And water, though now you should be able to find it on your own."

He somehow manages to grin, even as the skin around the gray burn on his chest weeps a few drops of tar. "Did you know the forest looks all the same? The cage has only gotten larger."

"That's not true." I set the basket down in a nook formed by a tree root. "Farther east it opens up into a sort of studded meadow. South, past my home, there's a waterfall. Just a small one, but it's beautiful in the winter. It makes thick icicles that shine with rainbows when the sun hits them." I pause. "Do you have that, in the monster realm? Rainbows, waterfalls."

"Rainbows, no," he rasps. "Waterfalls, yes. Most are not made of water, however."

The scholarly part of me wants to ask what they are made of, but the memory of that strange, horrifying substance Attaby had collected in a bowl on his makeshift worktable makes me pause. Besides, now is not the time for research.

My eyes drop to the thread of light ever piercing his chest. I wonder if that hurts, too. He doesn't show it, if it does. For a mysting and a trickster, Maekallus keeps his complaining to a minimum.

I lick my lips. *Half a soul.* "We'll break it, won't we?"

He rubs the poisoned flesh of his chest and stands with effort. "Somehow."

We face each other, silent for several seconds, until I feel strange inside. My mind blanks of words. Why should I feel awkward now? I've kissed him several times. Yet now, even with him in this deteriorated state, I feel . . . nervous. Like I did with Tennith.

Papa is waiting, I remind myself. I leave my basket and pick my way across the short space between us. Clench my hands into fists to hide the anxious quiver of my fingers. Say a silent apology to that deep space inside me. I can feel the warmth of what I lost radiating from Maekallus's broken body.

I lift my face toward his. Take in the slope of his nose, the curve of his mouth. I don't want to admit it to myself, but he is handsome. More so than before, though the exchanging of soul hasn't altered his face. It is the way I look at him that has changed, and that scares me most of all.

He hesitates. Only for a moment, but I notice it, and I wonder.

He doesn't touch me, save for his lips to mine. They are half-cold, half-warm. I crack with silent thunder even before feeling the break inside me. Hear my fractured soul's sorrow as yet more of it spins out of me and into him. At least this time I remain conscious.

Maekallus stumbles as though the extra piece of my soul struck him. He grabs my bandaged hand for balance. Almost instantly his skin clears, even the burns.

I don't feel any different, save for the sadness blooming in my gut like a poisonous flower. I squeeze his hand. He looks at me, and my mouth falls open.

"Maekallus"—his name is half breath—"your . . . eyes."

Their harsh yellow pigment has given way to warm amber. Not a common color by any stretch of the imagination, but a passable one, for a mortal. I marvel at them, at the humanness of that hue. Again my grandmother's voice surfaces in my mind: *What is a soul if not an extension of the heart?*

My lips part. Am I giving Maekallus a human heart, too?

"What—" he begins, but he's interrupted, and not by me.

"Enna?"

I'm so startled to hear the familiar voice I nearly collapse where I stand. Whirling around, I see Tennith coming through the trees. He's in his hunting leathers, but carries no game.

I glance back to Maekallus, then to Tennith, choking on my own breath. To be seen here, with a *mysting*, and in such a compromising position. Dear gods above, whom will he tell? Maekallus's eyes may be passable, but that horn gives him away! My father and I will be cast out completely, and I will be *lucky* if that's the only consequence—

The lack of judgment in Tennith's features confuses me, even as my pulse races faster than a mountain-fed brook. His countenance is gentle, concerned.

He pauses. "You look so pale. I'm sorry—I didn't mean to follow you. But I saw you go into the wildwood, and I've been meaning to speak with you."

Words fail me. Tennith's eyes only watch me, not Maekallus. He does, however, glance to my basket.

"Hmm." Maekallus puts his hands on his hips. "At least that part still works."

Tennith doesn't seem to hear him. To see him. "Enna?"

The instant he says my name, I remember the first thing Maekallus ever said to me. *You can see me?*

Breath rushes out of me all at once. Relief has never tasted sweeter. Somehow, Maekallus is hiding himself from Tennith's eyes. The Will Stone must have prevented Maekallus from remaining invisible the day we met. He had never meant to interact with me, only sate his curiosity, but his spell hadn't held against my charm.

"I-I'm sorry. Yes, you startled me." My heart is beating so quickly, perhaps I'll faint after all.

Tennith again glances to my basket. "Where are you going?"

I say the first thing that jumps to mind. "My grandmother's."

To my relief, he nods.

Maekallus steps around me, studying Tennith like he's some bizarre mortal creature. "Who is this?"

I don't answer him, of course. Tennith may not be able to hear Maekallus's voice, but he'll certainly hear mine. I try very hard to keep my eyes on Tennith.

He takes another step into the small glade. Runs a gloved hand down the leather over his arm. "Enna, I feel like . . . you've been avoiding me. I haven't seen you in town."

"I don't frequent town."

"That's . . . true. I visited your father yesterday. He couldn't remember where you'd gone."

"Tubers." I answer too quickly and try not to wince at the obviousness of it. Maekallus notices, however, and laughs. "I was . . . hunting tubers. Papa's memory isn't as sharp as it once was."

"Forgive me, I shouldn't pry."

Maekallus stands directly in front of me. "Seems like he's prying to me."

I sidestep to my basket and pick it up, if only so I can see around Maekallus to Tennith's face.

Tennith sighs. "But we're here now, and I should be direct."

Oh gods, no. "Tennith—"

"I've been baffled since we kissed."

Maekallus's brows shoot up. He glances at me. "Oh?"

I feel blood rising to my face. "Tennith, I—"

"Don't want to explain yourself, I know. So you've said."

Maekallus steps closer to Tennith, until he's practically breathing on the man. His horn looms above him like an executioner's ax. Tennith is a good deal shorter—the length of my hand, at least. "How old is he?" Maekallus asks. "Can he even fill out those breeches?"

I cover my face with my hand, trying to cool the heat beneath my skin.

"I've embarrassed you." Tennith's tone is apologetic.

I drop my hand and send a scathing look toward Maekallus. "No, no, you deserve to know. But . . ." I swallow my frustration. "I just . . . I truly can't explain to you right now. I'm sorry."

"I'm not trying to . . . force . . . you into anything, Enna." A single, dry chuckle escapes his throat. He rubs his hands together. "I'm not even sure what I want—"

"Oh," Maekallus chimes in, smirking. "I think I know."

"—but there was something there that night."

Even if Maekallus weren't extremely present for this conversation, making me feel a buffoon, I'm not sure what I would say to the sweet man before me. Honesty is impossible. Granted, there are truths I could share that wouldn't require me to reveal my entwinement with mystings. I could tell Tennith genuinely that I asked him to kiss me so he would be my first, because I fancied him—but to say such a thing in front of Maekallus . . . The idea makes my gut churn.

One truth I could never tell is that I haven't given much thought to Tennith since Caisgard. Shame trickles beneath my skin.

"Enna?" he asks.

"Uh, yes," I manage. I twist my fingers around the basket's handle.

Maekallus lifts a hand, perhaps to prod Tennith. I grab the Will Stone and silently urge him away. He backs off as though pushed and glares at me.

I clear my throat. "My grandmother is expecting me."

"I can accompany you, if you'd like."

"Ah, no. No, thank you."

"The wildwood is dangerous—"

Maekallus adds, "Very dangerous, Enna. Another mortal suitor could jump out at any moment."

"—but of course you know that. Gods, I sound like my father."

I clamor for the best response I can manage. "I like your father."

"Have you kissed him, too?" Maekallus asks.

Tennith smiles, but it fades. "I just . . . I don't want you to think ill of me."

I squeeze the Will Stone, then relax my fingers. "Oh, Tennith, I could never think ill of you. You've been nothing but kind to me."

Maekallus snorts.

Tennith shifts his weight to his back foot. "What I mean is . . . I never approached you—"

Maekallus barks a laugh, but there's a sharpness to it that seems to echo against my ribs. "This is intriguing."

"—but I noticed you. Of course I did, though you didn't go to school with the other girls—"

I feel like my very bones are curling in on themselves. "Tennith—"

"No, no." Maekallus folds his arms. "Let him continue. Please."

"*Now* you're being polite?" I hiss.

"What?" Tennith asks.

I clear my throat. "I, uh—"

But he goes on. "I won't press you, but I wish to know why you approached me *then*, on that night. Or why you'd prefer to forget about it."

"I haven't forgotten about it." My words are growing sharp, and my feet are freezing, for blood continues to rush into my face and neck. I squeeze the Will Stone. "Tennith, please, later." Harder. "Go home."

My fingers tingle.

"I will," he concedes. So easily. "Goodbye, Enna," and he turns back the way he came. I stand in mortified inaction until I can't see or hear him anymore.

"Your lover?" Maekallus asks. His shoulders tense; I'm not sure why. My soul should have cured his pains entirely.

"No."

He glowers at me. "But he wants to be."

"Spare me, Maekallus." I'm worn through, like I've run the length of the wildwood and back. That emptiness inside me gapes, refusing to be forgotten. "Tennith and I have no relationship to speak of."

One red eyebrow lifts. "He was speaking a great deal on it."

"Does it matter?" Venom laces my voice, though I didn't mean the words to sound so hard. "I've no ties to him, nor to anyone."

He turns, and in two steps he's standing before me, amber eyes ablaze, horn foreboding, and I curse the way my body thrills at his closeness. *He is a* mysting, *Enna!*

"Don't you?" he murmurs.

His hand slides beneath my hair, against the side of my neck, as though he's going to kiss me. I push a hand against his chest to shove him away—I can't lose more of my soul so soon, especially not for some game—

His horn dips from sight. His breath brushes my ear. His lips graze the side of my neck.

I'm frozen, shivers bursting from his touch and zipping through me in every direction. My hand stays pressed against his chest, but it's lost its strength. My heart quickens, beating a new pattern. Heat and chills do battle across my skin as Maekallus's mouth works down the length of my neck. What sensibility I have left tells me this is wrong, he's from the realm of monsters and I am human, but I lean into him, shocked at the sound that escapes my throat.

And then his teeth nip the valley between my neck and shoulder and I forget my own name.

For a moment—only a moment—I lose myself to him, closing my eyes against the sensation of his lips. I drop the basket and let my hand snake up to his shoulder and curl around the tail of hair spilling over it. A shaky breath escapes me; I can't get it back.

Maekallus dips lower, easing back the collar of my dress. His horn presses against my skull, reminding me of what he is.

Maekallus. A mysting. *What am I doing?*

I dig in the nails of the hand pressed against his chest and push him away, stumbling back into a tree. His eyes smolder with something I can't name.

I turn the question I've been asking myself on him. "What are you doing?" It's barely more than a whisper. I touch the side of my neck. I feel like a log before a weak woodcutter—half-split and waiting for a second swing. My body is alive in a way it very much shouldn't be, missing pieces of soul aside. "Because of Tennith? A kiss above all things should mean nothing to you."

His countenance darkens. "Enna—"

I gasp—the Will Stone has gone ice cold against my wrist. I drop my hand from my neck and clasp it.

Maekallus reaches out and wraps his hand around my fist. Bumps ripple across his skin as the chill travels up his arm.

He senses it the same time I do, for our eyes lock. Not with fear, but hope.

"Gobler," we whisper.

And it's close.

CHAPTER 19

Narvals have the ability to hide themselves from mortal eyes.
They are seen only when they want to be seen.

My body buzzes as if a lightning storm rages within it. My heart is weary from racing from one thing to the next without rest. My father, Tennith, the gobler. Maekallus, whose eyes look so utterly *human* they make the very marrow in my bones ache. I need to think. I need a dark corner to cradle my head and sort through the last quarter hour of my life, but the Will Stone pulses its bitter chill against my hand—his hand—demanding only one focus.

Freeing us.

"It isn't far," I whisper.

Maekallus leans forward, reaches into my basket to draw my silver dagger. He remains slightly hunched, his knees bent, ready for an attack.

"Bring it here."

I swallow, but my mouth has gone dry. "Be careful. We might not want to kill him immediately."

He glowers at me, pure mysting. "You can stop me whenever you want."

"I don't want to," I snap. "I've no desire to take away your agency."

He rotates the dagger in his grip, and it strikes me that the silver doesn't pain him anymore. Or if it does, he doesn't show it. "Don't you? With so much power, Enna, you can do almost anything you want. With me, with anyone."

I glance back to the space between trees where Tennith had been standing only moments ago. He will be safe; his leathers are marked with protective runes, and all the hunters of Fendell know the safest trails to take, none of which delve too deeply into the wildwood. Even Maekallus's glade it not so far from the tree line. I erase the awkward encounter from my thoughts and focus on the biting chill in my hands.

The Will Stone found the gobler, so surely I can control it. I close my eyes and focus on the stone's warning. *Come here. Do not fight. Come. Obey.*

My hands tingle. I open my eyes. The cold is strong enough to make my teeth chatter. I drop the stone and snatch my basket, hugging myself against the side of an old tree. "It's coming."

Maekallus remains in the center of the small grove, blade ready.

It doesn't take long. The gobler's footsteps, faster than a walk, slower than a run, announce its approach. My breath catches when it comes to the clearing, and I shrink away, fumbling for the stone. *Stay where you are. Do not fight!*

Maekallus curses, straightens.

My gaze jumps from him to the gobler. "What? What's happened?"

"Wrong one." His voice is low and hard. The voice of a stone.

I dare to step away from my guardian tree. "You're sure?"

He gestures to the docile gobler. "It's a *she*, Enna. The one that got me was male."

I gawk at the gobler before us, obedient and slightly confused, eyes glancing at my left arm, where my sleeve hides the print left by another of her kind. Perhaps my ministrations have only blocked its magicked call from afar. This gobler's skin is a light gray, her neck buried beneath rolls of fat. Thick arms and legs, pudgy fingers, large watery eyes. I see nothing to mark her female, but Maekallus would be the expert here, not I. Details for my book will come later.

The gobler begins to speak harsh gibberish that sounds like a threat, but with a thought, I will it silent. *Do not listen,* I add.

I step farther from my tree. Maekallus has lowered my dagger. The mysting remains silent and frozen, held in place by the power of the stone.

Maekallus is thoughtful. He quietly surveys the gobler, his first knuckle tucked under his chin. The tail of his red hair falls down the center of his back, reaching the base of his shoulder blades. It curls at the ends. I rub my warming fingers together, remembering its softness, then curse myself for thinking of such a thing.

"Is it alone?" he asks, not looking at me.

I clutch the stone. It remains cold, but not terribly so, perhaps sensing that the threat has been neutralized. "Yes."

"We can still use it."

Without words, I will the gobler to look at me. She does. It unnerves me how easily a wild mysting like this heeds my unspoken command. I keep my left hand, and thus the Will Stone, from her sight.

"Why are you here? Answer me."

She answers in garbled tones.

Maekallus translates. "To search for the stone."

My stomach tightens. "Do you know where it is?"

She replies. Maekallus answers, "No. Only that it is close. Here, in the mortal realm, in this wooded country."

I let out a small breath of relief. Had my father not killed that first gobler, I might not have survived to summon Maekallus. My soul might have already departed for Shava, whole.

Maekallus points my dagger at the mysting. "Do you know the gobler with the vuldor-tusk knife?"

The gobler replies, and as Maekallus lowers the weapon, his eyes widen.

I rush to his side and take his arm. "What? What does she say?"

"She knows him." His gaze remains locked with the gobler's. "His name is Grapf."

I spin toward the gobler, the remainder of my soul—less than half—stirring, warm. "You must bring him here, to us."

The gobler frowns, speaks. Maekallus says, "He will not come by my bidding."

"Convince him."

"He will not be convinced." Then Maekallus orders, "Kill him."

The gobler shivers. Speaks. Maekallus's expression darkens as if the corruption has consumed it.

"Tell me!" I beg.

"She says she will not succeed. She is too weak."

Tears tickle my eyes, but I blink them back and take a step toward the mysting. "Then bring me something of his."

"Enna?" Maekallus asks.

I turn to him. "The scrying spell. The one I copied in Caisgard. If this creature can bring us something of Grapf's—a shred of clothing, a buckle, *anything*—then we'll know the instant he comes here. We can find him, and with the Will Stone—"

"We'll break the spell," Maekallus murmurs, motionless. His lips press into a hard line. "Command her, Enna. Leave no room for error."

I consider this for a moment before looking back at the gobler. I wonder if she understands mortal speech, or if the Will Stone makes her believe my will is hers. But that is not pertinent. "You will return to the monster realm, the Deep. You will report your failure in locating the stone. You do not believe it is here after all."

Maekallus nods his approval.

"You will seek out Grapf's living space. If it is not near, you will seek out his person. You will subtly collect something of his—slough from his body, clothing, anything that he owns. You will bring that item back to this glade, and leave it by that tree." I point to the tree where

Maekallus cornered me earlier, and hope the light of the lowering sun is red enough to mask my flush.

"She should eliminate herself."

My belly tightens. The danger is real. If my will wears off in the monster realm, or if someone follows her, she could reveal us—and there's no denying she'd as soon kill me as not. She has no soul, just like the gobler who marked me, who would have torn me apart had my father not been there. But to will another creature to kill itself? What if I had done something similar with Maekallus? With Attaby?

Yet they are different. Attaby is harmless, and Maekallus has human origins. A partial soul. This gobler . . . she is a monster, through and through.

It doesn't matter. I can't curse her with such a fate, and so I pretend not to hear. "Then you will go into the monster realm and *never return*. Under any circumstance. You will die before you step foot here again. You will die before you reveal what has transpired here. You will forget ever coming here after you have brought something of Grapf's to this tree."

The gobler's eyes glaze over.

I glance to Maekallus. He nods. Thorough enough.

I squeeze the stone. "Go."

She departs. I don't move—don't breathe—until her footsteps merge with the dying song of the forest. I don't relax until the Will Stone returns to its cool state, whispering of Maekallus and nothing else.

Fatigue pricks me like angry hornets. I falter. Maekallus lunges forward and grabs my arm in a painful grasp to keep me upright. I force my legs to steady, to stay on my own feet. I will not lean on him. I can't.

"My father is unwell." My breath is too heavy, but I find my balance, and Maekallus releases me. "I need to go home."

"Can you?"

I laugh. It soothes that soulless hole inside me ever so slightly. "I'll manage."

"I can hide myself from mortals."

"And they'll only see a woman floating through the wildwood." I glance at him, but he is serious, and it dampens my mirth. I pick up my basket, trying not to stagger. Maekallus drops my dagger inside. "You are healed, and the gobler will return." *Please, please let her be successful.* If the spell wears off, or she is killed, I do not know how I'll ever free Maekallus and break the bond between us. We will perish together. "You can watch this place, and the stone will warn me when she returns." I cross the small glade and carefully step over tree roots. "I will come back sooner if it's more than a few days."

I slip and fall hard on my backside. I wince, and in the split second I close my eyes, I feel I could sleep forever.

Maekallus walks over, hands on his hips.

I sigh. "If you would be so kind."

He bestows upon me a wry grin that I want to slap off his face. *He is the reason my body is a century old beneath the skin. Why I am only a piece of what I once was.* But no, that isn't fair. *I am the one who summoned him.* The gobler—Grapf—is the one who bound him here.

Maekallus picks me up. Yes—he is warmer than he once was. Warm enough to be human. I rest my cheek against his bare shoulder. So tired, yet sleep doesn't come, even when he traipses across level ground.

"You'll need to show me where you live," he says after so long.

I open my eyes. "I suppose I must. But mark my words, Maekallus. One snide remark, one wrong move, and you'll be flying back to your glade so fast the falcons will squirm with jealousy."

Maekallus takes me nearly to the edge of the wildwood, setting me down when my home becomes visible, barely, through the trees. He watches me go—I feel his eyes—but when I turn back, he's nowhere to be seen.

I slip into the house, trying to shake my weariness. My heart nearly stops when I check on my father.

For a moment, I'm sure he is dead.

But his chest moves, and I rush to his side, energy restored. "Papa?" I ask, feeling his forehead. Still no fever, but his skin is clammy and gray. He looks twenty years older. I hurry to get him a glass of water and help him drink it. I've never seen such a sickness before. Grasping the Will Stone, I picture the town doctor in my mind and plead for him to come. It will be faster than seeking him out myself. And while I don't wish to force others to my bidding, I will not be refused in this.

I make tea and start stew, hoping to give my father something heartier than broth. I slice mushrooms thin and add them to the pot of water simmering over the fire. To my relief, only an hour passes before the physician arrives at my door.

He looks confused. "I don't recall making an appointment with you, but—"

"Here, quickly." I grab his arm and hurry him to Papa's bedside. I chew on my thumbnail as the doctor inspects him. Papa responds to his questions, though more with sounds than words. I clutch the Will Stone and pray. *Find what is wrong with him, please. Let him live. Live, Papa.*

Don't leave me alone.

The doctor frowns once he's done with his assessment. "It could be a number of things. Gray fever, though you've said he hasn't been feverish."

"Correct." My voice is small like a mouse's. Even as I say the words, doubt creeps up my neck. Was he feverish while I was away?

"It could be failure of the heart or kidneys," he suggests. My legs weaken, and I lean against the wall to stay upright. "Could be an ailment of the stomach."

"He's eaten nothing sour, and he hasn't thrown up." *Has he?* Could I have missed those symptoms, too?

The doctor stands. "Keep an eye on him, look for any changing or new symptoms. Lots of water and rest. Send me word."

I offer him payment. I don't see him to the door. Instead, I kneel at my father's bedside, stroking his hair back from his face. Trying to be strong, like my mother was. A few tears blur my vision.

"You'll be all right. Just rest." I can't believe it's a failure of his organs; Papa is so healthy. Gray fever? Perhaps, but I know little of the disease.

I devote myself to his care, body and fractured soul, even read to him while he slumbers, pausing every other page to watch his chest rise and fall. Night comes. I make up a pallet at my father's bedside and lie down, my weary limbs heavy.

I don't sleep.

I think it is fear for my father, so I lie there, listening to him breathe. There's only a light rasp to the sound, and it's even. Peaceful. I'm so tired. I close my eyes and wait for sleep to come, but it remains elusive. Hour after hour passes, and my body is so fatigued I could cry for lack of rest. It isn't until the blue light of predawn that I realize the insomnia might be my body's objection to what I've done to my dwindling soul. Yet would my own body truly torment me so?

Papa stirs as dawn breaks. I force myself out of bed, *will* myself to be alert. To my relief, the stone lends me its strength. I make porridge and tea, trying a different blend of herbs. My father is only partially lucid. I help him sit upright and feed him, but he only takes a few bites of breakfast, followed by a few sips of water.

"You need to eat if you're going to regain your strength," I chide him. He doesn't respond. I run my knuckles over his growing beard. "Papa?"

He sighs.

I help him back into his bed. Clean the kitchen. I should check on the mushrooms, but . . . I'm so weary. The thought of climbing up and down the ladder exhausts me. The little farm will be fine for one more day.

Near noon, my father begins to cough. I hurry to his side. He coughs harder without breath, until his skin's gray cast borders on blue. I lean him forward and beat my hand against his back. Mucous flies from his lips and onto the blanket. He gasps for air, then settles back down.

I grit my teeth, steeling myself. At least this is something I can tell the doctor. I take off the top blanket and launder it. I can hardly keep my eyes open as I scrub it and hang it outside.

I check on my father once more. He slumbers, peaceful.

I drop onto my pallet and will myself to sleep.

Everything is red as candlelight inside a closed fist. It pulses. Far off, an inhuman shriek fills the air.

The smell of rotting eggs stirs around me. I try to move, but my feet are caught in something—the floor is like a giant, spongy tongue, sucking against my shoes. My breath is too fast as I try to pull free. I stumble. My hand hits the tongue and starts to sink.

I hear their giggle—the grinlers. They're hungry. Their shadows blot out the red light.

I feel one sink its teeth into my neck.

I start awake, my throat aching as though I've been screaming. The sun is high; I didn't sleep long.

My dress clings to the perspiration coating my body. I stare at the wall, trying to calm my breathing.

Never in my life have I had a nightmare like that. So foreign, so *real*.

I pick my heavy body off my pallet and find some bread and tea to settle my stomach.

Papa coughs again.

I speed to his side and beat his back. He gasps for air between spells. I will him to breathe. More mucous comes up—ugly brown slime. I catch it in a handkerchief. Papa settles down, but his breathing is harsher, uneven.

"Papa." I sit on the bed beside him. Tears spill over my eyelashes. "Papa, please get well."

Another attack. His whole body heaves. I roll him onto his side and slap him between his shoulder blades.

"Please!" I cry through the hard, wet sounds.

He settles down. I press my forehead into his shoulder.

"Please, Papa," I plead. "Everyone I love has left. Don't you leave, too. Please breathe."

I clutch the Will Stone until my hand hurts, but I don't think it hears me.

I wake up with tears streaming down my face, wetting the shoulder of my father's shirt. I still see the muted red light. I hear the screams of creatures I can't name. I shudder as the twisted images recede too slowly from my mind.

I wipe my nose and eyes on my sleeve. Evening now. My hands shake. I'm so tired.

My father needs me. I drag myself to the kitchen and get yesterday's stew. Try to feed him. He gets perhaps two swallows down before refusing to take any more. The spoon shakes in my hand, like I'm trying to lift a horse instead of a utensil.

I start the fire, if only for the light. It takes too long. I cough as soot puffs into the air with my clumsiness. So tired. The flames build, and the rug before the hearth beckons to me. But even if I could sleep, I fear what sleep will bring.

Papa's coughs echo through the house. I force strength into my legs and hurry to him, help him through the fit. Try to force tea down his throat with little success.

I collapse at his side, imagining this house empty of him, another stone placed in the yard beside my mother's, grandfather's, and grandmother's. I take his clammy hand in mine and squeeze. "Please, Papa."

I'm so tired. I rest my head on the edge of the bed and close my eyes. Sleep refuses me. I roll onto my pallet as the colors of sunset dance through the window. I'm weary enough to hurt, weary enough to risk more nightmares, but even that unquiet slumber evades me. I cannot rest.

I stumble out of my father's room and toward the hearth. Stare at its patternless flames. I feel as though I could fall asleep standing up, but I know I will not.

The doctor. The doctor should come again. Maybe he'll have something new for my father. Maybe then my mind will grant me slumber.

More coughing. My feet are unsteady when I return to my father. This time, he's already finished when I reach him. I take another blanket to the wash, but can't bring myself to scrub it.

How will I have the strength to dig his grave?

There's a snap inside me, almost like the breaking of my soul, but this sensation is planted firmly in my chest, like my own heart has detached from the rest of me. I press the heel of my hand into it. The scar across my palm is pink.

Looking at that mark, I sense him. He's nearby, in the wildwood. I stare at the flames, inching closer until the heat is almost unbearable. I close my hand around the scar. He's coming. Nearer, nearer.

I move to the door, my tired feet scuffing against the floor. I open it. The night air feels cold compared to the hearth. Stars speckle the sky.

Hugging myself, I step onto the dirt path that leads away from the door. Suddenly, I'm at the ring of oon berry. Did I forget traveling here because of fatigue, or because my soul is too small?

I see him then, a shadow against the wildwood. I know it's him, but I don't know why he's here. Boredom, worry . . . Would he worry?

The oon berry won't hurt him. I know that instinctively. It's not a plant that would hurt a soul, and he has most of one.

Starlight glimmers off his horn. He comes closer, closer. Eyes the oon berry, steps over it. Looks at me and pauses.

"Enna?" he asks.

New tears spring from my eyes. Tears of sorrow, of fatigue, of hopelessness. I take one heavy step toward him before I fall into his arms and cry against his naked chest.

CHAPTER 20

The differences between a male and a female gobler are slight. Females have lighter skin, larger eyes, and tend to be slightly smaller than their male counterparts.

"Enna."

I blink, surprised to see the fire before me. I don't remember coming into the house. I sit in my father's chair, slouching, leaning toward the flames. Maekallus is near me, standing, hunched so his horn doesn't scrape the ceiling. Is it shorter? If it changed after our last kiss, I didn't notice.

I touch the side of my neck. Stare at the flames. "I can't sleep."

Maekallus is silent.

I drop my hand. "I can't sleep, but when I do, I dream of a horrible place. There's no sun, but everything glows dull red . . . and there are sounds I don't know. Screams. Monsters."

He shifts. "The Deep."

I meet his eyes. They're still amber, even more so in the firelight. I shiver, despite the heat. "That's it? That's the . . . other realm?"

I've always wondered what the monster realm is like. There's no literature on the subject. At least, not that I've found with my limited means. Papa has never spoken of it willingly, only in occasional mumbles when he's asleep. All I knew, until now, was vague and half-formed—that if the mortal realm is above, the monster realm is below.

If *that* is where they live, no wonder they come here. No wonder they visit our woods, our streams, even when lingering hurts them so. How they must long for relief from those sounds and smells.

I hug myself. "What an awful place."

"For one unaccustomed, yes."

His voice is soft. He stares past the floor for a moment, his thoughts elsewhere. I say, "Even accustomed, it's a terrible place."

He nods. I open and close my hands, feeling that squishy, sucking ground beneath my palm. "My father is ill."

"You said."

"Very ill." I shake my head, finding solace in the fire. It's easier to look at the flames than at him. "He barely eats. He has a horrible cough—"

As if to punctuate the statement, my father begins hacking in the other room. I grab the armrests of my chair to stand, but he calms quickly, and I relax. This chair has the indent of his body in it. Almost like he's holding me.

What if that's all I'll have left of him, come the morrow?

I swallow. "Do you have family, Maekallus?"

"No." He hesitates. "Not that I remember."

"Remember?"

He shakes his head. For a moment he's somewhere else, somewhere distant, but he returns within the space of two heartbeats.

"I told you about my mother." The flames dance, coiling around one another. The charring log beneath them splits in two. The light dims a little, turns redder, like my nightmares. "My father's parents used to live near here, but they're both gone." I can't believe there are tears left in me, but one builds in the corner of my eye. I wipe it away with a knuckle. "I'm afraid to be alone. I never have been. If Papa dies . . ."

I shake my head and wipe the tear on my skirt. Maekallus moves closer to the fire. The light spills across him, making his skin almost as red as his hair. He has human-shaped feet now, but they're the same color his hooves were. I look over him, finding a few black specks on his arms. Otherwise, he's safe enough from the devouring of my world.

"I know . . . the feeling." He speaks as though the words are iron, or his throat is too small for them. I stay very quiet, even in my breathing, not wanting to scare away his voice. He folds his arms and finds his own solace in the fire. "I didn't, before this. But your soul . . . makes me notice solitude . . . differently."

"Is that why you wandered here?" I ask. The red light at his chest is hidden by the firelight, but the string gleams in the shadows, piercing through the wall of my home as if the wood and stone didn't exist. "You were lonely?"

Maekallus scoffs. "Don't judge me by mortal standards."

"I don't know how to judge you, Maekallus." His gaze turns to meet mine. I will strength into my body, my heart. "You are a mysting with a soul. Almost a soul, at least. In a way, that makes you part of me."

My eyes are heavy, and I rub them. In the black behind my lids, I see unworldly creatures from the realm beyond. I jerk my hands away. Blink firelight into my mind.

"Enna." My name is so soft when he says it. Like a prayer.

I shake my head, wipe my eyes before tears can come. "I still see them," I whisper. I drop my gaze to the scar on my hand. "You're growing more human, but what's happening to me? Am I becoming one of them? A monster?"

The fire crackles, dims a little more. I should put another log on it.

"Do you think I'm a monster?"

I turn toward him. He no longer watches the fire, only me. As though I *am* the fire, and nothing else exists in the space around us. I open my mouth to answer, but I'm at a loss for words.

His lips quirk, but there's no mirth in the expression. He crouches before the fire, careful with his horn, and grabs a cooler piece of charcoal from the edge of it. Walking into the shadows before the door, he draws a circle on the floor, just large enough for him to stand in. Extends the lines, marks the eight-pointed star. The descent circle.

He tosses the charcoal aside and stands in the center of it. The lines flash blue. The light fades until it's dull as fog, but it lingers, and I realize Maekallus is pulling on tendrils of power.

His horn disappears. His feet smooth out and turn as peachy as the rest of him. The specks on his arms vanish.

I stand. "Maekallus?" A dull ache like a rusted rod pulses from the base of my neck to my navel. He's hiding the parts of him that mark him as a mysting. He looks perfectly human.

So beautifully human.

The fog fades, as does the power. Maekallus's horn returns, its peak a finger's width from the ceiling.

A question rises up my throat, and I almost dare not ask it, but I'm too tired to hold it back.

"Do you *want* to be freed?"

His gaze turns sharp. "Do I *want* to be a prisoner? Do I *want* to be caged and eaten by your ethereal demons?" He takes a step forward, smudging the charcoal. His voice has an edge to it that's almost frightening. "Do I *want* to *feel* this way?"

He winces and touches his forehead as though the horn is too heavy for it. "They never last this long." His rough voice is almost pleading. "They're not supposed to last this long, but you're keeping it alive." He rips his hand away. The fire in his eyes overshadows the one burning in the hearth. He lifts an accusing finger and stabs it toward my chest. "*You're* doing this to me, with that cursed stone. *You're* making me feel this way. For what? So I'll sympathize? So I'll serve you?"

The words strike me like an open hand. "Of course not! I've done nothing but help you!"

He growls. "You've done nothing but help yourself. You're using me like a puppet, just like you did that gobler."

"You're a fool," I spit. "You may have *my* soul, Maekallus, but anything you feel is entirely your own."

My pulse quickens, sending new energy through my blood. What am I making him feel, precisely?

I lift my wrist and tear at the clasp of my bracelet. It comes undone. I toss silver and stone at Maekallus's chest, where he catches it with both hands.

"There." He gapes at the stone before his eyes flicker to me. He's silent for a long moment, his expression a mix of surprise and sadness. I've given him perhaps the most powerful weapon known to mankind or mysting. He does not wield it against me, only cradles it in his hands, making it look small and unimportant.

My anger fizzles. I step toward him. "I promise I haven't . . . manipulated you, Maekallus."

"But you have," he whispers. Not accusatory. The fire in his eyes dies down to a smolder, the ruddy light fixed on me. I can't look away. There's a spell in their depths, different from my stone and his binding, different from the bargain we made. Stronger.

He palms the bracelet and reaches out, touching my shoulder, running his fingers up the side of my neck. Tucks a lock of hair behind my ear. I place a hand over his and lean into his touch, entranced by his eyes.

I whisper, as though my voice would sever the sorcery between us. "Are you afraid of being human?"

His gaze flicks to my mouth. "I wish I were."

I knit my fingers between his. He studies me like he's seeing me for the first time. Like he's waking from deep sleep and is out of place, out of time. The urge to hold him, to make promises to him, is so strong I could weep anew. I squeeze his hand. He comes closer. His other hand rests against my waist, traces the round of my hip. We breathe the same air, but now, in this moment, it's not enough.

I stand on my toes, tilt my face up to him. He looks into my eyes, and I wonder what he sees there.

His hand shifts to the back of my head and pulls me close, until his lips crash against mine.

He's warm, so blissfully warm. My fingers dance up his chest to find his soft hair, his neck, his jaw. My heartbeat swims in my skull. Maekallus tilts my head to the right to claim the whole of my mouth. I part my lips, welcoming him, sighing when his tongue traces mine. I foolishly cling to him, to his warmth, to his sweetness, to the scent of the wildwood that cleaves to his skin.

But even beautiful things must end, for even most of a soul cannot change what Maekallus is.

I kiss him, and another piece of myself breaks. In its wake, I'm left cold and hollow.

CHAPTER 21

*There is no sun in the Deep, also known as the realm of
monsters. Its source of ruddy light is unknown.
But it is a horrible place.*

She turns to ice in his arms.

Maekallus wrenches back from her as the new piece of soul collides
with him, fueling the passion and *need* devouring his insides, lacing
them with something sour, frosted, and heavy. He knows the sensation,
knows it in an almost nostalgic way, and hates it instantly.

Guilt.

"Enna?" He grabs her by the shoulders. She looks dazed and hangs
limp in his grip. Her skin is cold. Too cold.

His fault. What had he been thinking? Did he suppose this time
would be different, that he could kiss her and it wouldn't do . . . this?
That if he puts on the costume of a human, he can be like her? That he
can belong in a world that despises his kind? He doesn't even *need* more
of her soul, not yet, but he stole it from her, and now she—

She groans, his name a whisper on her lips. Her lips.

Spitting every foul word he can conjure, he picks her up and lays
her on the rug before the fire, spitting another curse when his horn
nicks the mantel. Even in the dim light she looks too pale. She curls in

on herself, turning toward the fire. Maekallus searches for a blanket, but finds none. Fumbling with the Will Stone, he presses it to her palm and forces her fingers around it. *Live, live.*

In the back room, her father coughs again. Enna's eyes flutter with alertness. After a few long seconds, the coughing stops.

Enna shivers and tries to pick herself up off the rug. "Is he . . . ?"

Maekallus turns for the hallway.

"Don't . . . let him see you."

Setting his jaw, he ducks and hurries through the halls, finding the room that held a middle-aged man. He stays only long enough to hear the rattle of his inhale—he has some sort of sickness in his lungs— before returning to Enna's side, again hitting that mantel. Narvals aren't built for human homes.

"He's fine." Maekallus grabs the edge of the rug and drags it, and her, closer to the fire.

The new piece of soul inside him bares its claws and rakes them from the base of his throat to his stomach. *Your fault. Your lies.*

But he hadn't wanted this. He hadn't meant to . . .

Idiot. Ka'pig.

Her teeth chatter.

"I'm sorry," he whispers, the words strange on his tongue. "I'm sorry. I'm sorry."

She opens and closes her hands. "I can't . . . feel my fingertips."

He takes one of her icy hands, the one not holding the stone, and places it on the side of his neck, willing his warmth into it. To his shock, she smiles. It's a barely there tilt of her lips, but there's no mistaking it.

"You're warm," she whispers.

His grip on her loosens. "Enna. I . . ."

The guilt claws him raw.

He swallows. "The bargain—"

"C-Cold." She shivers.

Pressing his lips together, Maekallus lowers her hand and scours the hearth until he finds quarter logs beside it. He throws three onto the dying fire, coaxing it into violent life. Then he lies down on the other side of Enna and draws her close. Her body is soft and fits well to him, something he might have lingered on were the damnable soul inside him not making his hands tremble.

Her shivering eases, but that grants him only a sliver of relief.

He holds her for a long moment, willing the warmth of her captured soul back into her. For a moment, he thinks she's fallen asleep, or lost consciousness, but she stirs the silence by asking, "Do you believe in Shava?"

The mortals' notion of an afterlife. "You're not going to die, Enna." Even if she loses her soul in its entirety, she won't perish. Not right away. She'll just be empty. Blank. Just like . . .

He shakes his head. No. He hasn't thought about *her* in years, and he won't start now. That had been . . . different. Enna won't meet the same fate. She can't.

He will guarantee it.

"I didn't . . . ask that," she says. She pushes her head back, resting the crown against his neck. "Do you believe?"

"No."

She turns her head just enough to look at him. The fire tries to cast her blue eyes green. "No?"

Maekallus doesn't know what happens to souls he consumes. Although he doesn't understand the workings of human theology, he imagines they just cease to exist. Can a partial soul still find purchase in its afterlife? "For you, perhaps, there will be something beyond mortality. But not for me." He lets out a long breath through his nose, lifting his gaze to the flames so he won't have to see the pain in her eyes. "I *am* the afterlife. I was created by death. I am the end. When I perish, I am gone."

He kneels by the young woman, her dark-blonde hair sticking to the trails of tears on her cheeks. He wipes the wetness away with his finger, crooked from that mishap with the ax in his boyhood. "Now, now, we'll sort this out."

The girl shakes her head. "It was the Factio. You don't resolve anything with them."

Maekallus shuts his eyes hard. A headache erupts in his right temple, like his brain is bleeding. The memories that have begun to awaken . . . and they aren't from this life. He doesn't have crooked thumbs. He doesn't—

"No god would be so cruel."

Maekallus opens his eyes. The searing flames fill his vision. "I don't have a soul, Enna. I don't have a god. I just am."

She shivers. He holds her tighter.

They lie in silence for a long time, until Enna's questions subside, until her eyes close and her breathing evens. It's a slumber without nightmares. She needs the rest. At least Maekallus can give her that.

The guilt carves her name over his heart.

When she's deep in sleep, Maekallus slowly pulls away. Moves the rug back from the hearth just enough to keep any sparks from hurting her, then wraps the side he'd occupied over her back. He stands, careful of the ceiling, clenching and unclenching his fist until feeling creeps back into his arm. The light from the gobler's spell burns into his chest, beckoning him back to the glade. Even though she's been left with a flake of a soul, her will had called to him. Not an order. A call. Almost like he was wanted.

He looks away and grits his teeth. Opens the door, ducks low under the entryway. The air outside feels wintry compared to the heat of the fire. He passes the oon berry, falls into the shadows of the wildwood. His eyes still penetrate the darkness. He wishes they didn't.

He walks and walks, over hills and streams, listening to the howl of a wolf and the hoot of an owl. Brush rustles nearby, but he doesn't heed it. He's a predator, after all. Enna is his prey.

No longer.

He reaches the clearing. Stares at the spot where the thread of light pierces the ground. By that light he studies his right hand, the newly healed scar on the palm. Enna believes their bargain has tied their fates together. He's convinced her the gobler's spell will destroy her as surely as it will him.

He presses the thumb of his opposite hand to the bottom of the mark. Slowly draws it up toward his fingers, erasing the scar as though it were merely a smudge of dirt or line of charcoal. When he pulls his hand away, the line is gone, his palm unscathed.

He's taken too much. Too much.

Kneeling before the thread of the binding spell, he closes his eyes, relishing the pain inside him, if only for its vigor, and waits for the mortal realm to devour him once and for all.

CHAPTER 22

Tapis root, though scentless, has some sort of aura that protects against the supernatural. I believe this aura to have a small range, but one can never be too careful.

I wake to a dead fire and early morning light. I shiver, colder than I should be. But the nightmares . . . there were none, only dreamless, black sleep. A long breath escapes me, stirring black dust that's tried to escape the hearth.

Pushing myself up, I groan from a shoulder made sore from pressing against the floor. The edge of the rug slips off my back and hits the floor with a soft *whap*. I twist around at the sound of it and scan the gray room.

"Maekallus?"

Nothing answers.

Finding my feet, I blink sleep from my eyes. Shudder. Touch my lips. My legs aren't ready to walk, but I hobble down the hallway anyway, past my room, to where my father lies. I hear the sound of his breathing before I see the rise and fall of his blankets. Praise the gods, there is a sound to hear. And does he breathe easier? Could the worst be over?

I move to his side and press my hand to his forehead. Cool, but not clammy.

A chill sweeps through me. The Will Stone is clamped in my hand, but it remains cool and distant. The charm is not responsible for my chattering teeth. Blearily, I fasten it around my left wrist.

Maekallus. I lick my lips. Last night is a blur, and my memory is dull, but I pick pieces from it. Large, sharp pieces. His human shape surrounded by the fog of the descent circle. His lips moving against mine. The breaking of my soul. The cold.

Stupid, stupid girl.

I hurry to my room, pulling open the bottom drawer of my small wardrobe, where my winter clothes are folded away. I tug my coat free and fasten it around my waist, then rebuild the fire in the front room. I'm so cold, despite the summer sun peeking over the mountains, highlighting a few clouds in the pinking sky. I rub my hands together. The tips of my fingers are numb, and no matter how I work them, I can't get feeling to return to them.

"Enna?"

I jump at my father's voice. Run to him, clipping my shoulder on a corner as I go. "Papa?"

He looks so weak and a little ashen. His voice is dry. "Water?"

A cup rests on his bedside table. I wriggle my arm beneath my father's head, lifting it to help him drink. His own hand steadies the cup. He drinks it dry.

"Thank you," he rasps.

"Oh, Papa." I blink away a tear and kiss his forehead. "How are you feeling?"

"Terrible."

"Not as terrible as you were."

He coughs, but has the strength to cover his mouth, and nothing comes up—nothing that escapes his lips, at least. He rests back against the pillow.

"Let me get you something to eat."

"Not broth."

"Broth won't upset your stomach."

"Not broth."

I smile and leave him for the kitchen. I warm water over the hearth, watching it boil so I can absorb the fire's warmth into my coat. I make ginger tea and take a heel of bread to his room.

"Enna?" he asks when I'm near the doorway. "Could I have something to—oh, you have it." He managed a weak turn of the lips. "Clever girl."

I set the meager meal on the table and adjust my father's pillows so he can be more upright. "Tiny pieces, followed by tea."

He smells the tea and wrinkles his nose. He hates ginger, but it's easy on the stomach. I bully him into taking a sip.

I tear off a half bite of bread, the texture strange to my numb fingers. My father starts to lift his hand, but I'm quicker and plop the piece into his mouth. He chews slowly, swallows slowly, but the food makes it to his stomach.

He sips the tea. I give him another piece of bread.

I freeze when I reach for the teacup.

My hand.

I open my right hand, splaying the fingers, and hold the palm to my face. No mark, not even a pale scar. The skin is unblemished. I run my fingers over it, detecting not so much as a trace of the temperamental wound. As if it never existed.

The bargain.

"Maekallus," I whisper. Has he freed himself? But . . . how? Even if our plan worked, he'd need the scrying spell to complete the next step.

"Enna?"

I look to my father, barely seeing him. Utter something like an apology and hand him the teacup, spilling some of its contents onto his shirt. He doesn't seem to notice.

I check my other hand, just to be sure. The Will Stone remains cool to the touch, just as it's been since Maekallus was bound to the mortal realm.

"What is it?" Papa asks. He tries to sit up, but the effort is too much for him, and he sinks deeper into the pillows.

I shake my head. "I just thought . . . It's nothing, Papa."

He hesitates, but nods. I feed him more bread. My movements are stiff, my thoughts tangled in the wildwood, but I give my due diligence until the bread and tea are gone. Until my father's eyes close once more in slumber.

I slip out through the kitchen door, toward the mysting garden, and scan the forest beyond it. "Maekallus?"

No answer. I don't know what else I expected.

I lean against the garden fence. Last night, he came to me of his own volition, not because I willed it. But why did he leave? When? Did something happen, something my damaged mind can't remember?

Empathy for my father surges through my chest. I pull my coat tighter around me, though crickets chirp that the air is warm. I fear to leave my father in case he takes a turn for the worse, but the scar is gone, and I don't understand what it means. For me or for Maekallus.

I choose my father. I kneel at his bedside, listening to his breathing, waiting for the wetness to return to the sound. It doesn't. A relief, but in the space between his breaths, Maekallus's name rings in my ears. I rub my right palm until the skin is nearly raw.

Papa wakes again, and there's a little more color to his cheeks. I make him a simple mushroom stew, and while he seems strong enough to feed himself, I take the liberty of doing it. I want to. I owe him too much not to take care of him. He is forgetful, sometimes distant, but he has been my caretaker all my life, and I his. My love for him runs deep, especially now that I understand the sacrifice he made to protect me.

We talk for a little bit; I read him a few passages of poetry. But my father is not well, not yet, and he slips into another restful slumber.

I roll the Will Stone between my hands. If Maekallus is near, I could will him to my side and get an explanation, if he even has one. But I know he bristles at being controlled, and the narrow bridge we're building between us is an unsure one. I don't dare shake it.

I take my coat and my dagger and trek into the wildwood as quickly as my body will let me. I don't wish to leave my father alone for long.

I squeeze the Will Stone, pretending it is just the Telling Stone once more, urging it to lead me to Maekallus. It weakly points me toward the glade, which surprises me. I've freed him to roam the entire forest, or at least a good league of it. Why would he choose to linger in the place he claimed was driving him mad?

Why didn't he stay with me? Was I so foolish as to imagine the intimacy we had shared?

I try to shake the thoughts from my head. Speculation is pointless when the answers I seek are so close. I will myself to keep going, to not need a break. I'm breathless by the time I reach the glade.

I pause at its edge. The binding spell remains just where I left it, glimmering and red, embedded into the ground just as it is in Maekallus's chest. Maekallus, who kneels not three paces from where the spell sinks into the earth.

I stare at his feet. Human feet. Peachy and wrinkled and filthy from the wildwood.

"Maekallus?" I ask.

He flinches, like I've stung him.

I take a moment to catch my breath before walking to his side. "I don't understand." I hold my hand out to him, but he doesn't look at it. Or at me. His gaze is pinned to the binding spell. "The scar, the mark of the bargain. It's gone. Maekallus?"

He is silent.

"Are you hurt?" I crouch beside him. When he does not answer, I grab his right hand and open his fingers. The scar on his palm has disappeared, too.

I touch his cheek, turning his head until he looks at me. I try to search his eyes. There's new depth to them, new darkness.

"You know," I whisper, guessing, but I feel the truth of it. "You know what happened."

He pulls from my touch. "Our bargain is broken."

I stand. Despite all the exercise I got in my trek through the wood, I hug myself for warmth. "How? The gobler has not returned, or the spell would be broken."

"You aren't bound to me, Enna."

"But the gobler—"

"You were never bound to me," he says, low and gruff, like he bleeds the words. "The spell affects only me, not you. Were I to perish—*when* I perish—it will have no effect on you. Nor would it have if the scar remained."

I loosen my arms. My heart's beating too quickly. "I don't understand."

"The bargain is merely a token. A token I could break at any time. Your life was never in danger."

I step back from him, my body reacting before my mind can unpack his meaning. A blackbird cries from a nearby tree. This would rouse my curiosity, as I thought all wildwood creatures had left this grove, were it not for Maekallus's words.

My throat is dry, and I tremble, but not from the cold. I stare at him, waiting for him to move, to do *anything*, but he doesn't, and that solidifies his guilt.

"You lied to me." The revelation burns like inhaled smoke.

He studies the line of the gobler's spell. The only change in his face is a crease that appears at the center of his brow.

"You *lied* to me," I repeat, louder. Even the blackbird quiets at the accusation. I clutch my stomach, as though I could reach that deep, unidentifiable part of me where what's left of my soul resides. That gaping hole that aches like a pulled tooth, only so much worse. Less than half remains. "You promised my peril! You said if I didn't . . ."

His stillness infuriates me. I charge him and shove my hands into both of his shoulders, forcing his attention to me. "You took my *soul*!"

Again he looks away. "I needed it to live."

"*I* need it to live!" My throat constricts around the declaration, forcing me to choke it out. "How could you?" Tears start to sting my eyes. I clutch the Will Stone and demand they leave, but they won't listen.

His jaw is tight, his shoulders taut, as he speaks. "I knew you would leave me to die. I told you, En . . ." He pauses, swallows, as though unwilling to say my name. "There is no afterlife for me."

"And are you so certain there's one for me? You have half my soul, Maekallus!" I'm shouting now, and tears stream down my cold cheeks. "More than half! How could I possibly cross into Shava with only . . ."

I push my fists into my middle and turn away, trying to compose myself, but anger is a beast inside me, pressing against my skin as though it could tear itself free.

What did I expect? That there could be a happy ending for this twisted story? That I could ever love a mysting?

That a mysting could ever love *me*?

I wipe tears off my face and fling them into trampled clover. Wheel on him. His stare remains fixed on that damnable magic thread.

"Can't you give it back?"

It's a weak plea, too heavy to carry far. A drop of rain hits the side of my nose, and it alarms me that it feels warm against my skin.

Maekallus finally meets my gaze. "I might."

Hope flares within me, hot enough to scorch.

"But not while I'm bound to the mortal realm." More raindrops fall, hitting my hair, my coat. They echo off leaf and branch, louder than Maekallus's voice. "Attaby had a theory once. I've never . . . but I can't, here."

He sounds defeated. Rain douses my hope.

I shake my head, wishing I could deny the truth, almost wanting to remain in ignorance. This, this is what they meant, the poets and bards who wrote and sang about heartache. I feel it now, so much sharper than those flowery words. Like my very chest is being rent in two by long, rusted knives.

"I'm sorry."

I laugh. It hurts coming up my throat. It's made of briars and gravel and poison. I wipe more tears from my face. "Bastard," I hiss.

"I am what I am."

It might be the truest thing he's ever said to me. I glare at him, clutching the Will Stone in my fingers, a violent array of possibilities whirling dark colors through my thoughts. But I release it, tired, aching, and defeated. Shaking my head, I whisper, "I wish I'd never summoned you."

He flinches again, granting me some sort of pathetic victory.

The rain comes down hard. I flee into the wildwood, clutching the hilt of my dagger in one hand, the Will Stone in the other. I break the power that allows Maekallus to roam.

Let him rot in his prison.

I'm too tired to cry, so the rain weeps for me.

It resonates all around me, pattering logs and earth and trees until it sounds like a mess of insect wings or the shushing of a thousand mothers. It thuds without rhythm onto my skull, soaking my hair. It drips into my eyes and runs down my cheeks just like real tears.

I shiver and grip the front of my coat with frozen fingers. Cold, because of *him*.

Fresh mud sucks on my shoe. I rip it free. I barely feel the iciness of the Will Stone as it warns me of grinlers. I will them back to the monster realm with a single hard thought, and in seconds the stone warms.

I breathe deeply, both to fuel my already sore body and to fill the open chasm in my chest. The air doesn't help the latter.

I curse him. I curse him with every obscenity I know, which isn't many. I curse him with every step of my feet and shudder of my shoulders, with every drop of rain that dilutes my path.

I needed it to live.

I shake my head and curse my foolish interest in mystings and the monster realm. Where would I be now if I had never crossed into the glade that night, where Maekallus was a heap of gasping tar? If I'd waited another half day, and let him perish? I'd have a full soul. I'd have been with my father when he fell ill. I'd be able to look Tennith in the eye, happily.

And Maekallus would have been consumed by the blight.

A dark, twisted image fills my mind until it's all I see. Maekallus, *melting*, devoured by a realm he couldn't escape. His skin liquefying into tar. His yellow eyes desperate and pained. The sound of his breathing . . . even my father's sickest breaths couldn't match that sound. My nostrils burn in memory of the smell. I trip over a stone.

I think of the blackness that oozed from the cut on my hand—the cut I *thought* tied my fate to Maekallus's—and imagine it seeping from my every pore. Imagine it bubbling and burning and popping, filling my eyes and ears and nose—

I gag, then choke on rain. It forces me to stop, to clear my lungs, to breathe until I can convince my weary legs to move once more.

Even then, Maekallus's suffering had moved me. It was my fault he'd come, at least partially. It was I who drew the summoning circle, who saw beyond his invisibility.

And yet . . . he'd been shocked to consume only *part* of my soul. He'd been willing to kill me, just for another few days of health. Had he also known a soul wouldn't break the spell? Undoubtedly, yes.

But he's changed.

I curse the thought just as I cursed the mysting, but it sticks to me, resolute. Yes, I can admit that much. Maekallus has changed. Every kiss changed him, and not only physically. I remember being shocked at his first thank-you, his first apology. Like I was single-handedly making him more human, inside and out.

But how much can a soul change a person? A *mysting*? For even a human soul could not recreate him into a human. He'd already been that once. *The blood of bastards.*

And what happens if he descends? Leaves? Consumes the soul I've given him? Will he not revert back to a pure narval, a monster from the other realm? Will he forget all he's felt here?

Will he forget me?

Do you think I'm a monster?

I remember the look on his face when he'd asked. The sorrow, the desire. The way he stepped into that circle and made himself look human to . . . what?

My steps slow. I'm so tired; I could lie right here in the mud and foliage and sleep, but the nightmares whisper from underground, and I rub wakefulness into my eyes. I force myself forward again, gauging the distance to my home. Rubbing the hurt in my chest through my coat, wishing I could reach the emptiness deep within and stuff it with . . . something.

I want to be whole again.

I want my soul back—all of it. He owes it to me for saving him, for giving him more time.

And yet the thought of Maekallus's yellow eyes and pointed tail and equine hooves makes this endless pain inside me hurt *more*, enough that I grit my teeth and hold my breath, willing it to pass. It does, a little. Only a little.

Do I lose the man Maekallus has become by retrieving my own soul? The man who bathed in my tears, who held me as I fell asleep, who kept the nightmares away?

Does that man even exist?

I look down at my hand, the palm glistening with rain. All this time he could have broken that bargain. Why now? It's almost finished. I've almost no soul left, if Attaby is to be believed. So why now?

What changed?

I turn, looking through the arrows of rain back up my trodden path. I'm unsure about so many things, except one.

There can be no happy ending for us.

CHAPTER 23

Mystings should never be trusted. Ever.

I'm wet and quivering when I break through the trees. My house looks darker, drabber, in the rain. I stop when I see Tennith walking away from it, a thin cloak draped over his shoulders.

I watch him, wondering if I should call out, but I'm cold and exhausted and broken, and what would I say to him?

For a moment, I let myself imagine. What if I had kissed Tennith but not Maekallus? Tennith would have approached me later, asking why, and perhaps I would have told him the truth, at least in part. Would he have been flattered? Would he have been bold enough to pursue me, despite the lack of gain?

Is he trying to pursue me now?

My heart flips in a tight, painful way. I'm silent at the forest edge. The rain should nullify the sound of my breathing, but Tennith glances my way and sees me. A moment passes, one I can't interpret, before he changes direction and strides toward me.

"Enna? Are you all right?"

I wonder what my face looks like for him to ask, or perhaps he's merely reacting to my winter coat or the fact that I'm strolling about the wildwood in the middle of the storm. I clear my throat to lend strength to my voice. "Well enough."

"And your father?"

I start toward my home. My legs are sore and heavy. "He is doing better, thank you."

"Let me help you inside."

I don't protest. I step into my home as Tennith holds the door for me. I ache to keep my coat on, but it's drenched and so am I, so I peel it off and lay it near the fire, which Tennith builds without prompting. Kind of him. He's always been so kind. So perfect. So human.

I slip into my bedroom, sitting on my bed for a moment to rest my legs. I want to sleep, yet I feel that my body will refuse me again. After several long minutes, I force myself up and peel my dress and underthings from my body and shake water from my hair. I dress in gray—it suits me today—and go to my father's room. He's awake, which eases a tension I didn't know I carried.

"Oh, Enna. A book, would you?"

"Would you like to sit in your chair, Papa?"

"Ah . . . not yet." He offers me a sad smile.

I retrieve a book from my own shelf, a fairy tale of a scullery maid who wins the heart of a prince. I wonder, briefly, what the story would be like if the prince were a mysting.

All copies would be burned in the town square, surely.

I hand him the book. "I'll be right back, Papa. Tennith is visiting."

"Oh, he is? Nice boy."

I return to the front room, where the fire is blazing. Nice boy. He is. A nice, mortal boy with a nice farm and a nice face. I let myself daydream again, just for a moment. Imagine waking to that face every morning. Imagine falling asleep in his arms.

Would he ever kiss me the way Maekallus did?

I shake the thought from my mind. Tennith stands near the hearth, perhaps thinking it impolite to take a chair.

"Can I get you something to eat or drink? Tea?"

He shakes his head. "You look ready to sleep on your feet, Enna. I don't need anything."

I sit in Papa's chair to spare myself the energy of standing. "My father is well. He had a hard turn, but he's mending. Reading now. He's too weak to come out, if you'll forgive him."

"In all honesty, Enna, I came to see you." He frowns. "You don't look well. Have you caught your father's illness? I could send my sister to care for you—"

I shake my head. "Trouble sleeping is all. Some rest will see me fit."

His countenance doesn't lift. We're both silent for a long moment. The fire cracks and dances in the hearth. I grit my teeth to suppress their chattering. I'm so cold I want to dive into the flames.

Tennith breaks the lull. "I wish I understood you, Enna."

I wish I understood me, too, I think. I meet his gaze, waiting.

He sighs. "You've been in my thoughts a great deal lately."

"I'm sorry."

"Don't apologize. But you have, and I hardly know what to think about you. And then I come here and see you looking miserable, if you'll excuse me for saying so, and I don't know what to say to you, either."

I roll my lips together. "Papa and I have had some struggles." I hug myself, clench my jaw. It might make me look angry, but I don't want to shiver and look a wreck. I don't want Tennith to feel he must stay and help me, especially when there is so little he can do.

Only Maekallus can mend my soul, if such a feat is possible.

Could Tennith mend my heart?

"I kissed you because I wanted to," I say, though I speak to the fire, not to him. "Some . . . family issues recently arose that . . . complicated a few things. And I thought that night might be my last chance."

A truth embedded in a lie. But vague lies are less harmful than specific ones, aren't they?

Tennith is quiet for a long moment. He sighs. "You're a difficult woman to court, Enna Rydar."

I look at him and raise an eyebrow. "Are you trying to court me, Tennith Lovess?" My breathing echoes in my hollow chest. Is it the slenderness of my soul that dampens my excitement? Yet it didn't stop my heart from tearing in the glade, or extinguish the fire of betrayal and the unyielding chill of sorrow that carried me home.

I want to cry all over again. Am I so broken I cannot find joy in the potential of a more-than-suitable match? A husband, a family?

What is a soul if not an extension of the heart?

Had I unknowingly given even my heart to him?

The edge of Tennith's mouth quirks. "If I am, I'm very poor at it."

A flame burns within me, something hot with rage and confusion and hurt. I want nothing more than to cast all of this behind me, to forget, to stop being a shell of who I once was. Couldn't I still have that dreamy life, even if I'll never be whole again? Am I not human enough to deserve happiness?

I stand on renewed legs and cross the small front room until I'm standing before Tennith. His eyes glitter with wonder, but he doesn't shy away from me.

"Then court me," I say, defiant.

His gaze lowers to my mouth, lingers. For a moment I think I'll have to do this myself, but just before I lean into him, he lowers his mouth to mine.

It's just as before, warm, his lips pleasantly rough. I push harder, and his hand comes up to cradle my cheek. I hold my breath from habit, but nothing breaks inside me. I'm filled with the scents of earth and fresh wood. The kiss is warm and sweet, and it makes me feel emptier than the hollow where my broken soul slumbers. I shrink away, parting from him, and I want nothing more than to be alone, to curl around the fire until my dress smokes, and weep. To escape into slumber, even if it's laced with nightmares. I clutch the Will Stone in my hand—then drop it just as quickly.

Averting my eyes, I manage, "This may be easier when health has returned to this home."

Tennith doesn't respond at first. When I gather enough courage to meet his eyes, he nods. "Can I . . . get you a blanket? Some water?"

I force a wan smile. "I will do well enough."

He hesitates. "Take care, Enna. I'll . . . be back."

He fastens his cloak around his shoulders and opens the door to the rain, casting me one last unsure look before stepping into it.

Alone, I let my wasted body collapse to the rug before the hearth. I lie against the hard floor, shivering, until my mind relents and takes my consciousness into the horrors of the monster realm.

In my dreams, the teeth of a great beast clamp down on my hand.

I startle awake, blinking red light from my eyes. The Will Stone sits in my open palm, burning cold.

The fire is down to embers. I drop the stone, not wanting to be any colder than I am. My coat is dry, so I slip it on before hurrying into the hall. It's dark. In my father's room, I see through the window that the sky has cleared enough for some stars to peek through.

"Papa?"

He slumbers, his book propped open on his chest.

Horrible images stir in my vision, sounds and smells foreign to me. I try to push them away. In the kitchen, I make a small plate of cheese and mushrooms and bread, and I set it on my father's bedside with a tankard of water. In the kitchen, I swallow a few morsels for myself and drown them in several gulps of mead. It warms my belly and drives some of the cold away.

Taking a deep breath, I clasp the stone.

Gobler. And I instantly know which one. The female, from the smaller glade. The one I willed to bring me something of her companion, Grapf.

My body sings with cool strength, like a dam has burst inside me. Like a portion of my soul has returned. I clutch the stone, trying to see her through its sorcery. I feel her moving through the wildwood to the north. If the gobler has returned as instructed, she's been successful.

I fasten a cloak over my winter coat, partially for warmth, partially for the dark color. I no longer fear the gobler or any of the mystings in the wildwood. If anything, they should fear me.

I slip out through the kitchen door with nothing but the scrap of paper I saved from the Duke of Sands's library and a lantern. I avoid the wildwood at first, for the ground beyond it is more even and easier to cover in the dark. Soon, however, the forest is inevitable, and I pierce its shadows, shivering under the touch of the Will Stone the entire way.

The stone's iciness recedes before I reach the rendezvous. The gobler has retreated, perhaps back to her realm, as instructed. By the time I arrive at the glade, the stone is merely cool again.

I clutch the stone as I enter the dark place, lifting my light. The shadows of this place, the smell of wetness and mud, the stirring of life in foliage and branches, should frighten me away. But I have the Will Stone. I've seen the monster realm. I am not afraid.

There, perched on the thick root of an aspen, is a tiny vessel, no larger than my pinky finger. It's made of a strange black glass, almost like obsidian, with a rough cork stopper. I pick it up and hold it to my light. There's some sort of liquid inside, thick and opaque. Something of Grapf's.

I'm cold and weary, but I cannot stop the smile that spreads across my face. Soon, Maekallus will be free, and I'll have my soul back.

CHAPTER 24

Narvals bleed red.

I hate how my entire being prickles, like pine needles pierce my veins, as I near Maekallus's glade. I hate that I feel anything toward him, when I could barely muster the strength to smile at Tennith. I hate how uncertain I feel, even with the black vial clutched in one hand and the Will Stone clasped in the other. Once upon a time, I wondered at the extremes bards sang about in their songs. Now I would cut the strings of their mandolins were I to hear them.

How, with but a portion of a soul, can I feel this way? So full of rage and sorrow and passion. Maekallus consumed the majority of my soul before losing his edge. I can only suppose the difference is that I am a naturally souled being, while he is not. Perhaps I must lose my soul in its entirety before my emotions relent. It almost sounds like a blissful end.

The lantern swings from my wrist, arcing back and forth through the nearly complete darkness of the wildwood. A few crickets chirp nearby—more proof that Maekallus is no longer a threat.

I hate the strange spark of hope the thought gives me. I hate feeling anything beyond contempt for the thief of my soul. I should stay away and let the mortal realm eat at him a little longer. Let it punish him for me. But human decency aside, the longer I wait to free Maekallus, the more of my soul I'll have to relinquish to keep him alive. And he must live, if I'm to retrieve the fullness of my soul. Neither of us has time to spare.

He's easy to find, for he's near the center of the glade, curled around the spot where the thread of the gobler's spell sucks into the earth. For a moment I think the corruption has already devoured him, and panic rises in a great bubble up my throat. But as I steady the lantern, I see that the smudges and streaks on Maekallus's exposed skin are mud. He is speckled with black, yes, but it's not bad.

I step lightly as I near him. A breeze through the leaves muffles the sound of my approach. A wolf howls, but the sound is distant, almost too far to hear. I lift my lantern.

He's sleeping. He looks more human asleep, save for that ever-shrinking horn. His breathing is unlabored, yet a line creases his brow as if he, too, dreams of the monster realm. I wonder if he dreamed at all, before meeting me.

I look at him too long. Standing there, staring at him, I feel directionless, like I've transported somewhere as foreign as the Deep and I'm spinning, spinning, unable to stop. I press my fist, the one holding the Will Stone, into my chest. I feel my ribs pulling apart, opening a bottomless hole in me—

I drop the Will Stone before I can do anything rash. I breathe deeply and grind my teeth. "Maekallus."

He is not a sound sleeper, for he wakes upon hearing his name. Slowly, his lids heavy, he opens his eyes. They dart from side to side as if he doesn't recognize where he is.

I wonder what his true name is. The name of the bastard that spawned him.

It doesn't matter.

His eyes find my lantern first, then my face. He sits up quickly, then presses a hand to his head. "Enna? What—"

I crouch down and hold out the black vial. "The gobler returned and left this. Unless something down there broke the stone's spell, this belonged to Grapf."

He blinks at the vial, then looks at me. Too long. *The vial!* I want to shout. *It's what we've been waiting for!*

I shake my hand to pull his attention back to it. Straightening, he takes it and turns it over in the light of my lamp. Uncorks it. Lets a bit of the liquid onto his finger.

His face twists. He corks the vial and wipes his hand on wet grass. "I think we have a winner."

"What is it?"

"Phlegm."

I frown, but I don't care what it is. It's something.

Uncaring for the condition of my dress, I touch my knees to the forest floor and pull the scrying spell from my pocket. "If this spell works, we'll find him at last."

"But if he's in the Deep—"

"I'll go into the monster realm myself and will him here."

His eyes harden. "No, you won't."

"You can't," I bite back. "I will do whatever it takes. I want my soul back, Maekallus."

He leans back as though I've struck him. Good.

His amber gaze shifts to the scrying spell. He takes it from my hand and unfolds it. Snarls. "I can't read this."

"You don't need to." I snatch it back. I get the feeling that Maekallus wants to do this himself. But why? To spare me? He should have thought of sparing me earlier.

He didn't have a soul.

I ignore the thought and read through the words. I'm no sorcerer. I've never cast a spell in my life, minus the circles that got me into this situation in the first place. I don't know where the magic comes from— what god, what place, what origin—but I want to make sure I get the spell right. I will myself to get it right, because if this doesn't work, I'm as good as dead. Both of us are.

The spell is in Horda, a dead language used by people who inhabited Amaranda before we did. Scholars still learn some of their tongue, and I know sorcerers used it. I'm fairly certain I can pronounce the words.

Clutching the vial, I say them. I feel a warmth deep in the hollowest parts of myself, but it fizzles out as I trip over the fifth word. Steeling myself, I try again, building the warmth up, losing it. My fourth try is the one that makes it stick.

Warmth shoots out of my lips, making me gag. A faint white shimmer hangs in the air, like dust caught in sunlight. It's the width of my thumb, and I watch, entranced, as it springs past the glade, winding east.

I stand up, blood racing, energy renewed. "Do you see it?"

Maekallus searches. "See what?"

Only the caster can see it, then. Something to document later. "A path. To the gobler." I turn back, almost taking his hand. Then I shiver, remembering how very cold I am, and keep my hands fisted at my sides. "Come."

We follow the trail a short distance before Maekallus hits an invisible wall. He says nothing, only waits.

You need to actively want my company, he said the first time. I don't want to want it, but I can't go alone. Can I?

I shiver and wordlessly will him forward. Maekallus takes another step and inhales like he's coming up for air after too long underwater. I should find satisfaction in the fact that I've made him suffer, however briefly, but I only feel the vastness of my cold and empty being.

I follow the trail, Maekallus half a step behind me, almost close enough to tread on my heels. The shimmering trail is about knee high. Sometimes it shoots through trees or over shallow ravines, forcing me to find my way around in the dark. The eagerness of the discovery keeps me going, but my body starts to fail me, and unnatural fatigue takes over. Maekallus touches my arm, but I slap him away. Moments later, my shaking legs give out beneath me.

I'm so close, I beg them. *Please.*

Not even the Will Stone will lend me the strength to go on. Maekallus crouches beside me, silent. I turn my head, refusing to look at him. Nod. The movement is small, barely detectable, but Maekallus sees it and slides his arms under my knees and shoulders. Lifts me like I'm nothing. My body acts against my will and curls close to him, savoring the heat of his skin. *My* heat, for it comes from *my* soul. In that closeness, I listen to his heartbeat. It's almost in sync with my own.

I squeeze my eyes shut, willing my thoughts to die.

Maekallus stops moving. "I can't see it, Enna."

I open my eyes and find the glimmer trail to our left. I point, choosing to remain silent rather than speak to him. In part because I believe this punishes him. In part because I don't know what to say.

He walks with me in his arms for about half a mile before he slows, though I'm still pointing the way and see no obstacles in the path marked by magic. I lift my head to question him, but he shushes me.

It's then that I realize I'm so cold, so distracted, that I didn't sense the Will Stone's warning. I feel its deep freeze now, and I clamp it in my hands. The ice it sends through my body hurts. Mystings. More than one.

Maekallus's grip on me tightens. He treads more carefully now, ducking to avoid brushing low branches with his shrunken horn. His red hair falls from his shoulder onto my forehead, but I don't move it aside. I don't ask the questions bubbling up in me, the most pertinent being *How many mystings will the stone control before its power stretches too thin?*

I shudder when I see muted red light between distant trees. When I hear the garbled, cryptic language of mystings.

Maekallus moves silently. Again I wonder how old he is, how much time he's had to practice such stealth. He sets me down two dozen meters from the grove of red light and whispers, "Will them not to see us. Not to hear."

I sense the mystings through the stone, each its own shiver of warning. I do as Maekallus asked, all the while clenching my jaw so my teeth don't chatter.

Maekallus presses his lips together. "Wait here."

"I will not—"

He grasps my shoulders. "Please, Enna."

It's the *please* that gets me, its imploring tone. It fuels the ache that resonates in my chest.

I nod, and he vanishes into the shadows. Not long after, the stone turns so bitter I have to drop it to save my hand. *Hurry. Please hurry.*

Maekallus isn't gone long—less than a quarter hour—but the stone never warms. When he returns, he motions me forward. The glimmer of red light before us, so like that of my nightmares, sparks my limbs back to life. Tugging my sleeve beneath my icy bracelet, I follow, matching Maekallus's footsteps until we've cut our distance from the grove by half. We duck behind a pine. If I crouch and lean to the right, I can see into the grove. That bloody light emanates from the odd, round lanterns ringing the space, but the forest floor glows as well—a whitish blue. I spy two short freblon near it, as well as a rooter, one much darker than Attaby. It walks with a hunch, back and forth, back and forth. When I squint, I can just make out the glimmer of the scrying spell, leading right up to that bluish-white light. Dipping down into it.

As if sensing my thoughts, Maekallus whispers, "Portal ring."

I look at him in question.

He crouches beside me, his mouth close enough to my ear that his breath stirs my hair. "Portal ring. I'm surprised to see one. It's . . . like a more permanent summoning ring. Used to summon multiple mystings at once. This one is big."

And the gobler is just beyond it. I can *feel* him. I roll the scorching Will Stone between my fingers, but Maekallus grabs my hand and murmurs, "Wait."

The portal ring's light brightens almost enough to hurt my eyes, but I can't look away. I stare, my legs cramping. My teeth chatter; I bite my tongue to hush them.

Something is coming through.

The body emerges, and from its silhouette alone I know it's not a gobler. Too tall, too lean. It's a humanoid mysting with dark-blue skin. Broad shoulders and ribs that taper into an alarmingly thin waist. Long black hair. Two thick horns that roll over the skull, crisscrossing like some ornamental plant. An orjan. My grandmother knew less of orjans than she did narvals.

Maekallus's grip on my hand tightens until I hiss in pain. He lets me go.

"This is bad." His words are heavy, almost solid.

"Why?"

Maekallus points toward the portal ring. "Because that is the previous owner of the Will Stone."

CHAPTER 25

*A portal ring is made of three summoning circles sealed together
inside an outer ring. Portal rings act as a more permanent door
between realms for mortals and mystings alike.*

I stare at the mysting haloed in light and forget to breathe.

I am far from him, too far to make out his facial features, but I see
from the breadth of his shoulders, the confidence in his stance, and the
cowering of the other mystings that this creature is powerful, strong,
and ruthless. At the same time, I am struck dumb with awe that *this* is
the mysting my father stole from.

My father is an even greater hero than I had realized.

But Scroud is here to take back what was stolen from him.

The orjan turns, and Maekallus jerks me back by the shoulder, putting his body between me and the glade, though the pine hides nearly
all of us.

"Don't breathe," he whispers, soft as the breeze. I don't. I squeeze
the stone.

His hand comes over mine again. He shakes his head.

I wait a long time, until my lungs begin to burn. Maekallus relaxes
a fraction, and I let air run slowly out my nose and back in. Maekallus
backs up so he's fully behind the tree. There's no space between us.

"Don't use it," he warns.

"Why?" I mouth the word more than I speak it.

"He owned it a long time. The stone. I don't know if . . . he might sense its power." His breath washes over my brow. "The trail?"

"Into the portal ring."

He considers. "That must mean he's close. Just on the other side."

"Does the ring work both ways?"

He hesitates, his shadow stiff. "Yes. But we can't risk using it. Not with—"

A voice like shattering granite washes over us. "Maekallus."

My heart seizes in my chest, and even with the protection of my sleeve, the bracelet burns my flesh. Maekallus jerks up to his feet, but the orjan still looms over him, nearly the same color as the shadows. My entire being jolts with fear. I can't breathe, I can't move. I am nothing more than an erratic pulse waiting to be snuffed out.

Scroud's large dark eyes look over Maekallus, but never once do they stray to me.

"You look different." His thin lips curl at the word, like Maekallus's humanified traits disgust him. "Fitting, for a deserter."

Maekallus is tense, a hare ready to spring. He does nothing to give me away.

And it's at that moment I realize I'm not being ignored. I am invisible. I'd willed it without even realizing. As far as Scroud is concerned, I am not here.

It offers me only a fraction of courage.

Maekallus bows his head in deference. "I am what I am," he answers. Exactly what he once told me.

Scroud snorts. "You are untrustworthy. Why have you come here?" He takes in the thread of light leading from Maekallus's chest. "What—"

He pauses, finally dipping his head to look in my direction. I could swear my heart stops under that gaze. *Don't see me. Don't see me. Don't see me.* Perhaps he's noticed the indentation in the wild grass where I sit. Perhaps—

Maekallus had told me Scroud might sense his Will Stone. Does he sense it now?

Panic stricken, I do the only thing I know I can. I *will* the mysting to go, to forget, to vanish back into the portal from which he came.

Not a noise escapes him when he turns and does just as I'd silently ordered. But even when he leaves—even when I can no longer hear his footsteps, and the stone warns only of his minions—I am paralyzed with terror. Maekallus, too, is afraid. He takes a moment before facing me. His shoulders, his chest, even the muscles in his face are tense. It makes me think of a corpse, after the hardening has set in.

"He sensed it." His word is more wind than whisper. "I know he did."

I manage to swallow, to wet my tongue enough to speak. "I willed him to forget."

Maekallus nods, but doubt shines in his amber eyes. I can't help but mirror it.

We sit there, alone for a time. I sense another mysting vanish into the portal. I wait for the gobler to come up, but he doesn't.

After what must be another quarter hour, Maekallus says, "We have to move forward. Scout the circle."

"We don't have time—"

He clasps my face in his hands. His fingertips are cold—not the cold of a mysting, but of a man shaken. I lean into them, yet the intimacy of the gesture pulls at my most broken pieces, like a knife cutting across burned skin.

"We have time. I promise. Two days. One for me to watch, one to make our move."

My gut sours. "But if you're caught . . . Scroud—"

Even in the darkness, I can see the glint of his smirk. "I won't be. I'm still a narval. And Scroud won't be looking for me, if you made him forget. Hopefully he was checking on his troops, nothing more. I'll stay to the south and keep the spell out of sight." He sounds like he's forcing himself to believe the sentiment.

I'm not sure if narvals can mask themselves from other mystings like they can with mortals, but I've no other realistic options available to me. I nod, and he drops his hands, and I hurt all over again.

We're motionless for a few minutes more. The portal ring activates again. Maekallus uses its flash of blinding light to scoop me up and move away from the red-lit grove. I don't ask him to carry me, but he does, through the depths of the wildwood, until even his breaths are short and his skin moist. He carries me all the way to the trees by my home and sets me down.

I think I feel his lips brush my temple, but when I turn back to him, he's already gone.

I spend the following day with my father.

He's well enough to sit upright in bed, and even gets up late in the morning to take a bath. I play fell the king with him, read to him, and listen to his stories. I chat with him while I darn one of his socks, and when weariness pulls him to sleep, I harvest mushrooms from the cellar farm and take them into town. It is Mrs. Lovess who mans the booth today. I'm grateful for that small relief. My heart has been stretched and knotted, and I can't pick my way through it for Tennith's sake. Not even for my own.

Maekallus is always there, lurking in my thoughts. I think of him in the half seconds between my father's breaths, in the spaces between sentences in my books, and in the silence between footfalls when I walk to and from the house. Maekallus isn't at the edge of the wood today—he's deep in the thick of it, watching the portal circle. I find myself searching the edge of the wildwood for him, and even trick myself into thinking I spy him, but the red glint is only the tail of a fox.

I grip my Will Stone and think, *Stay alive.* It might be too much to ask, however, for the stone doesn't tingle at my command. It flashes cold on and off, signaling the arrival and departure of mystings. Between flashes, it is cool, so I know Maekallus is alive enough to be considered a threat, if only a small one.

My body shivers with unnatural cold, and I continue to have moments of blankness as I work about the house. Feeling has not returned to my fingertips. Maekallus's betrayal still burns in my belly. Yet the kinder parts of me—perhaps the parts fueled by what bits of soul I possess—warn that I'm too harsh a judge. That I'm faulting a soul-filled Maekallus for the actions of a previous, soulless version of himself, and they are not one and the same. Yet even when I lean toward that reasoning, my heart aches. A rusted stake has been hammered between my breasts, and I'm without the tools to pull it out.

Perhaps what bothers me most of all is the fact that I feel so strongly about a *mysting*, whether or not he has a soul. I'm so sick with this that I can't even bring myself to write in my book, though I have so much information to record.

The day ends without event. My father complains about the fire being too hot, so I keep it down during the afternoon. As soon as he turns in for the night, however, I stoke it until smoke chokes the chimney, and I lie before its flames, willing my chills away.

I stay there, tortured by my thoughts, until dawn nears the horizon. Then I sleep for an hour or so, only to wake in a puddle of my own perspiration, the images of teeth and red, violent light seared against my eyelids.

My father is up and about again, much to my relief, though it will take another couple of days for his full strength to return. I chide him when I find him washing dishes after breakfast. He insists on working, so I set him to checking the oon berry for holes and steal away into the wildwood. Maekallus has had his day to watch, and I'm overeager to know what he knows. I clutch the Will Stone as I walk.

The Will Stone whispers of Maekallus's closeness long before I reach the glade; perhaps he is seeking me out, just as I am seeking him. I press my numb fingertips to the stone as I trek slowly through the wildwood and focus on keeping my breathing even so I might not tire so quickly. I change direction twice, the Will Stone guiding me, and find Maekallus near a brook. He scoops cool water into his hands and drinks before raising his head and noticing me. The sun shines off the point of his horn. It doesn't look as sharp as I remember it being. Black spots mar his body, some as small as a particle of dust, others as large as a grown man's hand. The right side of his chest and right shoulder are more black than peach, and a black smudge engulfs his left eye as though someone had hit him there. It makes the amber iris look especially bright.

His pants are dirty and torn, and his now-human feet are entirely mud stained. When I near him, I say, "I should have brought you clothes. And shoes."

"Won't matter soon."

He seems nervous, which prompts my question. "What did you find?"

He glances over his shoulder. Standing under sunlit trees, surrounded by bird and insect song, it's hard to believe anything evil could reside in the wildwood. Yet we both know better. Maekallus is tense; the melodies and brightness have no effect on him.

He says, "They're scouting. Just a few now, but there will be more." He glances to the Will Stone. "Let's hope it's only scouting."

My stomach tightens. I think of his stories of Scroud, of the War That Almost Was, and glance to my bracelet. What will happen if

Scroud manages to reclaim the stone? Will he attempt to resume his battle with the human realm? Half of me wants to sell it or find someone to cast it into the sea. The other half is terrified of being separated from it.

"If we're to strike"—Maekallus breaks me from my thoughts—"sooner is better."

"G-Good. Our time is limited." Rubbing my thumb against the stone, I try to focus on our immediate problem. I look at the blackness around his eye and frown. I hope we resolve this quickly. I have so little left to give.

"They have fewer guards during the day. More likely to run into mortals, I suppose. If we're going to find Grapf, the best time would be near sunset or tomorrow before sunrise."

"Tonight, then."

He presses his lips together for a moment before saying, "We'll go—"

"*I'll* go."

His eyes narrow. "You don't know these mystings like I do. You don't—"

"I don't have a telltale red thread announcing me wherever I go." I point to his chest, almost touching it. "I take it that even if your invisibility magic is up, they can still see the binding spell?"

His frown deepens, and I know I'm right.

"If we don't want Scroud to find us, we can't draw attention to ourselves. I can't merely tag along with you, willing others to look away."

Maekallus growls in response. "If you were a more docile mortal—"

He couldn't possibly be worried about my safety. I have the Will Stone. Still, doubt creeps into my chest. "How many can I control at once?"

He shakes his head. "I'm not sure. Several. Scroud . . ." He pauses, and I wonder if his memories are painful, even now. "He had a method to it. Shifts, clockwork, something. I wouldn't feel his pull constantly—it ebbed and flowed, but not consistently enough for me to find an easy way around it. Once I did, I ran beyond the reach of his influence. But Scroud's army was substantial, twenty years ago." He meets my eyes. "I doubt the numbers are the same now, without that rock's power, but . . ." He offers a half-hearted shrug.

"So he couldn't have controlled his entire army at once, only parts of it?"

"I don't know." He pauses, running his knuckles along the underside of his chin. "Don't go into the Deep. Bring Grapf to you. The scrying spell could sense him over the threshold . . . perhaps the portal ring will let the stone's power extend through the barrier between our realms."

I look away, gooseflesh rising on my arms. "Don't worry, Maekallus. I've seen enough of your realm to know to stay away."

"Nightmares again?"

I nod.

He sets his jaw. Silence stretches for nearly a minute before he speaks again. "Enna, had I known—"

I glare at him, and his words die beneath my scrutiny. For some reason, I feel the weight of each individual letter panging beneath my breast. A sore lump presses into my throat, and I swallow it down.

"I'm sorry," he whispers, crouching by the brook.

I sigh. Consider. "Maekallus."

He lifts his head until his horn points at my crown.

"What does it . . . feel like? My soul?"

He frowns. Doesn't answer at first, but I let the weight of silence press against him. His amber eyes look toward the water. "Terrible," he says, his voice gruff. "Wonderful. Strange. I've had souls before, Enna. I am what I am. But never like this. They've never been more than . . . food."

I consider this, unable to empathize.

"It makes me remember things that aren't mine to remember."

"My memories?" My face heats.

But he shakes his head. "No. This is your soul, but it isn't *you*. The memories . . . they're someone else's."

"Yours?"

He meets my eyes again, his amber gaze full of some strange emotion. "I don't know."

We stay like that for a moment, just staring at one another. I wish I could crawl inside his head and see what he sees, feel what he feels. I wish I could understand better. When I speak, my voice chokes to a whisper. "You'll give it back, won't you?"

The skin around his eyes tightens. "I will do anything to save you, Enna."

That hits my heart harder than the rest, and I glance away to prevent tears from betraying me. Once I've regained my composure, I say, "I'll meet you in the glade, near sunset."

"Let me carry you home."

"No. I have enough strength today. We'll make this work, Maekallus."

He nods, and I turn away. His gaze touches me like a feather across my neck, and despite my best efforts to stay strong, I glance back and meet it.

Once I'm home, I massage my chest and will the heartache to pass, but the Will Stone is not strong enough to obey me.

This will be the last time I lie to my father.

I tell him a woman—one whom I've invented—is in labor in town, and that the midwife is ill with the same ailment that plagued him, so I've volunteered to help her through the birth. I make sure he's fed and comfortable in his chair by the fire, and every window is lined with herbs to protect the house against mystings, before I set out into the wildwood. The sun hangs high over the mountains. Even with my slow pace, I should be able to reach Maekallus by the designated time. My mother's dagger rests in a belt over my hips. The Will Stone is cold in my hands, warning me of other mystings in the wildwood.

I'm surprised to see my scrying spell intact when I reach Maekallus's glade, its white shimmer hanging in the air. I drink water and take a bite from a peach I brought, hoping it will renew my energy. Though only a few hours have passed, Maekallus looks worse than before. The black around his eye is creeping toward his jaw. More of his stomach and back are corrupted.

It would take only one kiss. One kiss, and I could feel his arms around me, his mouth against mine. A moment of bliss for a piece of my dwindling spirit. It's absurd that the exchange tempts me, even if only for a breath. I might not make it tonight if I give up anything more, and he's hardly a tar puddle.

Still, I hate seeing him suffer, however much he might deserve it.

I swallow and wipe perspiration from my brow. "I . . . need you to carry me part of the way. It's . . . far."

He reaches a hand for me, and I'm about to insist I ride on his back—I shouldn't want to be in his arms—but the words jumble against my tongue. Maekallus swoops me up. I wonder how much of his own strength remains.

I point in the direction the scrying spell leads, but he says, "I know the way."

I turn my head, trying not to smell the scent of corruption on his skin. It makes his touch colder, more like the mysting he should be. I focus on the task ahead, on the portal ring, and on Scroud.

"What if Scroud is there?" I ask.

"Then we come back in the morning."

"But—"

"I don't know, Enna." I can barely hear him over his footsteps. "I don't know."

I clutch the Will Stone in both hands as Maekallus picks his way through the wildwood. It turns colder and colder, and I curl against him for heat. My pulse quickens with the stone's warnings. I remind myself that my father got close enough to Scroud to steal his most precious belonging and lived to tell the tale.

Over a mile stretches beneath Maekallus before I put my hand to his chest. "Stop."

He pauses. "We can get closer—"

"Put me down."

I don't will it, but he obliges as if I had. The brief rest granted me a little more strength. I look at the glimmering scrying spell ahead of me, then at the sun. I need to move quickly.

"Enna."

I meet his eyes and keep my voice low. "Go back to the glade."

"No."

I hold up my left hand and let the Will Stone dangle between us. He remains unmoving. Petulant.

I lower my hand. He knows I don't want to force him. And I won't. "I can do this. I have the stone. I can see the scrying spell. You can't."

He glowers. The heat of his gaze is stronger than that of the lowering sun. He lifts a hand and touches my jaw, sending pinpricks down the side of my neck. When I don't pull away, he leans forward and whispers in my ear, "Be ready for anything. Move forward only for your sake, not for mine."

He kisses me just beneath my earlobe. For a moment, in the back of my thoughts, we are two different people in a different place, free of the threat of monsters and the ache of betrayal. I blink, and the moment is gone.

Maekallus backs away, pulling the thin red light of the binding spell a few steps closer to the glade. I wrench away from his gaze and focus on the trail of mist. Steel myself. Will strength to my limbs.

I tread through the wildwood on the tips of my toes, creeping over the uneven forest floor as fast as I can without being too loud or wasting away my energy. Maekallus will not follow me, for he knows I am right—his spell would give him away. Give *us* away. I wonder if he discovered as much when scouting yesterday, without the power of the Will Stone to hide him. But my focus will need to be on the gobler—on summoning it and keeping it hidden from the mystings at the portal ring. I'm not confident I can do that and keep Maekallus masked, and I don't dare test the breadth of the Will Stone's power here.

The sky grows more orange as the sun sets behind me. I slip between two trees and around the thick bushes of blackberries, always keeping the scrying spell in sight. My breaths come heavier, my joints resistant. *Keep going,* I urge myself. This is the only way to free Maekallus. The one way to retrieve my soul.

Movement to my right startles me. I stop and stoop, listening, waiting for a deer to walk by. But it's no deer that emerges from the brush.

It's an orjan.

CHAPTER 26

*A vuldor-tusk knife is made by collecting a tusk from
the lower jaw of a vuldor, hollowing it out, and filling it
with mystium blood, which is usually sealed inside with a
bronze or copper hilt, as these mortal metals are harmless to
mystings.*

It is not Scroud. His hair is too light, too short. His horns too crooked. But he is large, far broader and taller than I am—larger, even, than Maekallus.

This is all I have time to think before the mysting's black eyes find me.

It doesn't roar or laugh. It's eerily silent as it darts forward, impossibly swift, the only sound it makes the parting of wild grass at its feet.

The beast has almost reached me when my mind cries, *Stop!*

My hand tingles around the Will Stone. I falter backward, putting space between the monster and myself. It's frozen, a puppet held up by hundreds of invisible strings.

My heartbeat is thunder. My throat burns, and my mouth is dry. The Will Stone is so cold, warning me of so many mystings that I had not heard its whisper about this one. Gripping its burning shape in my hand, I croak, "Sleep," and the orjan falls heavily to the earth, blue lids hiding its black eyes.

I'm shaking. I close my mouth, working it to get something to swallow. Remembering my canteen, I fumble with it, unwilling to release the stone, and drink. All the while I watch the orjan. His chest rises and falls as if caught in the depths of a dream.

"Forget," I mutter, stepping around him. The fresh vigor of fear fuels me when I run, putting space between the creature and myself. I acted too slowly. I must be quicker next time.

I pray Scroud is not nearby and does not sense the signature of his lost keepsake.

The sun is setting too quickly, and the new energy in my blood gradually dies. I push myself forward, forward—

The path of the scrying spell suddenly shifts, and the Will Stone whispers of a new mysting. A gobler.

I pause, staring at the glimmering white magic dusting my knees. It straightens, then curves southward.

The gobler, Grapf, is here at last.

I pick up my feet, following the light, my thoughts a whirlwind. If he is already here, I will not have to brave the portal ring and whatever mystings may guard it. I wonder what his purpose is in the mortal realm. His chill begins to fade from the stone—he's moving faster than I am, distancing himself. He must not sense his predecessor's print on my arm. Tonight, I am not his intended target. But he is mine.

Stay, I think, squeezing the Will Stone. It tingles softly against my skin. When I sense its power has worked, I beg it for energy to move. It heeds me only a little. Strength trickles into my legs, and soon I am weaving through the wild grass and trees, trying my hardest to be quiet. To come up on the gobler carefully, in case something happens against my expectations. The glimmering path holds true, no longer shifting in accordance with Grapf's movements. My legs burn. My lungs are on fire. My dress sticks to my skin as the sun dips behind the horizon, changing the sky from pink to violet to blue.

My body forces me to stop. I am not quiet as I gasp for air. My legs shake with exertion. I lick my lips and taste salt. I cannot go any farther, and change my plan accordingly.

I think of the corruption devouring Maekallus and force myself to stand tall. My knuckles ache from squeezing the Will Stone. It whispers, *Gobler.* The handprint on my left arm tingles as if to confirm the theory. I use the stone to search for other mystings, but none are close.

"Grapf!" I shout into the wood. His name does not sound the same on my lips as it does on Maekallus's, but it is close enough. Shoulders heaving with each breath, I take a step forward, and another. Stumble on the uneven floor. "Grapf!" *Come to me.*

The scrying spell shimmers. The edges of the wildwood are darkening as night creeps into the sky. Hair sticks to my forehead. I don't swipe it away.

Footsteps. Heavy, strong steps. Nearing.

I pause, fighting against my fatigue. Fighting my mind to stay alert. Urging myself to pretend my soul is intact.

He emerges from the trees. A gobler. I know it is him, for the scrying spell dances across his belly, then winks out as if it never were, its purpose fulfilled. I should be afraid to see him, my enemy, but my body is too spent to know fear.

He's large for a gobler. That is to say, he's about the height of an average human, a hand's length taller than I am. He is wide, his rolls of blubber thick. His head is five times the size of my own, bluish in color, hairless. His gaze dips to my arm, sensing the mark left by his compatriot.

His large eyes are glassy and blue. A curved dagger hangs on his belt. It looks almost like ivory and has strange, ugly etchings along its length. Its hilt is short and wrapped in leather.

He looks me up and down and asks, in my own tongue, "What mortal dares speak my name?"

I grip the stone in my hand. "Quiet."

He is.

"Turn east."

He does, stiff and doll-like.

"Take the tusk dagger from your belt and drop it on the ground."

He does. My arm shakes from the tingling of the Will Stone. My palm is slick with perspiration. "Step back. Again. Again."

He backs away from the dagger. I stare at it. My salvation, Maekallus's, lying right there in the clover.

And I comprehend how incredible the power in my left hand is. It takes my short breaths away from me for a moment. Long enough that Grapf turns his head to look at me.

"Face east!" I shout. His face snaps eastward, and I cringe at my volume.

"Are you alone? Answer me."

"Yes, for now."

"What is your task?"

"To find the Will Stone. To investigate the mortal hub to the west."

Fendell. My stomach knots.

I can make him sleep, just like the orjan. Make him forget, too. But this creature has been the ultimate cause of my grief. He's proven himself intelligent. He's working for a mysting who would use the stone to dominate my own people.

"Return whence you came and . . . kill Scroud."

The Will Stone does not react. Why? Is such a thing not possible? Fear makes itself known to me then, tracing my spine with the touch of ice.

I could order the gobler to kill himself, or, simply, to die. Yet I hesitate to do so. Perhaps I'm too soft a mortal. Perhaps it's because I've never before taken a sentient life. Or maybe the explanation lies with Maekallus, who has made me look at mystings differently.

I take a deep breath, letting it fill me to the brim before releasing it. "When I indicate, you are going to flee east, never faltering, until you reach the sea. You will never return to the forest. You will never harm a human. The sea and the Deep will be your only homes. You will never speak of this night or of the stone you seek." Then, to be sure, I add, "You will never speak again."

Grapf doesn't move.

I swallow. "Go."

He runs.

He sprints through the forest, grazing tree trunks, tripping over ditches and inclines. He runs, and I watch him until the darkness swallows him. My stone warms ever so slightly against my palm.

I can will the gobler to run, but I cannot will it of myself. My body is spent, and without the scrying spell to mark my path, I am hopelessly lost. I sway and drop to my knees.

I know he will forgive me when I hold the stone to my lips and whisper, "Maekallus, find me. And don't let anyone else see you."

Resting my head against the earth, I close my eyes, but sleep is far from me.

With the last of my strength, I crawl forward until my once-scarred hand wraps around the hilt of the tusk dagger. Then I lie inert, listening to the rhythm of my breathing and the song of remembered nightmares.

The moon is high when I hear another set of footsteps approach. These, I don't will away.

CHAPTER 27

Freblon are humanoid mystings that average about three feet in height. They are incredibly thin to the point of looking malnourished and wear a crown of bone across their foreheads.

The pull on his body suddenly stops. Panic rises. Does this mean something has happened to Enna? Is she . . .

But he sees her lying in the wild grass up ahead, her face pale in the moonlight. His stomach pitches as he runs to her and drops to his knees at her side. Feels for injuries, for breathing, for—

"Maekallus," she whispers.

Relief blooms as he brushes hair off her face. "Are you hurt?"

"Tired."

He lets out a long breath. "Gods below, woman." He expected the worst, especially when the tug of the Will Stone took him away from the portal ring. There are too many mystings this deep in the wildwood. He's already killed two, one who crossed his path and another who had followed the line of his curse.

He puts a hand under her head and helps her sit up. That's when he sees it.

He freezes, staring. The dagger. The tusk dagger, clasped in her hand. For a moment he doesn't breathe. A long moment. Until his lungs gasp for air.

A bubble of corruption rolls across his back, aching like a bad bruise. He ignores it. "You found it."

She lifts the dagger. Smiles. "I can free you, Maekallus."

He shakes his head, staring at his salvation. "But . . . how, when . . ."

She doesn't answer his questions. Instead she grabs his blackened shoulder, presses the tip of the blade beneath his pectoral, and slides it across his chest.

It crosses the glowing thread of light, and the spell vanishes.

It feels like a boulder lifting from his ribs. He gasps, air filling parts of him he'd forgotten he had. Muscles unwind and joints relax. He falls forward onto his hands, nearly whacking Enna with his horn.

"Maekallus?"

"I'm . . . fine," he says between breaths. He touches his chest, and the soul dances beneath his fingertips.

"I'm glad," she whispers.

He looks back at her. Even in the dark he can see bags under her eyes. Her touch is chilly. Taking her hand, he puts an arm around her and helps her stand.

"Your soul," he says.

"My soul."

"If there's a way, it's in the monster realm. Attaby had a theory. But . . ."

Moonlight glitters off her blue eyes. Blue like the mortal sky. "But?"

"But it may not—"

"We have to try."

He takes a deep breath, marveling at the freedom he feels. "You can only come to my realm unharmed if you're one of us."

She searches his eyes. "What do you mean?"

If you have no soul. He can't bring himself to say it, to ask for yet more from Enna. Her soul stirs within him, eager, waiting.

"Do you trust me?" he asks.

She doesn't answer at first, and he feels like a fool for asking. Of course she doesn't trust him. He's lied to her for his own gain, betrayed her, stolen from her—

"Yes."

The whisper shocks him like a bucket of cold water. He doesn't understand. How . . . ? But it isn't important now. He needs to act quickly. Once he takes it . . . he has only hours.

He puts a hand beneath her chin. Her skin is so soft, so fragile. He runs his thumb over her lips.

She closes her eyes and waits.

He leans down to her, pressing his mouth against hers. She meets him willingly, and it sparks a vigor in him that has nothing to do with her soul. Her ardor and trust make him feel human. *Alive.* It kindles a deep wanting only she can quench.

She whimpers against him, but doesn't pull away. Heat runs down his throat—another piece of soul, fiery and thrilling. The want becomes so much more. It courses through his blood, sings in his muscles.

He breaks away and claims her again, drawing her into his arms. She shivers, and he hates himself. When the final shard of her soul fills him, she doesn't make a sound. Her lips stop moving, fingers stop clutching.

It encompasses every last corner of him, illuminating shadows, brightening his memories. In that moment he knows Enna entirely, and he loves her. The whole of her spirit paints him—a flash of perfect clarity—and in it he sees a life left behind, a life that isn't his, not anymore.

He wipes the bar with a wet rag. The cloth is starting to smell of mold, but he'll scrub it clean, hang it to dry, and use it again. The little inn isn't much, but he got it by scrimping and saving, and the habit has stuck, even into his middle years.

The moment Ganter Kubbs walks in, he knows it is going to be a bad day. A bad week. Maybe even longer. Ganter is local. He doesn't drink here. None of the mobsters in the Factio do. But he pulls up a stool, spills a few coins on the bar, and says, "Stu, give me the strongest you've got."

He's never turned down a customer. And no one turns down Ganter Kubbs. So he pours him some ale and leaves to clean the kitchen.

But Ganter returns the next day, this time with two friends. Then it's three friends, then five, and he says, "Don't you have space in the basement? My boys would like space in the basement. Indefinitely."

Stu rubs the stubble on his face—a nervous habit. He catches himself and drops his hand. "Just for storage. I don't have the room—"

"We'll make it work."

He never said yes. The gang just makes itself comfortable down there, doing their busywork. Stu doesn't ask questions, and he doesn't get answers. He tries to move on like all is well, but mobsters are bad for business. Word gets out, and soon his only customers are the traveling variety who don't know any better.

But then there's Annalae.

Annalae, sweet Annalae. Like a daughter to him. Her mother brings him cheese for the kitchens twice a week in exchange for use of his fruit press. She brings her daughter, and the girl sits in the back while he cooks. Chats his ear off. He hated it, at first. But then he got to liking the company, so now that she's a little more grown and has found other things to do, it breaks his heart.

Sometimes Annalae still brings the cheese, and when she does he wraps her up in a story, and she pokes fun at his thinning hair and big ears. Then the cheese doesn't come for two weeks, and when her mother finally comes by with a delivery, he hears the hard truth.

Ganter Kubbs had taken a liking to Annalae, and he never takes no for an answer. It will only be a matter of time before he starts asking Annalae questions to which she can only consent.

Stu won't have it. Can't have it.

So he closes the inn the next day. Damn place hasn't so much as rested for a holiday in twenty years. But he goes off and sends a request to His Lordship, and the following week armored men come in and take the mobsters away. All of them.

Or so Stu thinks.

A moon passes before two come back. He doesn't even know their names. He never asked questions. But when it's so late even the sturdiest drunkards turn in, they come, and they drag him into the forest and rake a rusted blade across his throat, once, twice, three times . . .

The blood falls onto the grass. Seeps into it. Trickles down to another realm. Changes. Takes shape.

And Maekallus opens his eyes.

Maekallus winces at the memories, startling himself when he bites the inside of his lip. Blood dribbles from the corner of his mouth, and he wipes it away. His hand is free of corruption. The air around him is calm. Free of the pricks and nibbles that always engulf him on this plane.

The mortal realm sees him as one of its own.

Enna stands before him, staring straight ahead. She doesn't blink. Doesn't move. Barely breathes. Dull. Empty. Soulless.

The tusk dagger lies by her feet.

He picks it up and traces it across the earth, stumbling a bit. Off balance. He touches his forehead. The horn is still there, but it's shorter, perhaps one and a half hands in length. Never mind that.

He takes her left hand in his and unclasps the Will Stone bracelet—she can no longer use it. Without a soul, she doesn't have a will. He tries to fasten it around his own wrist, but the chain is too short, so he winds the silver around his middle finger and palms the most powerful thing he's ever touched.

Do not devour her, he commands himself.

He draws the mortal's descent circle, then takes Enna in his arms and stands at its center.

Blue light flashes, and the mortal realm falls away in one fluttering piece.

CHAPTER 28

*The mortal realm will devour a mysting's body. The monster
realm will destroy a human's mind.*

The ground separates.
  I fall.
  He's there.
  It's red.
  Too warm.
  I . . .
  I?

CHAPTER 29

*Narval horns make for excellent sorcery, or so a rooter
named Attaby has claimed. The extent of his meaning is yet
to be determined.*

Once, not long after Maekallus was made, before Enna was ever born,
he fancied a mortal woman.

He hid from her for a long time, watching, intrigued. Narah
worked at a brothel—those aren't too different across realms, save for
the customers. She was tall and lithe with hair like midnight that fell
in soft curls down her back. Her breath smelled like dying roses. Her
lips were stained red. She was coy and curious and bold, and Maekallus
learned how to charm just about anyone from watching her. He'd found
her during one of his scouting missions for Scroud; she'd been a diver-
sion from the orjan's dominating presence in the Deep.

Maekallus had already coaxed out a soul or two by then. Lost himself in the brief ecstasy of the vigor. So long as the mortal was willing,
the soul came. Willingness could come from lust, fear, or trickery. An
easy obstacle to overcome.

When he'd finally shown himself to Narah, she'd hardly reacted at
all. Perhaps it was the smoke in her lungs or the drink in her belly. It

didn't matter. She was kind and curious. Invited him into her home, and her bed.

It was a dark night, the sky congested with those strange white clouds of the mortal realm. She told him about things he'd never experienced—dancing and comedy and heartache—and he hung off her every word like they were drops of water in the middle of the Azhgrada.

It wasn't entirely his fault. She'd leaned toward him, smiling, reaching for his mouth. He'd kissed her, and he'd taken her soul—the entirety of it. He hadn't meant to. But intentions don't matter when one is a narval.

It burned brightly inside him, blissful and sweltering and agonizing. It made him *regret*. And like the other souls he'd consumed, it began to fade. He panicked.

Then he heard about Attaby. Sought him out. The rooter was interested, quiet, contemplative. Even now, Maekallus remembers their conversation. *The immortal waters might do it. Then again, once a soul leaves its body, the pathway is carved, isn't it? Who is to say it wouldn't leave again, and of its own volition? You'd need some sort of talisman to keep it in place. But it doesn't matter.*

Why? Maekallus asked.

The rooter shook his head. *Her soul is dead, dear lad. It died long before you found me.*

Just like that, he'd lost her. And the moment he digested her soul in the Deep, he'd stopped caring altogether.

The Deep has no sky, just endless red light that isn't really light at all, but somehow it enables the eye to see. It has trees, but they're ruddy and short with jagged limbs bearing fruit that will kill any mortal taster. Its soil is darker, where there is soil to be had. Much of the Deep, at least where Maekallus dwells, has uneven ground that's spongy with one step, steellike with the next. But there's water—brooks and streams and rivers of it, though not nearly as bounteous as in the mortal realm. Even mystings have to drink.

Sometimes, in the mortal realm, on a snowy night, one can experience pure silence. But it's never silent in the Deep. There is always something breathing, crying, laughing, feeding. Always something writhing, usually unseen.

It had bothered Maekallus at first, at the beginning of this existence. Then he'd stopped noticing it, stopped caring. But with Enna in his arms, he notices every click and whine, every shift of the endless red landscape.

Enna doesn't. She stares straight ahead, a puppet without a master. The light is gone from her eyes, captured inside his own body, burning inside a lantern that won't let it shine.

The Deep lends him the ability to digest what he stole in the realm above, and the mysting in him longs to do just that. His stomach growls with hunger. A strange thirst forms at the back of his throat, begging to be quenched.

He squeezes the stone and focuses. He has to be swift. He will not let her soul die.

Grabbing Enna by the hips, he throws her over his shoulder. He can move faster that way. She doesn't so much as peep at the discomfort.

Her reaction—her lack of one—spikes fear through him.

He runs.

Enna doesn't draw attention; she's soulless, a husk. But Maekallus does. He feels eyes, seen and unseen, follow him as he navigates through the Deep. His destination is the immortal waters, but no one can travel directly there. Its magic nullifies circles.

He passes through spiny trees, a poor imitation of the wildwood. Hears a low growl issue from the shadows between them. By habit he reaches his free hand for his horn—but his trusted "blade" won't come, even here. The soul cements it in place. It's barely a knife now, besides.

Then he remembers the stone, and he *pushes* toward the predator, and the pursuit halts before it begins.

He grips that stone until his hand aches, afraid to use it lest it draw attention. He doesn't understand how it works in the mortal realm; he certainly can't comprehend the consequences of its power in the Deep.

He nearly cries when he sees it—another absurd new sensation. The immortal waters. A great rusted hill with a crater where its crest should be, and in that open mouth laps an enormous pool of silvery water. It feeds the Deep, little by little. It's why Maekallus and his kind live so long, though he has no knowledge of its source.

He shifts Enna to his back and wills her to cling to his neck to keep from slipping off. The Will Stone goes into his mouth. He needs both hands to climb. His lungs burn first, then his legs, weak from so much travel. His arms throb last, but he climbs until his fingernails crack and bleed. Until his feet numb. Until his throat scorches like he's drunk acid-laced wine.

He comes up the lip of the crater and topples over it, sprawling onto the thick, almost beach-like ledge. Enna falls with him, losing her grip around his neck. He lies next to her for a moment, wheezing, staring up into the endless red. He grips the Will Stone. Can he still feel her soul inside him? He hurts too much to tell, but that very worry gives it away. Maekallus isn't accustomed to worrying.

Pulling himself up, he gains his bearings. Ahead, the ledge tapers downward into a lake. Two grinlers sit near the edge of the water, eyeing him, eyeing Enna. He ignores them; in the Deep, size and power trump all else. Without their pack, Maekallus can make short work of them with little effort.

Maekallus cradles Enna in his arms, balancing her across the crooks of his elbows. He wades into the waters. Something, an aquatic mysting, slithers by him. He wills it away. The waters calm.

"Stand up, Enna," he whispers to her, setting her feet down. The water reaches the tops of her thighs. She stands, but stares blankly ahead. Pale and sickly, quiet. The life has gone from her. She still breathes. Her pulse raises the vein in her wrist. But the thing that had truly made her alive has vanished.

Reaching around her, he pulls the silver dagger from her belt. Silver, a metal nowhere to be found in his world. Deadly to all mystings.

Narval horns make for excellent sorcery.

Grasping his horn in his left hand, he squeezes the hilt of the dagger with his right and swings with all the strength he can muster. The silver does its job. It hacks halfway through the horn, which is likely weakened from his borrowed soul. He hits it again, and this time the tip comes off. Two-thirds the length of his hand.

Something quakes below the hill. Not uncommon here, but it sets him on edge. In the lake, he can't see over the ridge of the crater, so there is no telling if the tremor is natural or not—it merely reminds him to hurry. He fastens the Will Stone around Enna's wrist. The wrong one, but it doesn't matter. As his fingers move, his mind pulls up Attaby's decades-old theory, the one he initially sought out in the hopes of saving Narah.

He takes Enna's hands in his own and kneels in the water. It rushes up to his chest. Bending his head down, he pulls water into his mouth and holds it there. Stands again. Places the Will Stone in Enna's hand, putting his own over it. Wills this to work. Wills her to live.

He thinks he feels the stone shiver.

With his other hand he cradles Enna's head and covers her cold mouth with his, letting the water trickle between their lips. Kisses her like it will be their last . . . for it will be. It needs to be.

The soul within him ignites. Enna gasps against his lips. The tearing sensation hurts, like something deep within him has broken. It rushes out of him like water, or perhaps like blood, leaving him cold, empty, and unfeeling.

Remember, he tells himself as the last tendrils of bliss flood from him to her. He squeezes her hand, squeezes the stone. *Remember your task.*

He pulls back from her. Her eyes shimmer. Her body trembles.

"M-Maekallus?" she whispers.

He wraps her in his arms and plunges the tip of the horn into her back.

CHAPTER 30

The "immortal waters" is a great lake in the monster realm that
fuels the longevity of those who call that horrid place home.

I wake with a start, hot and cold all at once. I squint at the uneven light before me, yellow and white and green. The familiar sounds of birds and insects filter through air that's warm yet slightly crisp—summer morning.

Something creeps over my hand. I shake it off, pushing against moist earth and weeds to sit up, groaning at the pain in my head. My back is damp and covered with bits of old leaves. Trees stand sentinel around me.

The wildwood. Morning. I know this place—it's not far from my home. A good area for rabbit snares.

I lift my hand and press it to my forehead, trying to calm the ache there. The Will Stone swings before my eyes. I stare at it, a trickle of sunlight glinting off its dark edges. It hangs from my right wrist, not my left.

I gasp, and when I do, a sharp pain sparks in my chest just below my breasts. I cough and touch the tender spot. The ache is deep, traveling clear to my spine.

Gods above, I remember. I remember the gobler, I remember the tusk dagger. Then there is a hole, my thoughts plucked free, but I'm used to that now, used to—

I pull my hand back again and flex the fingers. Warm fingers. And my fingertips . . . they're not numb.

My soul. It's there. It's *there*.

Tears spring to my eyes. I stand up, sore but not fatigued. I laugh and leap and hug myself as I would a long-lost friend.

But then the blank spot in my memory fills in, and the joy distills into sobs. Great heaving sobs that make that sore spot in my chest burn.

The last thing I saw down there was Maekallus standing over me, watching me with vivid yellow eyes.

I clutch the Will Stone in both hands, but its surface is warm.

He is gone.

I was truthful when I said I had lied to my father for the last time, for when I arrive home, I cannot even bring myself to speak.

He follows me to my room, worried, but when I softly shut the door, he doesn't intrude. I stand there for a long moment, head resting against the wood. I reach up a hand and rub dried tears from my eyelids. The sun pours through my window, making the room too warm. It's almost silent within, but even these walls can't block out the noise of the forest.

Pulling away from the door, I reach around and unfasten the three buttons at the back of my ruined dress. I let it puddle on the floor, my punctured underclothes with it.

There, just over my diaphragm, is a small circle, almost like scar tissue. No larger than a pinhead. I touch it. The skin feels bruised, but it's not discolored. I find another circle at the center of my back, barely missing my spine. This one is bigger, the size of a gold farkle, our largest denomination of coin. I recognize it, although I don't know how. Maybe by the size, maybe by the color. Maybe by the feeling of it inside me, hard and unyielding and magicked, for anything else would have taken my life.

His horn. The tip of it, plunged through me. Why? Not to return me to the mortal realm. I trace the small scar beneath my breasts, thinking again of the pinhead. Pinned.

And what else would he have need to pin, except my soul to my body? So it could not escape?

A new surge of sorrow erupts. I cover my mouth with my hands to muffle the sound and drop to my knees. Tears spatter the pile of clothes. The too-warm Will Stone brushes my wrist.

I think of his yellow eyes. Without my soul inside him, what has he become? Unfeeling, unknowing, uncaring—

Mysting.

I am renewed. I am returned. I am everything I once was. I am whole.

And yet I am useless.

I feel as though my own home is a dream, faded around the edges, and I have become a specter within it. I am complete, and yet my heart is so broken I can't find its pieces. I remind myself that he is a mysting, that he lied to me, that he betrayed me, but the words are no salve to the deep and unrelenting ache. All I know for certain is that he is gone, and that, beyond all reason, I love him. Loved him, for my mind is clear enough to know Maekallus is no longer the being who shattered me so completely, and that makes it hurt so much more. I cannot even lure him back to me, for the powerful Will Stone cannot reach into the monster realm to find him. I cannot even bring myself to worry for the portal ring deep in the wildwood, save for when I clutch the Will Stone and pray Scroud's scouts will pass over this place.

I know how pathetic I am, yet I can't seem to heal myself. I place one handkerchief in the laundry and take a second to wipe my eyes, which are growing sore from the constant application of linen. My dear, kind father does not ask after my troubles or try to make them right. He merely remains silent, feeds me when I forget to eat, and places a kiss on my head when I sit on the rug before the unlit hearth, where Maekallus had once lain beside me.

It takes another day for me to realize the gobler's mark has vanished from my arm. Whether it was nullified by my entrance into the monster realm or vanquished by the power of the narval horn, I'll never know.

I sleep a sleep without nightmares. Without dreams at all. I am still broken and sore in the morning, but I force myself from my bed and put a broom in my hand, determined to reclaim the life he so selflessly returned to me. Whenever I pass the east-facing windows, I look out into the wildwood, wishing and hoping, but the stone tells me he is not here. The bracelet remains fastened around my right wrist. I haven't the heart to move it.

I tend my garden, pulling weeds without a thought in my head, trying to will the sweet summer air to mend me. I make dinner and burn myself on the pot, then guide my father through the steps of finishing the meal.

All this time, the stone hangs from my wrist, not cool, not hot. But after we've eaten, when Papa is setting up a game of fell the king, the stone turns cold, chilled as snowfall in an instant. My broken heart leaps, and I clasp the charm tightly against my palm.

But it is not a narval it warns me of. It warns me of many things, many mystings. The first name it whispers is *orjan*.

It is with utter despondency that I realize Maekallus was right. That it wasn't safe to use the stone near Scroud. That he is intimately familiar with it. That the moment I unleashed its power in his presence, I confirmed what the first, dead gobler had known.

The stone is here. And now the great mysting lord has come to reclaim it.

"Papa."

My voice is hoarse, though I've barely spoken the last two days. I rush from the house, leaving the front door open. The sun is half-set, casting everything in shadow. "Papa," I say, a little louder. I run around to the cellar and call down into its darkness. *"Papa!"*

"Enna?" he calls back.

"Papa, mystings. In the wildwood. They're coming this way. We need to leave."

"Mystings?" he repeats, and his face appears at the bottom of the ladder, a basket half-filled with mushrooms in one hand and a lantern in the other.

"Please, Papa. Scroud is coming."

There's a glint in his eye, and not just from the lantern. A moment of recognition, and then it's gone.

He sets down the basket and climbs up with the lantern. "I should have kept a horse."

Regrets do us no good. I grab his arm and pull him into the house, grateful he's hale again. I grab a sack and load it with whatever food I can find. The Will Stone brushes my arm and stings. I hiss, but refuse to take it off. Instead I wrap a cloth around it, tucking the ends beneath the bracelet.

I fear I'll need it.

"How many?" My father takes his sword off the mantel.

"Too many." I'll hurt myself if I grasp the stone now and attempt to count. Never has it been so cold, so acidic to the touch. They'd felt so close. Closer than the portal ring. Had a scout discovered my home without my knowledge? Had another mysting seen me, or Maekallus, the night I freed him?

Thoughts of Maekallus stab through me, making the broken horn in my breast ache anew. I throw the sack over my shoulder as Papa buckles his scabbard to his belt. He's donned a cloak as well.

He pauses and studies me. "Elefie, where are we going?"

The backs of my eyes burn. I rush to him and take his hand. "Away, Anchal." I call my father by his first name, as my mother would have. There's no time for corrections. "Away." But though I'm eager to flee, I can't just abandon Fendell to its fate. The townspeople will think I'm crazy when I ring the warning bell, especially midday. But the wise ones will heed me.

"But the baby—"

"She's here," I assure him. "Come."

I take his hand in mine and bolt out the front door, flying down the dirt path into Fendell. It seems forever away, and yet I reach it quickly. Odd looks assault me as I push through the crowd to the bell tower looming above the well. I have to stand on the well's lip to reach the rope. It's heavy, but Papa grabs the length just above my hands and pulls it down.

The bell's toll is emphatic and reverberates through my body like a living thing. My ears rattle with the sound, but I pull again, and then a third time. Townsfolk are gathering around; I see the apothecary and Tennith's mother among them.

"Prepare to fight or flee," I say, ears ringing. "An army of mystings is coming."

Several stare at me, fear slipping into their countenances. One man actually laughs.

I don't have time to convince him.

Taking my father's hand again, but before I can pull him through the crowd, I hear my name over the murmuring of the others. "Enna Rydar!"

I whirl back, panicked, only to spot an unfamiliar face among the townspeople. He is tall, with a strange beard and—

Gods above, I know that face. He is one of the scholars from the library. Jerred, wasn't it? I drew the vuldor for him.

The horn piercing my middle throbs as memories threaten to sink me into the earth.

Jerred runs up to me. He is *elated*, his eyes wide, his mouth smiling. "I've finally found you! You said a day's ride, but I didn't know what direction! My search led me—"

"Run," I interrupt. There is no time. "If you want to live, run."

I turn my back on the scholar, on opportunity, a second time and hurry my father out of town, ignoring the questions and jeers that fall upon me from the locals. I answer only, "There is no time!" We head west, parallel to Fendell and away from the wildwood. We do not cover even an eighth of a mile before the shrill giggle of a grinler raises the small hairs on my neck.

My father stops and turns back, drawing his heavy blade.

"Papa, please," I beg, but his clear eyes narrow at the great forest behind us.

They emerge in broken lines—grinlers, orjans, goblers, freblon. Another serpentine slyser like the one who appeared from the summoning circle in Maekallus's glade. Even two dark-haired narvals march among them, and the sight of their menacing horns and switch-like tails hits me like a blacksmith's hammer. They look nothing like him, yet they are so similar. The woman is taller than the man, her hair brushing the ground, her chest exposed.

They leak from the wildwood like mortal corruption, and I wish our realm would devour them faster and turn them into sludge. A strange part of me feels betrayed by the wildwood, that it would let so many of our enemies trespass. Yet I've always known what the wildwood was. I've always been told to beware it, even when its sun warmed my skin and its land fed my belly.

I hear a scream in the distance, followed by shouts. Some in Fendell have seen the monsters pour from the forest. The small army, at least seventy-five mystings, does not move toward the town, however. They march toward me and my father, and at their head is a tall orjan wearing a gold-plated sash, from which hangs what I assume to be large teeth. Scroud.

He is far more menacing in the sunlight. His black eyes hold eternal depths. His tusked scowl, a thousand promises of suffering.

My father crouches, his sword ready. I grab his elbow. "Stop."

"We will die valiantly, Shenard," he whispers. I don't recognize the name and can only guess it belongs to an old fellow in arms.

The army passes my home. In the distance I see a smattering of men armed with knives and pitchforks on the road from Fendell, but they hesitate. They are outnumbered. Never have we seen so many of these creatures at once.

A chorus of grinler giggling fouls the air as the setting sun turns the sky red, filling me with memories of the Deep. I pull the rag from my wrist. I feel Scroud's gaze like a poisoned arrow in my cheek.

I grab the stone, gasping as chilly agony shoots up my arm and into my shoulder, instantly immobilizing the joints. It webs across my back, tightening the muscles and twisting bone.

In response, somehow, the conical horn in my breast warms, driving back the worst of the pain. Still, my teeth chatter and my palm burns. I clench my jaw until my head aches.

"*Stop.*"

Scroud hesitates. The narvals slow, and most of the others do the same. A few grinlers continue forward, shoving each other and making that horrendous screeching, laughing sound. Scroud growls loud enough for the sound to carry the distance between us. He takes one labored step forward, then another. He bellows at me, and I cannot tell if it's in my tongue or his, for the words are too low and harsh. They are nails in my ears, hammering down into my brain.

I squeeze the stone harder. The broken horn heats to a feverish temperature.

"Stop."

My entire body tingles with the power of the Will Stone. It's as if I've shot an invisible wall out from myself and the army has collided with it. The soldiers freeze and look about in either anger or confusion.

My body is shaking, as though the Will Stone draws its energy from my own soul. Beside me, Papa says, "Enna?"

I don't answer him. I don't dare break my concentration.

The goblers inch forward.

"STOP!" I bellow, and my voice echoes against the wildwood. The mystings hit my wall again. The horn burns so hot I fear my body will crumble to ash around it. The Will Stone is so cold in my fist I can feel it searing a hole through my flesh. I meet Scroud's dark gaze head-on.

"Go. *Go!*" I scream. "You will not come back here! You are *banished!* You *will not come back here!*"

The wall pushes at them. I can't feel my legs. The simple act of standing is excruciating.

The army doesn't move. Scroud balks at me, but he does not look away. I can *feel* the intensity of his will. Of his desire, his hatred, and I am its focal point.

My father gasps with what I can only assume is clarity. Recognition. And I believe Scroud recognizes him as well.

"Leave!" I stagger. My father grabs my arm, the one not paralyzed by the stone, and holds me upright. I lean into him, pushing what strength I have into the stone. My breast is on fire, driving back the ice in my shoulders and gut. "Return whence you came. Leave this realm and never come back. Leave. *Leave. LEAVE!*"

A bolt of the bitterest winter spikes through me, filling every crevice of my body. I gasp and collapse into my father's strength.

He drops me to my knees. The cold has abated, but I tremble with the memory of it. The fire has left, too, but my body tenses as if run through by a sword. I lift my eyes to the wildwood just in time to see the flicking tails of the two narvals as they vanish into the trees.

They're gone, all of them, as if they never were. Folk from the town begin filling in the almost battleground, lowering their weapons, exclaiming and whispering all at once. They look back at me, their eyes astonished or bewildered. I am grounded enough to recognize Tennith among them, dressed in soiled farming clothes, a scythe in hand. His dark eyes meet mine. He is confused, yet his brows draw together as though he is angry. As though I've removed some sort of mask and he doesn't like what's underneath.

Trembling, I manage to stand and take a step forward. "T-Tennith—"

His father, behind him, sets a heavy hand on his shoulder. Tennith allows himself to be pulled away, his expression never lifting.

I was clearly the target of the mystings' attack. I rang the warning bell. My voice shouted mad commands at them. Mad commands they *heeded*. I have given the townspeople good reason to reject me. I know instinctually that they will no longer buy our mushrooms or sell to us. They will close off their conversations when we venture near. Were I to knock on Tennith's door again, it would not open to me.

Something sharp bites my right fist. I wince as I open stiff fingers. I can barely see for the tears in my eyes.

The Will Stone, the dark gem my father risked his life to secure for me, rests in a dozen pieces against my palm.

CHAPTER 31

Two Months Later

The town of Crake is a modest one. I had thought Fendell small, but Crake is half its size, barely large enough to be called a town. We have a wisewoman, a biweekly farmers' market, and little else. One must travel to Caisgard for supplies that cannot easily be homemade.

It was Jerred, the scholar, who helped us find the place. He was the only person who would speak to me after Scroud's army vanished. It was he who bartered for our supplies, he who found the abandoned blacksmith's cottage half a mile from the tiny town. It is a small home with three rooms, nestled against a bend in the wildwood, about seventeen miles south of the home my father had built with his own two hands. The house meant for his sweetheart, before the mystings killed her. The house that now stands as a great tombstone for the three loved ones buried on its grounds. A painful loss, but the time had come to leave the dead behind.

Jerred has left us to rebuild our lives, with a promise to return. He saw me turn away the mysting army with his own eyes. His interest will not be deterred. And were I of a more sound mind, I would be thrilled at the prospect of studying with an accomplished scholar. But for now,

I must focus on securing this new life, and repairing the damaged pieces of myself.

There is a comfort to this new home, this new patch of forest, and I'm grateful for the endless list of tasks that need completing to make the cottage a suitable place to live. I've cleaned cobwebs and spiderwebs, hammered new boards into the floor, filled holes in the roof with mortar while Papa hammered shingles. I've even cleared a plot at the back of the house, facing the wildwood, and placed my delicate transplants in its soil. Tusk nettle, lavender, rabbit's ear, aster leaf, tapis root, and oon berry. It will take time before they grow hearty enough to harvest, but I can wait. I've gotten rather good at it—it's what I've done all these weeks since the mystings vanished into the wildwood.

Time is the best healer, my grandmother used to say, but it is a cruel master that takes pleasure in my torment and withholds its salve. The pieces of my heart are as shattered as the Will Stone, and they are so heavy that when I cannot occupy my mind with a distracting enough task, I can barely breathe for their weight. I cannot forget, for the horn lives inside me, keeping my soul where no other can take it. But if I cannot forget, then I cannot heal, and thus I find myself trapped in an endless loop of sorrow and self-pity.

My mother never cried, or so I've heard. I always thought myself like her, but my time without my soul made me weak, and the tears come easily now, especially at night when I am alone to dwell in my regrets. It worried my father, at first. Now I think he's made his peace with it, though I have not.

After a wearying day of helping Papa dig out the cellar to make space for mushroom shelves, I collapse onto my bed, dusted with filth. Yes, time is cruel. I weep just as much as I did the morning I found Maekallus gone and my soul restored to me. The pin through my breast no longer pains me. On occasion it warms, as if speaking to me the same way the Will Stone once did, but it cools down just as quickly, leaving me unable to interpret. The foolish part of me searches for him in those moments of warmth, imagining that he's calling to me, but he is never there.

Maekallus holds very still until the pesky dragonfly hovers a little closer. Then he flicks his tail, slicing through the insect's long body with its sharp point.

He gives the halved insect a cursory glance before ducking his long horn under an oak branch and continuing on his way, hoofing softly through the edge of the wildwood. He's spent way too much time here. At first, he told himself he was fleeing the unrest in the Deep. Scroud had lost another battle—this one before it had even begun—and his remaining followers had abandoned him for good, hating him for their banishment from the mortal realm. While Maekallus is glad to see his former tormentor so diminished, he doesn't want to partake in the ensuing anarchy. So he returns to the wildwood, following memorized paths.

But when Maekallus finds her house empty, he searches farther, sneaking through the streets and taverns with his invisibility up, listening and watching. It takes a week to find her, though she has yet to see him. He wonders if she even can—the Will Stone no longer hangs from her wrist.

The things he could have done with the thing . . . To think he'd given it back to her. Twice.

That was a different Maekallus. One he remembers but doesn't understand. He recalls loving the mortal woman, enough that he'd do anything for her, but he can't . . . comprehend it now. Yet he finds himself pulled to this place, as though she made a binding spell all her own. Perhaps she *is* a witch. This new spell tugs at him in the same spot the first one had.

He hates it. Yet the memories eat at him. Enna is different than Narah, the brothel woman. Enna had been a part of him once. She made him mortal, for a moment.

He hasn't eaten a soul since expelling hers. He wonders if doing so would bring the emotions associated with his memories pouring back. Does he *want* to feel that way again? Those feelings had come with a heft of miserable emotions. He also knows that Enna would hate him if he consumed another mortal's soul just to remember the connection they once shared. That makes him hesitate.

And he hates it.

CHAPTER 32

One Month Later

The trees in the wildwood whisper of autumn. Some seem to crave it, their leaves already tipped yellow and orange. I hate the cold, but the beginning of autumn is my favorite time of year. The ancient trees are brilliant in their symphony of color. A person can walk among them and feel as if they've walked into the sunset itself. Ash trees will soon wear crowns of gold, and maples will burst into tangible flame. Then the leaves will drop, and for days it will be like a rainbow of snowfall, and it will be beautiful. It's no wonder my mother could not resist crossing through the wildwood the day the grinlers found her. I was born at the peak of the leaves' vibrancy.

I crouch outside our little home, tending the oon berry I'd uprooted in the wildwood and transplanted here. I had to wait for the moving sickness to wear off the plants before I could meddle with them, and today I weave their slender, thorny branches together, creating a loose braid between the small bushes. Thorns stick to my gloves, and an occasional burst berry stains them. The winter will strip them of everything but the thorns, but they will continue to dissuade mystings, even in a frozen and withered state. I do not yet have enough to surround the house, but thus far we've seen no mystings in these parts. I make sure to follow the rules—staying inside at night, washing my clothes in lavender, carrying silver, never straying too far into the wildwood.

I no longer have the Will Stone to warn me, so my days of frivolous adventure have come to an end.

I finish my work, wipe my hands on my apron, and tuck hair behind my ears. I've always preferred my hair short, but I haven't taken the time to trim it in a while. It sits on my shoulders now. A piece falls forward again, and I brush it away, jangling the silver band I still wear on my right wrist. I've never taken it off.

Walking back to the house, I wave to my father, who's gutting a doe he caught near dawn at the edge of the wood. He's turned his focus on building up our stores for winter, and I'm glad. Not only for the food and security, but because Papa seems to be the most himself when he's working with his hands.

I scoop up my basket from the doorstep and venture into the wild-wood, toward the thicket of oon berry I discovered not long ago. It's warm enough to pull up more plants, move them to our land, and coax them into the growing hedge. I pull dried lavender from my pocket and sprinkle it beside me as I walk, staring up into the trees to see which welcome the change of season and which resist. A jay calls from a nearby limb. The air smells of rain, though it hasn't rained for two days.

When I reach the thicket, I kneel down and examine the plants. The old ones are too thick in root to upend with any ease—I hunt for the offshoots, the daring ones that fell away from their parents last winter and sprouted in the spring. I gently ease my spade into the earth, loosen the soil, and scoop my protection from its home. I set one in my bag, then another, wincing when it pushes a thorn through the seam of my glove. The spike in my chest warms again, but perhaps that is just from the exercise. Ignoring it, I stand in the thicket until I find three more young plants to uproot. My work done, I set my tools and gloves in my basket and walk the rest of the way around the thicket, over a fallen tree branch, and—

I hear the hiss of the viper half a heartbeat before it lunges from the foliage ahead of me. Enough time for my heart to plummet, but not enough for me to act.

But the snake stops midstrike, midair. Nothing holds it, and yet it lingers there as if frozen, its long neck compressed, its mouth agape, revealing dripping fangs and a struggle for air.

I stagger back from my near death, struggling for air myself. I lift my eyes from the snake to the invisible being I know holds it. I fight to speak, to act, for I'm stiff as the ancient trees around me and cold as the depths of winter. A deep ache radiates through my chest, and I wonder if the snake had sunk its fangs into me after all.

I manage a wheezy "Maekallus."

His invisibility drops at his name. His fingers are coiled behind the serpent's head, and his yellow eyes regard me, narrowed and wary. He slowly stands from a crouch, the viper writhing in his grip. He wears a cloak of strange make, fastened at his left shoulder, and pants of layered leather pinned together by small metal studs. They end at hooved feet.

Save for the blunt end of his horn, he is the same mysting I summoned the day after the first gobler attacked.

I'm at a loss for words. A lump hard as granite sits in my throat. I feel my pulse around it, quick and hard. My eyes burn without tears. The horn in my chest—the one that once protruded regally from his forehead—feels like an ember.

I lift a hand, not quite reaching, and take a step forward.

The viper writhes in his grip. Frowning, he moves to strike it against the nearest tree.

"No!" I call, staying him. "Please don't hurt it. I . . . I was trespassing in its territory. It was only protecting itself."

Maekallus raises an eyebrow at me before shrugging and flinging the snake far to my left. I don't see where it lands, but it will survive.

I swallow, my mouth dry as week-old bread. My pulse thumps hard against my chest and neck. Does he hear it? "Do . . . you remember me?" I ask.

He scoffs. "I gave you back your soul, not my wits."

There's an edge to his voice. Not an angry one, but . . . one I don't remember him having, even before he took that first piece of my soul. "I-I'm sorry. I don't know exactly . . . how it works."

Yet I *do* know, but I try not to dwell on that knowledge, because I desperately do not want to fall apart before this man, this mysting. I don't wish to show him the weakness I've been harboring like poached meat for too long.

He does not feel the way he once did. He remembers, but he isn't . . .

Tears threaten my vision, and I blink and shove the thoughts away, clawing for composure. "W-Why are you here?"

He gives me that narrow gaze again, then a shrug. "The Deep isn't a friendly place."

"No, it's not." The lump has reformed and chokes my words to a whisper. I swallow again. Take a deep breath. "I—"

"He is not me."

Four simple words. They would be nonsense to anyone else, but they rake across my skin like briars. Even with the fullness of my soul, I don't have the strength to hold back the tears that pool in the corners of my eyes.

He shifts awkwardly, averting his gaze. His inhuman gaze. "I shouldn't be here," he grumbles as a tear streaks down my face.

I cross my arms over my chest, as if I could somehow keep more of me from breaking. As if I could squeeze out the hurt like pus from a wound. I tremble within my own arms, wishing I did not want so badly to be in his.

He turns and walks deeper into the wildwood. I can't bring myself to watch him go, yet I feel each footstep as if my body were the forest floor. Before he gets out of earshot, I croak, "Maekallus."

He pauses. Looks back.

I don't dare to meet his eyes again. I won't be able to say the words if I see his eyes, but I have to speak them. No other opportunity will present itself. I will down that lump in my throat without the aid of any otherworldly charm.

"I forgive you."

He doesn't reply. A moment later, his footsteps carry him away, and the warmth from the horn embedded in my chest dies.

I break like a dam, rooted where I stand.

Not even the threat of serpents can move me.

Looming night finally drives me from the wildwood. I have no protection against the predators that lurk in its shadows, monster or otherwise. Uneven steps take me to the house. I drop the basket and the collection of oon berry by the woodpile and retreat inside. My father reads by the fire. He calls my name. I continue to my room. Not to punish him—no, he has been nothing but good to me all my life. But I can't face him. I can't face anyone or anything, even myself.

I thought the heartache was terrible before. Now I would sacrifice my whole soul just to make it stop.

I barely have tears left to cry, yet they come, pulled from some awful reservoir inside me. I should never have gone into the wildwood. I wish I had never seen him.

I grab fistfuls of my hair and drop to my knees, sucking air into my lungs, forcing my breaths to be even. I am a fool. Three times over I am a fool. Four times. Ten.

Fumbling for flint, I light the single candle on the bedside table. I wipe my nose on my sleeve before reaching under my bed. I find the wooden box there, the one that once held my mother's wedding ring. I open it and hold it toward the light. The shards of the Will Stone sit inside the container like scabs of blood. I pour them into my hand and crush them against my fingers until the skin threatens to split.

"Can't you make it stop?" I plead to the lifeless charm. "Can't you make me hate him? I can handle hate so much better than this. Can't you grant me so much?"

Two tears splash against my knuckles. I don't bother wiping my eyes.

Bending over, I press my forehead to the floor. "Can you not give him what he lost? Bastards have souls." I whisper the words, not wanting my father to hear me, not wanting him to know how pathetic I've become. "Please. Make me forget, or bring him back to me. *I want him here.*"

A few more tears escape and join weeks' worth of long-dried sisters against the wooden floorboards. The sting of the broken stone in my hand lessens. I lift my head, blinking my eyes clear, and open my hand to see blood streaking my skin. I sit up in alarm, only to realize my hand is undamaged—the pieces of the Will Stone have somehow liquefied against my palm. The droplets slide off my hand like oil and mix with the tears on the floorboards. They seep into the woodgrain and vanish, leaving not so much as a smudge of crimson behind.

I run my hand across the wood. Dry, save for my tears. Enough pieces of my heart fuse together to leap within me, and I run to the window that faces the wildwood, searching the darkness beyond.

I am there hour after hour, until the morning sun illuminates the trees. There is no sign of him, or of any other mysting. The spike in my chest never warms.

Of all the injury I've suffered, none of it compares to the misery of that disintegrating hope.

CHAPTER 33

*A human soul can change the behavior, and even the
appearance, of a narval. One might conclude it could do
the same with any human-made mysting. This is a question
that may never be answered, however, as no man, scholarly
or otherwise, should ever tinker with the nature of souls.*

The day after the incident with the viper, I pull my great tome of mysting notes from my shelf. I haven't opened it since before . . . before Maekallus lost his soul, and I gained mine. I haven't needed to. Haven't wanted to.

I hold it carefully in my hands as though the pages are much older than they are. Turning them carefully, I read my grandmother's words mixed with my own, tracing charcoal over faded letters. I add detail to the sketch of the grinler. Darken the eyes of the orjan. Turn to the passage on narvals. I write in the margins, detailing the magic potential of their horns and the long-term effects of harboring a human soul. Or part of one. In the bottom corner of the page, I draw a picture. My drawing is not as refined as my grandmother's, but it's a decent likeness.

I fill in other notes as I remember them, sketch the profile of a slyser. I draw pictures of a descent ring and a portal ring, adding beneath them, *For educational purposes only. Do not recreate.* Even if this book is never published, it will someday be passed on. I want another to have this knowledge, but perhaps future generations can learn from my mistakes.

I consider adding the scrying spell, but I do not remember its words, and have since lost the paper. Should I ever desire it again, I know where to find it in the Duke of Sands's library.

I close the book and return it to the shelf, tracing my finger down its leather spine.

It happens then.

Warmth blooms in my chest like a sunflower unfolding its petals. Subtle, but powerful enough to make me pause. It has been cold since Maekallus saved me from the serpent.

Thinking the sensation a trick, I cough to dispel it, but the orb of heat only grows stronger. Not uncomfortably so, but undeniable.

Leaning back on my heels, I press my hand to the spot, centered just beneath my breasts. I feel the hard nub of the horn. It tingles beneath the dark fabric of my dress.

Holding my breath, I wait. Feel. Listen. The horn grows warmer. If I close my eyes, I almost feel . . . a tug. Light as a whisper, but it's there.

I stare at the leather of my book. Why has he come back? Is he just passing through? Does he mean to speak to me? Or is the horn whispering of something else entirely? I struggle to understand it, but the spike only responds with heat and that faint, gentle tug.

I cannot follow it. I cannot tear myself open again. I cannot—

I run.

I swing around the corner of the house and burst through the front door, startled by the cool evening air. I stop, straining to find that tug over the hammering of my heart. It pulls me toward the wildwood. I'd sworn never to return to it, but I break that promise without a second thought.

My boots pound ungracefully against the tamed earth of my father's land. I pass the first trees, shoulders tense, searching, searching. A tug.

I follow its lead. Two mice scurry from my path. I duck under a tree branch, swipe away a cloud of gnats. I focus on that feathery pull, on the heat stirring inside me, stronger and stronger and stronger, guiding me south, close to the tree line. It fuels my legs, and I run faster than I ever have before. It's as if the wildwood were no longer there, just a straight, even path ahead of me, and I must reach its end. I *must*.

I sprint, stepping through a dried stream, picking my way over rocks. A beehive sings above me but allows me to pass. A breeze pushes against my back, urging me faster, stirring the debris around my footfalls. I'm pulled deeper into the wood, then closer to civilization.

I stop ten paces from the tree line, gasping for air, sweat dancing across my hairline. I lean on a young oak for support and stare, heart pounding over that blossom of heat. A cry rises up my throat and dies at my lips.

He looks up at me, hair red as the changing maple, eyes amber as topaz. His feet, his *human* feet, are bare and muddy. His shortened horn extends a hand's breadth from his forehead before ending at a flat break. Its point radiates in my chest.

"Enna," he says. That edge is gone from his voice. I've never heard a more beautiful sound. His expression droops. Lines etch his forehead. His gaze drops to the earth. "You should never forgive me."

Tears frame my vision. I shake my head. "How?" I whisper. "How are you . . . ?"

A soft smile warms his eyes. He pulls back the edge of his cloak until he bares the center of his chest, the flesh over his heart. There are strange markings there. At first I think them corruption, but as I take a staggering step forward, I see the color is wrong. It's the color of old blood, or perhaps wet rust. Shaped like droplets of ink splattered on parchment.

The Will Stone. The drops that melded with my tears and fell through the floorboards.

"There I was, sitting at the edge of the immortal waters, and it started to rain." He drops his cloak. "It doesn't rain in the Deep. Just a few drops, right here"—he points to his chest—"and suddenly . . ." The corner of his lip quirks up, but the half smile is mournful. "Enna, I'm so sorry."

A tear escapes my eye and traces the edge of my cheek. "But . . . ," I choke out.

I recall what Maekallus said the Will Stone was—the petrified heart of the god who first created the mystings. And if Grandmother taught me anything, it is that the heart and soul are forever intertwined.

The Will Stone heeded me to the last.

It gave Maekallus a soul. It gave him *its* soul.

"I'm not asking anything of you." His voice is warm and lovely and draws me toward him like a baited snare. "I only wanted to . . . see you once more. To tell you that. Don't forgive me. Ever, Enna. I hurt you."

I shake my head, moving closer, closer. "You didn't."

He lifts a hand. He's close enough to touch my face, to wipe away a tear, but his fingers hover in the air. "Now you're the one lying to me."

I laugh. It's a pitiful laugh, half-chuckle and half-sob. He smiles at it nevertheless, that wicked grin I've grown to adore. I'm glad to see his transformation has not dulled the sharpness of his canines.

"I promise to only speak the truth," I whisper, leaning into his hand.

"You should never make a promise to a mysting."

"I did before. It worked out, in the end."

He cocks an eyebrow. His voice is even smaller than mine when he asks, "Did it?"

I take his hand in both of mine. Step around him. Pull him toward the tree line. Toward *my* world. "It did."

He hesitates. It's so slight I almost don't feel it. Drawing a thumb across the skin where horn meets head, he says, "I'm not one of them, Enna."

Reaching up, I measure his horn with my hand. He could cut off what remains of it close to the skin, claim it as a birthmark, but this protrusion is part of him. I don't want him to lose it, and I doubt he wants that, either. "No, you're not," I whisper. "But neither am I." I squeeze his hands. "You and I, we'll always be different. There will always be something wild in us. Others will see what they want. It's always been that way. But for now"—I can't help the smile that pulls on my mouth—"it's short enough to hide with a wrap. You're obviously not from Amaranda, and who knows what your native customs dictate?"

He grins and reaches for me. I leap into his arms, taking his jaw into my hands. His skin is warm and blissful beneath my touch. He holds me tight against him, and I seize his mouth, kissing him with all my hurt and all my glee. He is almost savage with the kiss, claiming me and parting my lips, seeking permission with the tip of his tongue. I wholly give it to him.

I kiss him, my tears wetting his skin, my laugh dancing across his lips.

Beneath my singing heart, the horn burns a brilliant heat.

And so does my soul.

Erna's Wildwood

C.N. Holmberg
©2014

ACKNOWLEDGMENTS

Another adventure concluded. Another one to put in the books, literally. This is the first novel I've ever written that was based off a dream. A bizarre dream, but many aspects of it were so intriguing to me that I knew I had to write it. So I did. At the same time I was drafting *The Plastic Magician*. Never have I written so much so quickly in all my life! But as all books before and after this one, this was not a one-woman show. Hardly.

Thank you for my critique partners and first readers, Caitlyn (who made the ending of this *way* better), Rebecca (who rounded out my protagonist), Erin, Katie, Rachel, Kim, and Cerena. Your help and patience as I made this story something worth reading is never forgotten. Many thank-yous to my fantastic husband, Jordan, who is not only an early reader but a great sounding board. Not to mention, like Tennith, he is wonderful to look at.

Thank you to Jason and Marlene for making this book happen. And to Angela, who was very patient with me and all the back-and-forth we had during edits! My gratitude goes to Rachel McNeill, whom I texted for twenty minutes over a problem with this book, thinking she was the above-listed Rachel. While that must have been a confusing conversation, she took it in stride and proved quite helpful.

Many thanks to Tacket Brown, who graciously reviewed my hand-scrawled sheet music in the back of this book to make sure it was legible and playable. (And for indirectly letting me know I'm still competent in that area!)

And once again, thank you to the Guy in White, the Big Man Upstairs, the Head Cheese of the Universe, that Divine Being who keeps my heart beating and gives me ideas in the same breath.

Never knew He liked kissing books.

ABOUT THE AUTHOR

Charlie N. Holmberg is the award-winning author of the Numina series, *The Fifth Doll*, and many other books. Her *Wall Street Journal* bestselling Paper Magician series has been optioned by the Walt Disney Company. Charlie's stand-alone novel, *Followed by Frost*, was nominated for a 2016 RITA Award for Best Young Adult Romance. Born in Salt Lake City, Charlie was raised a Trekkie alongside three sisters who also have boy names. She is a proud BYU alumna, plays the ukulele, owns too many pairs of glasses, and finally adopted a dog. She currently lives with her family in Utah. Visit her at www.charlienholmberg.com.